CASTLE RIDGE
Small Town Romance
BOOK FOUR

THE
Playboy
SWITCH

"If you're looking for small town romance that tugs
at your heart, Allie Burton's Castle Ridge series delivers."
– Romance Author Caro LaFever

BESTSELLING AUTHOR
ALLIE BURTON

Other Books in Castle Ridge Series
Where small town love takes you higher.

The Romance Dance

The Christmas Match

The Flirtation Game

The Playboy Switch

The Billionaire's Ploy

The Heartbreak Contract

The Marriage Merger (*coming soon*)

The Runaway Royal (*coming soon*)

THE
Playboy
SWITCH

ALLIE BURTON

Chapter One

The ground shook like an earthquake.

The snow-covered slope trembled and roared. A rumbling, thundering, cacophony exploded. The wind stopped blowing for a second and then switched to gale force with an almost supernatural ability. Tiny snowballs raced past speeding skis.

And Dax O'Donnell knew…

Knew an avalanche had been triggered.

Knew it stalked him from above.

Knew his life was in danger.

His heart stopped for a second and zoomed faster than his skis. Frigid air hit the back of his throat trying to suck oxygen into his lungs. Glancing over his shoulder, he spotted boulders of snow barreling toward him in a race to death. The narrow gulley funneled, pushing the snow between the carved walls and crags, creating the snowball from hell.

Thoughts of his brother Reed, his sister Isabel, and his parents flooded his mind. Would Dax ever see them again?

An adrenalized rush took control of his body. He dug in his poles and pointed his skis downhill. He had to outrun the avalanche. He was an avalanche expert, for shit's sake. He wouldn't dare let one kill him. What would his ski patrol friends say?

Determination raced the panic in his bloodstream. He couldn't die now. Not when he'd finally realized he had his entire life to live. He leaned into the hill, urging his chattering skis to go faster, heading toward the flank of the avalanche. Toward safety.

The small balls of snow got bigger, continuing to rush past him, hustling to the finish line. What the hell? He'd performed the avalanche hazard evaluation checks. He'd skied here a million times. The area wasn't known for avalanches.

The roar grew louder.

He was being chased by a large locomotive made of snow and rocks and ice. Digging in his edges, he swerved right. The narrow valley gave him no escape. His heart pounded and the echo stuck in his throat. This was open backcountry. No one knew he'd come out here.

Snow overtook the back of his skis.

He tried to go faster, but the avalanche was too fast. Too powerful. The slope too steep. The blanket of snow came to his knees. Similar to skiing in deep powder, except at mach speed.

The avalanche won the race.

His ski patrol training kicked into his brain. He needed to stay on top of the snow, to ride the avalanche like a wave. He switched on the emergency beacon his sister had insisted he carry. He gulped down a large, cold breath knowing it might be his last.

He slid into the frigid embrace of the snow.

The snow covered him, turning day into night. Hysteria bubbled in his stomach. He tried to keep his head up, to stay close to the surface. Snow surrounded him, appearing the same in every direction. The bubbling rose, burning his chest. He tried to keep the panic down. He didn't know which way was up. The entire time he was sliding, sliding, sliding.

His skis twisted beneath him. One ski broke free. The pole straps around his wrists tried to tug him under. He lost a glove.

Holding his arms over his head, he punched at the concrete snow as it sealed him in a coffin of white. A moving coffin. Dread weighted him, taking him down farther. His body slid with the force of nature. Moving him, burying him, until he finally stopped.

Silence.

The avalanche had come to a stop, covering him under who knew how much snow. The only thing he heard was his breathing, filling the small space with carbon dioxide and stealing the oxygen. Opening his eyes, the sparkling crystals of snow blinded him. His hands were stuck in front of his face. His legs couldn't move. No pain. He wasn't injured. Only pinned into an immovable position.

His lungs spasmed in and out. The exact opposite of what he should be doing. He needed to conserve oxygen, not waste it. Using his fingers, he scraped at the snow, trying to carve out an air pocket.

He shouldn't have been backcountry skiing alone.

The number one rule of skiing.

He'd broken several rules, today and many other days. His reckless nature was as much a part of him as his frostbitten hand. Not that he'd die of hypothermia. Suffocation was the primary cause of death in an avalanche.

The red of his exhaled breath filled up the small space he'd carved for his head, filling the pocket. The air wasn't really red. Hallucinations. *Oh, man.* He was going crazy.

The redness fought with the fresh blue air. Just like he'd spent the last few months fighting with his emotions. His mind and his heart were finally in agreement. He was over his ex-girlfriend Phoebe. He'd realized it had been more about loneliness than love. Everything had clarified in his head, and instead of moving on and living his life, he was going to die.

Idiot. He'd gone out skiing in celebration, and taken the usual precautions when skiing alone. He might take risks, but they were prepared, calculated risks. Skiing was a dangerous sport. Risk was part of the fun. From falls and injuries, to getting stuck on a chairlift.

To avalanches.

"Stay calm." He tried to slow his panicked breathing. "You're not going to die."

The tomb of ice didn't respond. A shiver wracked his body.

The frigid cocoon appeared so much different than from above an avalanche. His job was to start avalanches to make the slopes safe for other skiers. He knew the signs to search for, he knew how to trigger with his skis or set an explosive device. He would've noticed if the conditions were bad. One miscalculation or overlooked slight detail could doom a man.

What did he miss?

"Ahh!" His screams echoed in his coffin. "If I get out of this I'll quit being reckless." His pledge pounded in his ears. "I'll pursue becoming a paramedic." His nerve endings tingled with the goal, stimulated and yet scared at the promise. "I'll grow up and get serious."

His friends would laugh at his near-death oath.

More silence. Complete and utter silence. He never knew the world could become so silent and still.

He used the nails of his bare hand to claw at the snow in front of him until his fingers bled. He punched out with his elbows, hoping to make a crack in the concrete. He wiggled, and he kicked, and he shimmied. The icy snow didn't budge.

Swallowing, he closed his eyes, trying to be comforted by the fact if he died, he'd die in a place he loved. In the mountains. On the slopes of Castle Ridge Resort that he considered home.

Swish, tetcha, swish, techa.

His ears perked. His pulse *rat-a-tat-tatted*. Hope soared in the small, enclosed space.

Swish, tetcha, swish, tetcha.

An avalanche probe.

Dax tried to temper his hope, yet his spirits flew free. "Help! I'm here!" Except, where was here? He didn't know which way was up or down. He listened again.

Shouts. Crunching boots. The probe again.

He smashed his fists against the snow. "Here! I'm here!"

The metal stick probe pushed into his small cavern. He pressed his lips to the hole, trying to suck in air. The hole wasn't big enough. His breathing went shallow again and his mouth numbed. What if they found him, but couldn't dig him out in time?

The probe etched away at the size of the hole. He'd have to give his sister a big kiss for the beacon. It was the only way the ski patrol could've located him. He sucked in cold air, and his lungs quivered. He could breathe. He wasn't going to suffocate. His body started to shake, from cold or reaction, he didn't know. He didn't care. He could feel again.

Hope exploded, lighting a fire inside him. He was going to live. He was going to survive. His heart flailed. He was going to have to get serious as he'd promised. A shiver, not from the cold, traversed his entire body.

The hole grew wider. A tube of water was pushed through. Things happened fast. He heard shouts and shovels. He saw light. The air hole got bigger.

"Are you injured?" His boss Chuck's voice boomed into the hole.

Dax's body sagged. Just his luck his boss was on the rescue team. "No."

"We'll get you out in no time." His boss' authoritative tone gave Dax a sense of peace. "Stay calm and relax."

He'd have a lot of explaining to do once he was rescued. He'd broken the ski patrol and resort rules. And even though he'd had his beacon, shovel, and other gear, he'd needed rescuing. Even though he'd lived, he'd never live this down.

Pulling on his cocky armor, he said, "Just chilling under the snow."

Too tired, cold, and thankful, Dax didn't notice time passing. Shovels dug around him, snow flew, hands reached in, and rescuers pulled him gently from his almost-coffin. The rescue blurred and whirred. The reddish-orange coats of the ski patrol, the glint of metal shovels, the cheering as they pulled him out from beneath the snow.

"He's alive." His friend Bode imitated Frankenstein. Sweat dripped from his reddened face and onto his blond beard. He wrapped him in a tight hug. He'd been working hard to save Dax.

Thankfulness had him clinging to his friend.

"He'll live another day." Aiden shoved his shovel into the hard snow and gave Dax an embrace. His red hair stuck out from his knit beanie.

"Another day to steal the girls away." Laughter followed Matt's declaration and a hard slap on the back.

His friends had been on ski patrol shift this afternoon. They must've heard the beacon and hurried to rescue him, saving his life.

A few other patrollers hugged Dax or gave him a high-five. It was his friends' job as members of the ski patrol, but it also meant more. They hadn't given up on him like so many others in his past. They'd heard the beacon and found the avalanche location. Found him.

Standing on weak legs, he raised his hand in a wave. "Thanks."

He couldn't find more words. Normally, he was a talkative-always-joking type of guy. Not now. Relief and post-adrenaline tiredness kicked his butt.

A blur of turquoise blue with flowing, fiery-red hair ran toward him. Two warm arms wrapped around his waist and he leaned into her for support. A rich, passionate smell infiltrated his frozen nose.

Lexi.

She always wore the scent.

Not that he'd noticed much. She wasn't anything to him. A fellow ski patroller, a casual friend.

Her tremulous smile quivered. Her bluebird-sky eyes shined with something he couldn't define. His mind tried to analyze, but his brain wasn't thinking quick enough. Her lips moved closer to him. And then he couldn't think at all, too dazed by her hot lips pressing against his.

His cold mouth melted against her assault. The atmosphere went more silent than when he'd been buried under the snow. He didn't hear the other rescuers or the blowing of the wind. He heard nothing.

Only felt.

Felt her body molding against him. Felt the seam of her mouth open. Felt the heat transferring between them. The kiss was the most incredible kiss he'd ever experienced, and he'd kissed lots and lots of women. The kiss melted every shiver of coldness. Gave him the fire of motivation. Ignited his body and his soul.

Suddenly, his lips were cold. His arms empty. She'd abandoned the kiss and the loss was physical. Blinking, he opened his dazed eyes. He couldn't believe his response, or the fact she'd kissed him. Stunned, he stuttered her name. "Lexi?"

Lexi Henderson's cheeks steamed.

By Dax's question, he hadn't even realized who he kissed. His confused gaze suggested shock that she'd dare kiss him, not a gorgeous model type. Her mobilizing fear went into low-energy mode. What had she done?

"Woo-hoo!" The crowd continued to cheer, making her want to disappear from her surprising actions. Their lecherously-boisterous shouts and whistles were what brought her out of the sensual haze of the kiss. An amazing kiss, a kiss she'd yearned for since starting on ski patrol. A kiss she'd never expected, and couldn't believe she'd initiated.

His frozen-red cheeks were probably less bright than her own.

She purposely kept to herself at work, and never went out afterwards with the group of ski patrollers. She'd go for coffee one-on-one with a couple of them, never to a wild party, because she didn't want them discovering her secrets.

It had started as an innocent hug, a-thank-God-you-were-rescued embrace, similar to what the other patrollers had given him. And then he'd peered into her eyes, and she'd been unable to stop herself.

"If I need to get caught in an avalanche to get a kiss from Lexi, sign me up." Bode, a ski patroller and one of Dax's good friends, gave an exaggerated wink. He slapped her on the back because she was one of the guys.

Because that's how they saw her. One of the guys, a team player, a coworker, a friend.

The heat from her cheeks spiraled down her spine,

warming her from limb to limb. She couldn't believe she'd kissed her coworker in front of her boss. In front of the entire team. She didn't take risks. She twisted the ends of her braid. What had she been thinking?

She hadn't been thinking. Desperation had clawed in her lungs. When she'd heard Dax's beacon had gone off and he was trapped in an avalanche, she'd joined the rescue attempt. She'd already clocked out, and had planned to take a few turns down the mountain. Instead, she headed to the backcountry, because she needed to know when he was found. When he'd come out from being buried in the snow she'd needed to touch him and make sure he was okay.

Not that Dax could be anyone special. He was a friend and coworker, and a total playboy.

She plastered a flat smile on and glanced at her boss. "I must be woozy from the altitude."

A total lie.

Chuck's gray arched eyebrows showed he didn't believe her. "Right."

Her invention could've saved Dax from being buried. An invention desperately needing funding. Funding she wasn't going to get from her brother or her trust fund.

The rescuers helped Dax onto the litter, and strapped him in. His longish blond hair had been freed from his black helmet. His ruddy cheeks highlighted the light-blond stubble on his face. His green gaze appeared dull, possibly in shock. She choked on an internal snort. From the avalanche, or her kiss?

Because she'd attacked his mouth like a mugger on Fifth Avenue.

Lexi could only watch the patrollers prepare to ski him out. Her body refused to move, as if flash-frozen. Numb. She'd made a fool out of herself.

The workers wrapped him in a yellow safety blanket, and checked his vitals. As a ski patrol member and paramedic, she did this type of work all the time, and it never affected her. She was always calm and efficient and capable. Except with Dax, she'd manifested more than a rescuer helping a *rescuee*, and she didn't want to analyze the emotions charging through her. Emotions too similar to echoes from the past.

The echoing expanded, striking her brain and vibrating to her heart. She remembered another time. Another avalanche. Another rescue. With a completely different outcome.

"The training is arduous." Paul, the paramedic program director, tapped the application sheet against the desk. His serious and weathered expression showed his commitment to the paramedics.

Dax nodded firmly, even though his conviction wavered. He was happy with his life. Skiing, work—which was also skiing—partying. What more did a guy need?

Paul leaned against the hospital gurney stored in his tiny office. "The classes are tough."

School. Dax had always hated school. Why had he made the promise while buried under snow? He'd been under pressure, and his promises shouldn't be held against him.

"Your EMT qualifications will give you a head start. You can join the program in its second semester."

The beeping of medical equipment in the hallway distracted him. He tried to focus on the explanations of qualifications and training to become a paramedic, but the *beep, beep, beep* timed with Dax's pulse.

You can do this. You promised you'd do this. He kept his promises.

"Here's the application, and you can email me your references." Paul pushed the paperwork forward. "The deadline is next week."

"Got it." Dax understood the deadline, didn't mean he'd apply. He'd gotten along fine being an EMT on ski patrol. His specialty was avalanche control. Did he really need to go back to school, endure hours of physical training, just to get another couple of letters after his name?

And the cost would constrain his tight budget.

"After your application is in and your references checked, including your current EMT functional position description," Paul's long laundry list weighed heavier and heavier on Dax's shoulders, "there will be personal interviews with me and others."

Interviews? This kept getting worse and worse. Dax hadn't interviewed since he'd joined the ski patrol team. He didn't think he remembered how to put together a resume.

"Classes are held at the community college and online." Every word coming out of the program director's mouth hit Dax like an ice-packed snowball. "Labs and training are held here at the hospital."

The final snowball smacked him in the face. He listed to one side. Working ski patrol, he dropped off his rescuees in the Emergency department and got out of the building fast. He didn't hang around.

Even after being buried under the avalanche and rushed to Emergency, he hadn't stayed. Nothing broken. No frostbite. He didn't need observation overnight.

Enrolling in the paramedic program would put him in the hospital all the time. The imagined snowball on his face melted with the heat flaring inside him.

After shaking the program director's hand, he scurried out of the tiny office in the basement of the hospital near the Emergency department. A shiver tiptoed across his skin. He hated hospitals. The smells, the sounds, the dying. He'd spent hours roaming the hallways and visiting his grandfather as a middle schooler, the one person who had time for him and totally believed in him. The memories had etched into his soul.

Being a paramedic on the ski patrol team, he'd spend more time in the hospital, yet this same seniority would give him a higher pay grade. He'd be able to carry extra equipment on patrol. He'd have a career and not just a job. A career that kept him on the slopes most of the time, doing what he loved.

A couple hugged in the hallway, sadness permeated their body language. This was the type of scene he wanted to avoid. He didn't want to see other people's misery and loss. The woman lifted her head.

Lexi.

Her bright hair had been up in a tight bun, not the usual pigtails or braids. She wore shimmery pants and a cream-colored sweater. The pants hugged her curves. She never dressed nice when they occasionally hung out. The time they'd strolled through Main Street, and he'd introduced her to his sister-in-law and her dance studio, she'd worn jeans and a jacket.

A streak of green dashed through his veins. He knew he had no right to be jealous of her hugging another man. And yet, he was.

Memories of their kiss seared his mind. The most incredible kiss ever. He'd had a hard time getting the post-avalanche kiss out of his head, finally reasoning the kiss had seemed so incredible because he'd thought he was going to die. He'd just been rescued, and the kiss had been a shock. The only reason he couldn't forget.

His promise to get serious and the kiss had haunted him the past two days. He'd followed up on his promise, he was at the hospital picking up the application, but the kiss he didn't know what to do about. He'd hung around the ski patrol locker room hoping to bump into her, wanting to see her smile, and possibly kiss her again. He shook his head. What was he thinking? Lexi was cute, and too straitlaced and cautious for him. She was nice, but where was her fun?

He was about fun. That's what people expected of him. The relaxed one, the partier, the joker. That's the only thing that made him special.

Tears fell from Lexi's eyes, and his stance softened.

She was crying in the hospital. There must be a lot more going on in her life than he'd realized. Including a boyfriend.

The guy kept his arms around Lexi. They whispered back and forth. He had long hair tied back in a short ponytail. He wore designer jeans and a nice sweater fitting his muscular body. Even though the guy appeared to work out, Dax knew he could take him. Not that there was a reason to fight.

Dax had never thought to date Lexi. By her buttoned-up attitude, she probably didn't sleep around. And he didn't do permanence. His on-again-off-again fling with Phoebe had been his longest relationship. At least, he'd thought they had a relationship. Until she'd slept around.

He and Lexi were two opposites, who happened to share one incredible kiss.

Her boyfriend probably didn't know about the smooch.

Dax pulled back his shoulders and narrowed his eyes, watching the two of them. If the guy was her boyfriend, why did she kiss Dax with such passion? Blood rushed to his head. He wanted to taste more of Lexi, even knowing she was off limits.

The engagement party was in full swing when Dax arrived at the Castle Ridge Lodge. A small band played dance music from the stage. Bars were set up near the back.

"Dax." His sister Isabel rushed toward him, and hugged him a bit too tight. Ever since he'd been buried in the avalanche, she called and texted *a lot.* Her hair hung down in curly waves, which was rare because usually the strands were tied up and under a chef's hat.

He was fine and didn't need coddling. "Where's the chain?" Teasing, he kissed her on the cheek.

She wore a silky pink dress and heels, making her taller than usual. "Michael, my fiancé," she emphasized the title, correcting the chain moniker, "is by the bar."

Michael Marstrand flashed his television-personality smile, as if sensing he was being discussed. Or maybe there was a special connection between he and Isabel. Except, Dax didn't believe in special connections, or even marriage. At least, not at his age.

"You clean up nice." She grabbed the lapels of his blue sport coat.

Dress shoes, khaki pants, a button-down blue shirt, and jacket. Things he never wore, especially on a Sunday. "Why're you having your swanky engagement party on a Sunday night?"

"Michael and I work every night except Sunday and Monday." She waved around The Heights dining room. "We're chefs. You know that."

Chefs who became embroiled in a sex scandal on a reality television show. The image of the secretly taped sex video burned Dax's eyes. A shot of anger pumped through him, remembering how he'd felt when he'd punched Michael. Dax knew now Michael hadn't meant to cause the scandal. He and Isabel ended up together, so Dax didn't hate the guy.

Her fiancé waved at her. "Gotta go. Michael invited

people from Los Angeles, not expecting them to actually visit Castle Ridge. And they did." Isabel shrugged before heading to her fiancé and his friends.

Letting his sister go, Dax turned toward the bar.

A woman with long, long legs in a short, short red dress bent over. The woman's back was to him so he couldn't see her face. Still, he enjoyed the view.

Dax liked legs. He'd always been a leg man, and these legs were trim and muscular, in sheer tights and high black heels. Fuck-me pumps. The puffy skirt of the dress ended above her knee revealing powerful thighs meant to squeeze a man.

The woman picked up a cocktail napkin, as if worried someone might trip on it, and straightened, facing the other way. The puffy skirt trimmed and tightened at her tiny waist, and molded her womanly shape. Fiery red hair flowed and curled down her back.

Maybe she was from out of town, staying at the lodge for a few nights. Engagement parties were always a good place to meet women. Single women dreaming of their own engagement and willing to take a chance on him.

At least for the night.

His pulse picked up pace. He swished the beer in his mug and took a step forward.

Red-dress pivoted toward him. The swish of her skirt over toned legs mesmerized. His perusal slowly moved up her body. The low-cut bodice snagged his attention. The large diamond pendant hanging between her breasts had his own chest pounding. His gaze traveled up and up and up, more pleased with each aspect of the lady.

The clear, shining skin, from her pointy chin to the slight parade of freckles across her cheeks, captivated. And her eyes, her sky-blue eyes, sharpened at his stare. The pointed, familiar glare jolted him out of his lustful ogle. Because he recognized the sharp gaze, and had been at the receiving end of her scowl of disapproval at work because of his lax attitude.

Lexi.

His shoulders slumped, reacting to his disappointment that the red-dress lady was Lexi. Soon after, a slight thrill charged through him *because* the red-dress lady was Lexi. He'd never seen her dressed up, or her hair down. At work, she wore her hair in pigtails, resembling a little girl, no make-up to enhance an angelic face, and padded ski clothes hiding the delectable body and the long legs.

But this was Lexi.

His coworker. Someone he patrolled with, talked to at work. No one he could initiate a fling with. Not with her cautious nature. She'd want a relationship.

But, wow, Lexi.

His knees weakened, and he leaned against the bar to observe. He'd never thought of her as hot. Boy, was he wrong. Ever since she'd kissed him five days ago when he'd been rescued, he hadn't been able to get his mind off her lips. The way her heat had infiltrated his cold body, enflaming something inside him. He'd believed the flare-up of attraction had been caused by his near-death experience, yet he still felt the spark. A spark he'd tried to smolder. Until now…

Lexi's glare changed to an unsteady smile. Either she hadn't recognized him at first, or didn't enjoy his ogling. Now, she seemed unsure about how he'd greet her. Her bright-red lips drooped.

He hadn't talked to her since his rescue, avoiding her at the hospital. It must be fate she was at the party, resembling a fiery goddess, changing his impression of her from buddy to sexy lady. Another kiss would be a way to test his theory.

He set the beer on the bar with a thud and took a second step. A big step.

Except testing his theory meant she might think he wanted to get involved. And he didn't. He really didn't. So, no kiss. Didn't mean he couldn't talk to her and appreciate her beauty up close.

Lexi's attention shifted to the left. Her uncertain smile brightened, and his breath caught. Her megawatt grin could stop a speed skier in his tracks.

A broad-shouldered man in a designer suit pulled her into his arms, as if he had every right. A streak of something swooshed inside Dax. It wasn't jealousy, couldn't be jealousy. He didn't do jealousy.

The man kissed her on both cheeks and tilted back, holding her forearms.

Recognition hit. This was the same guy holding her in the hospital hallway. She'd cried in this man's arms. He'd hoped the guy was a friend or a relative. But seeing them together again, he determined this must be Lexi's boyfriend.

The streak shot into a spike, hitting Dax hard. He didn't poach, even if it was for only a kiss. He'd been on the other end of a similar raw deal, and he'd never do that to another guy. Her having a boyfriend would stop his temptation.

The couple strolled toward the dance floor, and he followed with his gaze. Lexi moved on the small parquet similar to how she moved on the slope, with grace and caution. She was the total package, and he couldn't believe he'd never even thought about her in that way. Now, he couldn't take his eyes off her.

Forcing himself to turn away, he spotted Chuck at the other end of the dance floor, hitting on a much-younger woman. He was probably twenty-five years older than Dax, and single. The guy was old and alone and still trying to be a player.

"Hey." His brother Reed knocked against his shoulder. Besides their green eyes, they didn't look much alike. "Why're you so glum?"

Dax forced a jovial smile on his face. He was the free-spirit and joker in the family, and it was time to put on a show. "Happy to be alive."

Which was true.

Frowning, his brother ran a hand through dark hair. "Hopefully you've learned a lesson."

When his siblings had heard about the avalanche, they'd hurried to the ski patrol base, and once they received word he was fine, they met him at the Emergency room. They'd coddled him the next couple of days, until he was cleared for duty, and he'd moved back into the ski patrol dormitory. For a few days he'd felt special.

"Lesson learned." He swished a hand horizontally and vertically across his chest, not sure if it was true. Elbowing his brother in the ribs, he didn't want to talk about himself. "How's married life?"

"Excellent." His brother's satisfaction and wide

smile gave him that weird, couldn't-be-envy feeling. "Isn't that one of your ski patrol buddies Ryder Croft is hitting on?" Reed pointed at Lexi dancing with her boyfriend.

"Ryder Croft? Why does that name sound familiar?" The name left a sour taste in Dax's mouth.

"Croft Industries. Ski bum in a multi-billionaire family. Playboy extraordinaire."

Dax's muscles tightened and he took a defensive stance. Lexi shouldn't be dating a playboy. She was too nice and innocent. That's one of the reasons he'd decided not to pursue her. She didn't do flings.

Protective instincts he didn't realize he had bristled, setting him on edge. The need to be her champion hardened inside him. For some unknown reason, he didn't want to see Lexi hurt.

Not by Croft, and not by him.

Chapter Two

Lexi sensed Dax's gaze follow her onto the dance floor. Nerves tumbled in her tummy as if starting the dance before her. He'd never looked at her like he wanted to lick her from top to bottom, making heat flare throughout her entire body. He'd never looked at her, period.

And he'd never looked so good. Creased khakis, a blue shirt making his green eyes stand out. She'd done a double take when first spotting him.

Her stepbrother Ryder had arrived, breaking the spell between her and Dax. She hadn't seen him since the kiss. Did he believe she'd kissed him because she liked him?

She didn't.

A piece of her protested. Okay, she'd always been attracted to him, but didn't agree with his wild partying ways. It wasn't simply going out for drinks. The rumors she'd heard about the ski patrol ragers filtered through her mind: binge drinking, drugs, and orgies. She'd heard that's how Dax and Phoebe, another ski patroller, had hooked up. Lexi didn't want to be a hook up. And if she socialized too much with the other patrollers, they might figure out her secrets.

She'd been burned by that before.

Ryder stuck his thumbs out in an over-the-top dance move. His roughly-shaven face gave a rugged and untamed appearance. He'd put on an actual suit for the party, not his usual torn jeans or sweats. His casual attitude displayed his comfort in any type of attire, because he'd been raised attending fancy events in designer clothes.

When first joining the Croft family at the age of twelve, she'd wondered how two brothers, Ryder and Jackson, could be so different. Jackson always wore a suit, and was stern and serious about the Croft family business. Ryder was a ski bum and volunteer coach. Never serious, and always wanting a good time.

She and her mother had moved from Denver into the Croft family mansion outside of town, and Lexi had immediately been enrolled at a small, private school with her new brothers. Never really meeting any of the kids from town and never befriending the kids from school. She'd always been an outcast. Being on ski patrol wasn't any different.

Wiggling her hips in a poor imitation of a dancer, she glanced at Dax. He stood in the same spot and stared, causing her stomach to do a backflip. Too bad her dancing lacked luster, compared to her brother's. Tightening her muscles, she threw her arms in the air and moved her butt back and forth. She needed to prove to Dax she was having fun, show him the kiss meant nothing.

"Woo-hoo, Lexi!" Her brother grabbed her hands and spun her around. He unwound her, imitating a spinning top. He'd always been a great dancer. "You go, girl."

Her cheeks heated. Had Dax heard her brother? "I enjoy dancing." She hated how she sounded prim and defensive. To prove her point, she twisted low to the ground and up again.

"You're usually not so flamboyant." Ryder put his hand on her lower back and guided her hips in a salsa beat.

A beautiful woman wearing a clingy dress approached Dax, and he shot her one of those sexy-and-he-knows-it grins. The woman's flirty return smile stabbed into Lexi's side.

"I can be flamboyant." Sure, she analyzed every move in life because she was cautious, not because she was dull. She bent down and shook her booty while watching Dax move onto the dance floor with the woman.

The stab in her side steamed through her bloodstream. Guess he didn't feel anything after their kiss.

Just. Like. Her.

Taking her brother's hands, she twisted toward him. "Dip me."

Ryder's gray eyes flashed with a tease, and he dipped her low. She pointed her heeled foot in the air with a flourish. Taking dance classes at Quinn's studio had helped her flexibility and her moves. With her head upside down, she spotted Dax watching her, not his partner. Her blood cooled with satisfaction.

Her brother brought her back to standing and she stuck her arm out. "You're sure nothing's bothering you?"

Ryder might not be her real brother, but he'd always acted like one. She hated how he could read her thoughts so easily. "I'm fine." She wasn't about to tell him about her foolish and desperate kiss with a guy who slept with many women and never once asked her on a date. Never even noticed she was a woman.

She remembered how crazy both her brothers had behaved when her ex-fiancé's true personality came to light. Or should that be, came to dark?

"Have you talked to Mom?" At her stepbrother's question, she tripped.

Ryder and Jackson had been calling her mother *Mom* for years, although it was still strange to her ears. Her mother had adopted both boys, after marrying Stephen Croft. The man had adopted her, too. She preferred to go by her father's name, because she loved her real father, and missed him terribly. As she got older, she'd realized the notoriety associated with the name Croft, and been glad she'd stuck with Henderson.

Her brother swung her into a slow dance when the music changed. "*Have* you, Lexi?"

Guilt curdled inside her. She'd been so wrapped up in thoughts of Dax, she hadn't given her mother's decision much thought. Maybe because she didn't want to think about the decision that could shorten her mom's life. "I talked to her this afternoon."

"Did you talk about the experimental treatment?"

His never-serious expression was serious. Stern. And watched her way too closely.

She ground her heel onto the floor, barely missing his shiny leather shoes. "Mom is not a monkey."

"Experimental, not quacky." He wheeled them expertly around.

Lexi wasn't paying much attention. Not to him or to Dax. She'd already lost one parent, and a stepparent. The thought of losing her mother caused the curdling to explode in her lungs.

"Experimental means risky." Risk-taking was not her thing. "Mom could die sooner."

"You know what happens if the doctors do nothing." His sad tone tried to soften the blow.

It didn't. The blow struck her chest. Her throat went dry. "I can't lose my mom."

He held her close in a brotherly hug. "I know."

She let his strong arms comfort her. His strength, and Jackson's, had helped her get through her mother's treatments so far. They'd been supportive and caring. They'd done whatever needed to be done, including bringing in renowned specialists in the cancer field.

The slow song came to an end, reminding her Mom's life might end. The dance ended on a depressing note.

"I need to find Michael and congratulate him, and then find a drink." Ryder dropped his arms from around her. "Do you want something?"

"Sure." Nodding, Lexi wandered to the edge of the dance floor. "I'll wait here." She didn't want to deal with the crowd around the bar while her thoughts were occupied with her mom.

Besides, she needed more than a drink. She needed a spine to agree to the terms of the experimental treatment. Her mother wouldn't sign the paperwork until the entire family agreed. Right now, Lexi was the only holdout.

"That guy will break your heart." Dax eased up next to her with a drink, but no woman in hand. His carefree expression was gone, and the light had dimmed from his green gaze.

"Will he?" She was curious to see where this was going. He must not realize Ryder was her brother and would never hurt her. Not like others in her past.

"Ryder Croft is a playboy with no serious career or goals."

She glared. Her brother loved coaching the kids on his ski team. Sure, he was a little lost when it came to a career, but Dax had no right to judge. "Really?"

"Croft is a gazillionaire." Dax sounded as if his beer went sour. "If I had as much money, I'd quit my job and ski around the world."

"Sounds as if you want to be just like him." His sour tone filled her mouth with a bitterness that burned down her throat. He was jealous of Ryder's wealth, not because he'd been dancing with her. Dax reminded her of her ex-fiancé Andrew, who had only been interested in her money and her family's connections. Pursing her lips, she tried to control her annoyance. "You don't care about your job?"

She had a passion for saving people, which was why she'd joined the ski patrol and become a paramedic. She didn't want anyone else to unnecessarily lose their life on the mountain. The invention she'd been working on and trying to get developed would help her mission.

"I care about my job. I don't want to see you get hurt." He took her hand and patted it like she was a cowering puppy. "Croft's a playboy."

"And you can say this because you have the greatest dating record?" Overplaying her sarcasm, she let her pessimism come out in her voice. She'd always been attracted to Dax, yet kept her distance, knowing his true personality. "You're a playboy."

His eyes morphed into chipped emeralds. He gripped her hand tighter, and pulled her against him. "Then go out with me, instead."

The whispered words sent a tingle down her spine.

She'd longed to hear a declaration from Dax. A sexual tease or an invitation. Except this was a declaration of competition, because he was jealous of her brother. The moment he learned about her background, she wouldn't know if he liked her or her money. Plus, what exactly was he asking for? A date or a night in bed?

Stopping the tingles before they reached her heart, she forced a sappily sweet smirk. "So I should dump Ryder and start dating you, doing a playboy switch?"

"O'Donnell! Henderson!" Chuck yelled from his small office at the ski patrol base, and from the tone, Dax wanted to hide. "Get in here."

Oh shit. Did Lexi squeal he'd hit on her at the engagement party? That she'd said no?

Dax scuffed his ski boot on the ground. He

wondered if she'd told her boyfriend and they'd had a good chuckle. He didn't know what had possessed him to ask her to make a switch. To him.

Because he worried about how Croft would treat her. And desire. Dax admitted he thought she was sexy.

It wasn't Chuck's business. He couldn't judge, when he'd hit on every single woman at the party between the ages of eighteen and sixty.

Besides, Lexi had kissed Dax on the slope. She'd started this sexual awareness.

He sent a sly glance her way. She took off her ski patrol coat and hung it in her locker. Her expression appeared surprised, too, and Dax blew out a breath. She gave a shrug, slammed her locker shut, and headed toward the conference room.

Following, he noted her legs covered in ski pants still looked long. Why hadn't he noticed before? He could picture her in the red dress she wore Sunday night. Her long hair down and calling to him. He remembered her laughter when he'd asked her out, the sound grating in his ears. He'd never been laughed at by a woman turning him down. Lexi hadn't take him or his question seriously. And she took *everything* seriously.

She stood rigidly inside the door, and he jammed in next to her. There wasn't a lot of room in the tiny office, with its big metal desk and two guest chairs. The walls were covered with ski patrol flyers and posters.

"Hey, boss. How'd you make out at the engagement party?" Dax figured if he hit his boss with evidence of his own infractions, he couldn't come down too hard.

"Fun party." He scratched at his full head of gray hair and shuffled papers around. "Sit. Both of you."

Dax whipped a chair around and straddled it backwards, balancing on two of the chair legs. Lexi perched on the edge of another chair, crossing her ankles, imitating a prissy princess. He wasn't attracted to prissy, but something about the way she held herself straight and upright had him wanting to see how far she could bend. Literally and figuratively.

"What's up?" She gave him a quick perusal, sensing his attention before focusing on their boss.

"You two," Chuck pointed at both of them. "are going to be our safety committee."

Dax screwed up his face in disgust. He didn't want to sit behind a desk discussing things. He was a man of action.

She glanced his way again. "What would be involved?" Her precise tone and perfect diction scratched at his nerves. Her patience and acceptance made him wiggle in his seat.

Their boss tapped his fat fingers on the desk. "You two will inventory our patrol's safety equipment. Research what's out there, and with a budget, decide what we need to purchase."

"I don't need no stinkin' safety equipment." He faked a slow drawl, and slipped his hands to his sides, pretending he wore holsters. When he'd first started on junior ski patrol there'd barely been any safety equipment. It had been you, the mountain, and the elements. "I'm the last one to care about safety, so wouldn't someone else be better on this committee?"

Her mouth dropped open and she glowered. "You of all people need safety equipment. You were pulled from under an avalanche and almost died." Her voice picked up strength, as if she really cared about him.

His heart thudded. The kiss tattooed in his mind, followed by the image of her dancing too close to Croft. "Didn't know you cared so much. Especially after Sunday night."

She'd turned him down. Joked about a playboy switch and gave him a flat no, before going back to Ryder Croft's side. And leaving with the rich playboy. Dax had gone home alone, not even interested in the other women at the party.

Her face reddencd, and her mouth moved, about to rebut. She regarded their boss, and closed her mouth into a thin line.

"Stop fighting." Exasperation screeched in Chuck's voice. "I believe you two will balance each other out perfectly."

What was that supposed to mean? Dax's recklessness compared to her overcautious nature. Her smarts versus his dumbness. He glowered.

She wiggled her shoulders and pursed her lips. "How much time will this involve?"

"Not a lot. And your time is on the clock."

Extra cash would be nice to pay for the paramedic training, if he decided to go that route. Still, he'd be locked up indoors when the mountain called, and he'd be working closely with Lexi. Tempting and taken Lexi. "Can I get out of it?"

"No." His boss handed a bunch of papers to Lexi.

"You two will work on this together. A system of checks and balances. There's the last inventory and the new budget."

If he said he was considering applying to paramedic training he might get out of the committee, but he didn't want to share that tidbit with anyone. Not until he decided for sure. There were too many factors to consider. Working so closely with Lexi might prove interesting. He'd love to see her get riled up about rules and safety like she'd just done on his behalf. Love to experience her anger and her passion. Love another kiss.

No, not a kiss. She had a boyfriend and he didn't steal. But teasing her and ruffling her pristine feathers would be fun.

She stood and headed toward the door, her hips swaying with a tempting tease. "I'll put a folder together and organize the inventory."

"Dax." His boss' tone stopped him from standing.

What had he done wrong now?

His boss leaned forward over the large desk. He frowned. "I want you to take care with Lexi."

He let the chair legs fall onto the floor with a thud. His boss must be able to read his dirty thoughts. "What?"

"I saw the kiss she gave you, and I saw you watching her dance at the engagement party." Chuck kept his voice low so it wouldn't carry out of the office.

"You didn't see anything. We're coworkers." Dax puckered his lips and blew. "Besides, she has a boyfriend."

His boss tilted his head in an angle of surprise. "Really?"

"She was dancing with the guy all night." Remembering caused his chest to burn. She hadn't danced with anyone else.

Chuck's eyebrows rose. "Is that so?"

The question poked and prodded Dax's mind. Did his boss know something he didn't? His thoughts spun with *what* and *ifs*. Having worked with her for two years and hung out with her several times, he really didn't know much about Lexi.

Was there more than she showed?

Lexi plunked down at one of the desks the ski patrol members used to fill out incident reports. There were two desks at the end of a row of ski patrol lockers and before the oval-shaped conference table. A counter divided the table from where the general public entered their building. Not a lot of space or a lot of privacy.

She yanked an empty folder open and shoved the paperwork inside. She didn't want to work closely with Dax. He was too dangerous and too tempting. She sucked down a large breath trying to control her racing pulse. He'd actually asked her out the other night.

Only because he was jealous of Ryder. Once he found out Ryder was her stepbrother Dax wouldn't look at her twice. He never had before. They'd worked together for two years and he'd always treated her as one of the guys. One of the boring and not-worthy-of-being-asked-to-happy-hour coworkers.

Which was fine. Truly it was.

Ski patrollers going out after the mountain closed, getting drunk, and picking up on each other, or snowbunnies and snow-buns—as the patrollers referred to the male of the species—wasn't her scene. She had better things to do with her time. She didn't want or need to sleep with everyone and anyone. Her body heated. There was only one person she wanted to sleep with…

Stop. She refused to think of Dax that way. So what if she'd been attracted to him since the moment they'd met. He wasn't the one.

She was an adult and had to stop believing in romantic fairytales. She should've learned that lesson with Andrew. He'd acted good and was bad. Dax was a bad boy who wouldn't change. She respected herself too much to be a fling. Besides, she had other things to worry about, for example, getting an investor for her avalanche safety prototype, and her mom's illness.

Her eyes prickled. She squeezed them tight stopping the tears from falling. She refused to think about her mom's situation at work, refused to think about the decision she needed to make. Her job kept her busy. The other patrollers didn't know her second last name or know anything about her personal situation. She liked it that way. She didn't want to be known as a Croft.

She grabbed a pencil from the drawer and twirled it between her fingers.

Coming from a big city, she'd learned not to trust strangers. Once she'd moved to Castle Ridge and the Croft mansion, she'd realized great wealth had great impact. Positively and negatively. Determining who liked her for herself and who befriended her for her new money had been a painful experience.

"Where should we start?" Dax slouched against the desk, interrupting her pity party. His delectable butt sat only inches from her itchy hand. Even in ski pants and uniform sweater, he looked good.

She fisted her fingers together and drew her hand into her lap. "Inventory first."

"Yo!" He called to the room in general, where several ski patrollers were changing by the lockers or taking breaks at the large table. "Everyone put your hand up if you have a safety beacon."

The patrollers surveyed them strangely and raised their hands. Of course, they listened to Dax's weird request. If she had asked the same question, only more politely, they would've ignored her. She shrank in the chair.

"One hundred percent." Dax made a check mark in the air with his finger. "Done."

The man tried to simplify everything. There wasn't a shortcut he didn't take. Which she admired and hated at the same time. She never took shortcuts. "We need to mark down the serial numbers of each unit, and who its assigned to, check the batteries, etc."

"Back to no-fun Lexi." His disappointed voice slapped.

The imagined slap stung. She refused to show offense. "I'm fun. Just cautious."

"When was the last time you took a risk, or went wild?" His doubting eyebrows arched in a tease.

The stinging spread across her skin. He had no

right to judge. He didn't know everything about her. "At the engagement party." She'd danced crazier than she'd danced in a long time.

"Ha. You left early."

He'd noticed when she'd left. Why? She'd only danced recklessly because he'd been watching. "Ryder had an early morning."

"What will he think of us," Dax leaned closer to her, "spending time together," he took one of her pigtails and wound it around his finger, "doing inventory?"

His scent of pine and fresh air twirled around, helping to weave the atmosphere with intimacy. She swallowed. "We're just working together."

"Together." His deep tone throbbed with sensuality, making it sound like a sexual proposition. "A lot."

Her heart stuttered and she melted. Was it?

Dax surveyed the mountain scenery on a lesser-traveled expert slope at the Castle Ridge Resort. Another blue-sky Colorado day. He smelled fresh pine and cold air. The view encompassed the town of Castle Ridge nestled against the side of the mountain, and the frozen lake he'd skated on as a kid. This was one of his favorite spots in the resort. The view brought back memories of skiing on the high school ski team, and skiing with his friends. A good place to think, even while on ski patrol duty.

The radio at his side crackled. The paramedic paperwork crinkled in his pocket. He'd carried it with him to fill out during break, and hadn't touched the application. Wasn't sure he was going to.

He'd made a promise to himself before he'd been rescued, but he'd been under duress. Surely, the promise could be taken back. Yet, paramedic training had always been in the back of his mind when he'd joined ski patrol after college. He'd never gotten around to it. With his sister Isabel engaged and co-head chef at a nice restaurant, and his brother Reed married and not only head of a growing business, but writing music again, Dax had been thinking it was time for him to do something with his life. Being caught in the avalanche had been the impetus to get a move on.

Yet, what if he wasn't smart enough or disciplined enough to go through the schooling and training? Life held too many distractions.

His mind flickered to Lexi. Speaking of distractions.

The radio crackled again before the dispatcher said, "Medical emergency at Sunnyside, near Delilah's Dash. What's your location?"

"O'Donnell here. Top of Sunnyside." He slipped on his goggles and pole straps, awaiting further instruction.

"Affirmative, O'Donnell. Go to site. Henderson and Rock to assist."

Great, Lexi would be his backup. He'd been avoiding her since the meeting with their boss. At the desk, he'd wanted to get under her skin, similar to how she'd gotten under his. He wanted to peel back the layers of her personality and discover what their boss had hinted at. He wanted to peel away her clothes.

Which he wouldn't and he shouldn't. He shouldn't even be thinking about her in that way.

Dax headed down the slope, tuned in to the radio and trying to keep his mind on the job. "En route. What's the situation?"

"Adult male collapsed on side of slope. Son called in incident." The radio cackled louder than normal. "Henderson bringing litter."

The trail became more crowded the lower the elevation. Dax whizzed past skiers and boarders while keeping control. Traversing the trail, he assessed his path while thinking about his plan when he arrived on scene. Medical emergency could mean anything from a broken bone to a concussion. He had to be prepared.

He enjoyed the unknown element of the job. Of helping people. Of being outdoors on the mountain.

A kid around fifteen flagged him down. A man's body lay on the white snow at a steep angle. The man wasn't moving.

"My dad!" The kid's voice screeched.

"What happened?" Dax stepped out of his skis and placed them in a crossed position to signal the emergency. He didn't want any skiers crashing into them. He pulled off his pack and kneeled by the man. Moving with deliberate actions, he assessed everything about the scene, from the marks in the snow to the position of the victim. The man hadn't had an accident. There were no sudden break marks in the snow and no collision debris.

"Dad stopped to rest." The kid kneeled on the snow beside him. "And then he collapsed to the ground."

Dax took off his ski gloves and unzipped his first aid pack. He slipped on latex gloves. "Any medical conditions?" He unzipped the man's black ski coat, trying to keep his voice calm and professional.

"No." Tears fell from the kid's eyes and slid down red cheeks.

Sympathy swarmed inside. He wanted to comfort the kid, except his first job was dealing with the victim.

Bending over, he listened for the man's heartbeat. He took his pulse. Nothing. Dax's adrenaline spiked. Efficiently, he took out the CPR mask in the poly bag and ripped it open. If he'd been a paramedic, he'd have more equipment.

"Is he going to be all right?" The kid gripped his dad's coat bunching the material between his gloved fingers.

"Step back." Dax sounded brusque knowing seconds meant life or death. He checked the air passageways and put the mask on the man.

"Dad," the kid wailed.

Starting CPR, Dax pumped the resuscitator assessing every move and reaction. He put his hands together and pressed on the man's chest. "Did he hit his head?"

"No." The kid spoke through gasps. "Not hard anyhow. He clutched his chest and slumped down."

Adrenaline backed up in his veins, keeping his panic low. He was a professional. He'd practiced CPR hundreds of times. Practicing and actually doing were completely different. He switched between pumping the resuscitator and pressing on the man's chest.

"Breathe, dammit," he muttered, trying not to let the kid hear. He pounded on the man's chest again, using his anger for extra strength.

Skis slid to a halt beside him. Lexi and Rock snapped out of their skis. Both were full paramedics. Feeling less than capable, Dax pumped again.

"Defibrillator." She assessed the situation correctly.

The other patroller, Rock, dropped to his knees. He set up the machine and cut the man's sweater. "Switch on my count."

If Dax had been a paramedic, he would've carried a defibrillator, and could've started the process immediately. The situation might not have been so dire.

"Clear." The patroller worked the machine, and Lexi assisted with CPR.

The man's body jerked.

Dax's arms hung to his sides, his useless hands weights on his body. He stood helplessly by while the paramedic patrollers took control of the medical situation. There was nothing he could do. He moved to the kid's side. "What's your name?"

"John." The kid sniffled.

"How long?" Rock yelled to him.

Dax didn't need to ask what the patroller meant. The victim had stopped breathing a while ago. "At least five minutes."

"Time?" The patroller stopped the machine, his tone cold.

The coldness snapped something inside Dax, making his body frigid. His muscles contracted and he wanted to scream. He took a deep breath, letting the frozen air hit his lungs. He needed to be numb. The man had died on his patrol.

"Eleven thirty-four." His voice cracked.

"No! No!" The kid's cries grew louder, breaking the silence on the side of the slope.

He hugged the kid trying to provide warmth and comfort. "Who else are you skiing with? Where are you staying?"

Even though his questions were controlled and compassionate, he was in a total daze.

Lexi gave him a horrified look. She must believe the death was his fault, and the guilt chilled him to his bones. If he'd been a paramedic, he would've been carrying the defibrillator, and might've saved the man.

He'd been pressured for the last several years to become a paramedic, and he'd put it off. He'd believed he was doing his job fine without the extra training. He'd thought schooling and training would take too much time. The deepest reason he'd never applied was because he didn't think he was smart enough.

And because of it a man had lost his life.

Chapter Three

Lexi was used to being in hospitals on a daily basis as part of being a ski patrol paramedic. She was not used to being in them on a daily basis visiting someone she loved. Until recently.

Since her mom had been diagnosed with pancreatic cancer, she'd seen a lot of hospitals. They'd traveled for specialty treatments and clinical trials. Her brothers had spent tens of thousands of dollars, possibly more. And they'd all spent hundreds of hours at doctor visits and hospital stays.

Lexi dragged her heavy feet, shuffling down the white and antiseptic corridors. Tired, she felt as if she'd aged through the process and couldn't imagine how her mother felt. Yet Mom stayed upbeat and positive. The woman was amazing.

Entering the private hospital room, she peered at her mom. Her tiny frame took up such a small amount of space. She'd lost weight with the illness. Lost her once-glowing red hair. "Lexi, come here."

"Hi, Mom." Lexi gave her mother a kiss on the papery-soft skin of her cheek. "Hi, Ryder." She waved at her brother sitting on the other side of the bed and holding her mother's hand.

"Hey." His tired and sad expression matched his wrinkled pants. He'd obviously been here for a while and it was comforting to see how much he cared.

"How're you feeling today, Mom?" Lexi slipped off her coat and hung it on the back of the door. She moved to the side table and fiddled with the flowers in a vase, avoiding the topic she knew Ryder wanted to discuss.

He'd been pressuring her on a decision for a week.

"Good." Mom didn't look good or sound good. Her blue eyes never held a sparkle anymore. "How was work yesterday?"

Sadness at the thought of the man's death on the mountain penetrated her professional shell. She wouldn't share the details. "Okay."

Ryder flashed a knowing glance. He heard rumors from the local resorts. He must know about the death, and probably knew she'd been around when it happened.

Surveying the equipment hooked to her mom, she interlocked her fingers and tried to hold on to her emotions. Every time she entered this room one single thought punched: her mother was really sick, and the thought of losing her last remaining parent darkened her soul. She held back the tears. Crying was better done alone.

"Good morning." A nurse hustled into the room. "Would you two excuse us for a few minutes?"

Nodding, she and her brother left the room, and walked at slow pace down the corridor.

"We need to make a decision soon." He didn't need to add, *Mom doesn't have a lot of time.*

Lexi knew. Time was constantly ticking in her head. She tried to push it aside and live life like her mom wanted, but the worry was constant. The swirling in her stomach and the tightening of her muscles were never-absent companions.

In an older-brother gesture, he put his arm around her shoulders as they walked. "What are you thinking?"

She heaved a shaky breath. "It's such a big risk."

"Life is a risk."

A harsh laugh choked out of her. She'd lost her father at a young age. She'd ended an engagement in college. She knew about life's risks.

"If Mom doesn't try the experimental treatment, she'll die." He softened his voice, trying to lessen the blow. "The doctor says the single-patient investigational drug is the only option left."

Meaning Mom was dying. How quickly she died depended on the experimental drug.

"And if the new biologic drug doesn't work, she'll die sooner and with more pain." Lexi's lungs constricted. Agony sliced across her midsection. "I don't want Mom experiencing pain."

"Neither do I." Ryder squeezed Lexi's arm in support, his expression grim. "We've tried everything else. Researched every doctor and treatment. We've used our resources to do what's best."

Ryder and Jackson had used the family's influence and resources to help her mother. If she didn't have them, she didn't know how she would've dealt with her mom's illness. Her and her stepbrothers had always been close. Mom's health issue had brought them closer.

"I know. And I thank you—"

"It's not about thanks." Ryder's terse response signified his hurt. "She's mine and Jackson's mom, too."

Mom had taken care of and counseled both boys during their trying teen years. Their real mother had left the country the moment her divorce settlement money ran out. She'd not cared about them, only about the money their father provided. Lexi had witnessed the boys' anguish and had empathized. As a new, younger sibling there wasn't much she could do. "I know."

"Then quit thanking us. We'd do anything we could for her."

Lexi's mind swirled with options and complications. There was so much to consider. The experimental drug could help. It could also kill. "The risk is so high."

"Some things are worth taking a big risk." Ryder repeated his earlier claim, a saying she didn't live her life by. He sounded mature, not his usual joking and carefree self. He'd aged in the process as well.

She stood on the edge of a cliff with her skis hanging over. If she tilted forward she'd ski down the face of the mountain and either crash at the end or have the best ride of her life. If she tilted back she'd stay safe on the edge, never knowing what could happen, or how wild the ride. Staying still, she could also freeze to death.

They continued roaming the halls, her steps keeping pace with her wild thoughts. She didn't know whether she should take the plunge and go down the cliff or not. Should she give her approval to her mother's experimental treatment or not?

Rounding a corner, Lexi saw Dax heading in their direction. His jeans and nice shirt pointed out he wasn't working. Why was he at the hospital? Ryder's comments about taking a risk applied to Dax, too. What if she'd said yes to his request for a date? Where would the two of them be now?

He lifted his head and his eyes widened when he spotted her. Stopping, he raked his fingers through his longish blond hair before sliding toward them. "Lexi." He always said her name with a certain reverence.

She didn't like it. She didn't want to be put on a pedestal. Untouchable and out of reach. "How're you doing, Dax?"

His skin seemed paler than usual, probably experiencing shock from yesterday's death, and she wanted to hug him. "Fine."

She shifted on her feet, hoping her eyes weren't puffy. No one on ski patrol knew about her mother's situation, except her boss. Between the different last names, the size of the town and outskirt populations, and her keeping her real identity a secret, she'd kept her two lives separate. She didn't want Dax asking awkward questions.

"This is Ryder Croft." She purposely left off the

brother part. "Ryder, this is Dax O'Donnell. He's on ski patrol with me."

Dax spread his stance and ruffled his shoulders. His chin tilted up in a look of defiance. "Hey." He shook her brother's hand. "Lexi and I are on the safety committee together. Hope you don't mind."

Her brother's eyebrows screwed up. "Why would I mind?"

She knew why Dax thought her brother would mind. The kiss.

"No reason." She should confess Ryder was her brother, except she didn't want anyone learning the Croft family was her family, and she was wealthy. A chill traversed her spine. Her relationship with Andrew had altered her trusting outlook.

Her brother grabbed his cellphone. "I need to make a call." He walked back toward her mom's room.

She stood, awkwardly shifting from one booted foot to the other, knowing Dax was tormented by the man's death on the mountain, and not knowing what to say. She understood the helplessness he was going through. She'd been on a scene where someone had died. She'd been with her father when he died. She was with her mother now, watching her slowly die.

He kicked his hiking boot into the tiled floor and saluted her with a large envelope. "I should get going."

"If you ever want to talk about what happened on the mountain…"

"Talk?" He fluttered the envelope in his large hands. "You think it was my fault the man died." His tense tone matched his tense body.

All her blood drained to her feet. "No."

He gripped her shoulder with his free hand, applying pressure. "Are you sure?"

"I'm sure you did everything you could."

"Yeah, everything *I* could." He strode away, not giving her a chance to respond.

Not giving her a chance to help or comfort. She understood being upset about a victim. Understood the anger and the confusion and the doubt. Between her personal life and her professional life, she had way too much experience with death.

Everything I could. Everything I could.

Lexi's words taunted Dax later in the evening, as he climbed the back staircase to his brother's old apartment above the dance studio. He had done everything *he* could, but what he could do wasn't enough. If he'd been a paramedic, he might've been able to save the man. Having the certification to carry a defibrillator could've been the difference between life and death.

He'd never forget the expression on the kid's face when they'd stated time of death for the father. The kid's eyes had gone as wide as saucers, and his mouth had gaped open like the image in *The Scream* painting.

The incident would go in the final report, on the death certificate, and possibly ruin his chances to become a paramedic. Did he want it to?

Shoving open the door, he found Reed painting the small living room walls. His paint-spotted jeans and white T-shirt hinted he'd been working for a while.

"Don't you have enough work to do at your and Quinn's house?" Dax forced a jovial tone, pretending to be his normal casual self.

His recently-married brother had unknowingly bought his new wife's grandparents' house. Now they lived there together, while Reed worked on the fixer-upper, ran his remodeling business, and wrote music. His brother was a multi-talented guy.

Unlike Dax.

"Figured we'd rent the two apartments over the dance studio. Earn a little extra cash before the baby comes." His brother's grin spread from ear-to-ear lightening the mood.

Reed was so happy with Quinn, and now thrilled a baby was on the way. For himself, Dax didn't understand the whole settling down and raising a family thing. There were too many things to do in life. While he'd believed he'd been in love with Phoebe, over time he'd realized it was more lust and availability. When she'd lived here, their relationship had been easy and convenient. Once she'd moved, he'd been lonely and thought he'd missed her, until she started taking advantage of him.

His experience with Phoebe proved he wasn't ready to lock himself to one woman yet. "Whatever floats your boat."

Reed's wife had floated Dax's boat for a short time. Nothing serious. She was attractive and new to town. He'd recently broken up with Phoebe, and needed a distraction. He could see now how Quinn and Reed were perfect for each other, even if it took him longer than most to recognize.

"What's this about a reference?" Reed rolled paint on the wall.

Dax twisted his lips. He hated asking his big brother, or even letting anyone know his plan to apply to paramedic school. What if he failed to get in? His brother never failed. Not even after a serious car accident and losing his first career.

He yanked the knit beanie off his head, and turned toward the kitchen, hoping a cold beer waited inside the refrigerator. "I need personal and professional references for an application."

"What kind of application?"

Dax knew he was making this more difficult. It was like opening the beer bottle in his hand with his eye socket. "Paramedic training," he mumbled.

"What?"

Taking a long sip of beer, he raised his head and stared straight at his brother. Saying it out loud to someone important to him would make it real. The quivering inside shook faster. He planted his feet firmly on the floor and stopped the shaking. "Paramedic training."

Reed stopped rolling. He raised his brows. "Wow. That's great."

The beer settled cold against Dax's throat and sank to his gut. "Is it?"

"Of course, it is," His brother set the roller in the tin, swaggered to the kitchen, and slapped him on the back. "A little late, but better—"

"You're right. It is too late." His voice cracked and he slammed the empty bottle onto the counter. "I was too late."

"What're you talking about?" His brother placed a comforting hand on his shoulder.

Nothing could comfort.

He'd held the guilt in. On the outside, he'd been the same cocky Dax the world knew. His boss mentioned a psychiatrist, but hadn't forced the issue. His coworkers treated him the same. His friends joked and went out drinking with him last night. Only the denial of accusation from Lexi at the hospital had caused the simmering guilt to boil over. The death was his fault.

He might've been on ski patrol for years, but he'd only ever dealt with sprains, broken bones, and bleeding wounds. Simple injuries. His first death hit hard.

If Lexi or one of the other paramedics on the ski patrol team had been the first on scene, they might've saved the man.

He placed his forearms on the kitchen counter and cradled his head in his hands. "A man died because of me." He couldn't hold it in any longer.

"What happened?" Reed's quiet tone oozed with concern, reminding him of his grandfather's unfailing support.

Dax appreciated how his brother didn't automatically say it wasn't his fault, how he asked for details. This gave him the strength to confess.

"A man had a heart attack on the mountain. I was first on scene." With stinging eyes, he heaved a quivering breath. "I initiated CPR, but...the guy was gone."

His brother opened a second beer. "You tried. You can only do what you can."

Lifting his head, he snagged his brother's beer and took a long pull. "What if my trying hard enough wasn't hard enough?"

"If you did everything at your disposal..."

He rolled his shoulders trying to gather his thoughts without the confusing guilt. "I did everything I could. If I'd been a paramedic I would have had other resources."

"That's why you're applying now." Reed's voice used an *ah-ha* note.

"I should've applied years ago. My boss wanted me to." Dax's body dipped with defeat. "You're right. It is too late."

"It's never too late." His brother's conviction zapped him into action. "Because you never want the situation to happen again."

The zapping gave his backbone strength. His brother was right. Now was the time to do this. To change his life. To get more serious, like he'd promised himself under the avalanche. At twenty-eight, he certainly wasn't getting any younger.

"I'm going to finish the application." Emboldened by the conversation, he took another long swallow of beer. "And you'll be one of my references, right?"

"Best reference ever." Reed wrapped his thick bear arms around Dax's much thinner body. "Come down and say hi to Quinn. Her dance class should be over."

Dax followed his brother down the narrow stairway leading from the apartment to Quinn's Social Dance Club. Quinn opened the studio a few months ago, and had a successful business, catering to kids and adults.

Tonight the class featured adults. Women. Wearing tight leggings and tops of varying colors, they stretched in front of the mirrored wall. Quinn stood out front, with a slightly rounded belly.

He skimmed over the women again and stopped at long legs in skintight black leggings. Her fiery red hair drew him. The strands flowed past her shoulders covering her face. He knew it was Lexi by how his body reacted. His jeans tightened, and heat flared up his skin. Thoughts of their kiss and how he'd love to do more with her, *to her*, spiraled his lust. He couldn't tamp down on this unwanted attraction. Frustration at his reaction tied his conscience in knots.

Class done, Quinn sashayed over and kissed him on the cheek. "Sorry to hear about what happened at work yesterday."

His gaze narrowed, knowing she could only be talking about one thing. "Lexi told you."

Quinn's eyes softened. "Not the details. She said to be nice to you."

"You're nice to everyone." Reed gave his wife a sloppy kiss.

Dax couldn't hold back a smile. The two of them were perfect together. "I'll catch you guys later." He headed to the bench where Lexi was putting on her coat and boots. "Dance class, huh?"

"It's good for stretching your muscles and tendons." Her haughty tone tried to explain something that really didn't need explanation.

"So, you're not doing it for fun." *No surprise there.*

Why was he even interested in her? She was his opposite in almost every way.

She bent down to grab her bag, and he realized some opposites were a good thing. "You should try it for the exercise."

"No way. Quinn already has Reed in the men's dance class." Dax put his fingers on his head and did a silly spin. His charade of pretending to be okay continued. He didn't want to be alone, or go back to the ski patroller's dorm to get caught up in a drinking game. "Have you eaten dinner?"

Her forehead wrinkled. "No."

"Are you meeting Croft?" Dax spit the name.

"No."

"Have dinner with me." He couldn't believe he asked. Only as a friend, and because he didn't want to be alone. She'd said she didn't blame him. He wanted to be sure.

Her mouth started to round with the word no, and his worn-down heart couldn't take the rejection.

"You told Quinn she had to be nice to me, so why aren't you?"

Her blue gaze flashed with what appeared to be guilt. "I…"

"It's just dinner." Hooking her arm through his, he wasn't going to take no for an answer. He walked her to the door.

She opened the door for herself. "Not a date."

"No. Not a date." He held back his disappointment. They had nothing in common. She wasn't his typical type of date. She was quiet and reserved. Structured. Not spontaneous. The other ski patrollers never asked her out for drinks after the resort closed, because she'd never come. And yet, he couldn't stop this strange attraction.

Maybe if he spent more time with her, his body would catch up to his brain and realize they weren't right together.

They strolled down Main Street, her gloved hand tucked in his elbow. The stars shined in the night sky, and the air had turned frigid and sharp. He appreciated the calmness of the atmosphere. No drama like his usual dates, who needed constant laughter and alcohol.

Not that this was a date.

"Where to?" She asked, not insisting they go to a specific place, not being controlling as he'd expected for a rigid rule follower.

"The pub." He crossed the street by the ice cream parlor.

She wrinkled her cute, little nose. Her fresh face with freckles was cherubic—an angel. Except his thoughts about her were anything but holy. "Everyone goes to get drunk at the pub."

"The food is good. Come on, live a little."

Her jaw dropped and her gaze stabbed.

What had he said? Was it his tease to have fun or the word live? She'd been at the hospital twice recently, and both times she'd appeared upset. Was someone she knew having health issues?

If she was worried, fun is what the doctor ordered. And he was the fun physician.

They strolled past the small park and noticed the fresh field of snow. He stopped. "Snow angels."

"What?" Her lips pursed together.

"Snow angels." He placed himself at the edge of the sidewalk with his back to the snow. "Let's make them."

"No." Shaking her head, she stepped back, horror etched on her face.

"It will be fun."

"We'll get soaked, and end up sitting in the restaurant with wet clothes."

"Clothes won't get that wet." He let his body fall backwards and his stomach swooped like being on a carnival ride. Or falling in love. No, he wasn't ready to fall in love. "Come on."

"No."

Before even swishing his arms, he jumped back on his feet. He was going to force her to make snow angels and have fun. He grabbed her around the waist. "Yes."

Her coat slipped through his fingers. "No!" The shrill scream followed by her big grin and thrilled laughter had his stomach swooping again.

He lunged and grabbed her again, bringing her close so they could fall together. Except when her body pressed against his they fit so well. He didn't want to tumble in the snow with her. He wanted to tumble into bed.

Her rich scent surrounded, calling to him. Her eyes softened and desire swirled in their depths. His cock roared in response. Her mouth positioned close to his, all he'd have to do is pucker and they'd be kissing.

Temptation tickled, taunted, and tantalized.

Chapter Four

Blood surged in Lexi's veins and raced to her heart. Dax was going to kiss her. Anticipation shivered across her quivering lips. Fear and desire heated her body. She closed her eyes and moved closer to meet his mouth halfway. Her foot slipped on ice. Falling backwards, she grabbed onto him. "Ahh!"

She tumbled into the snow and took him with her. Landing on her side, she let go of Dax and flipped onto her back. Falling had never felt so good.

Giggling, she raised her arms. "Snow angels it is."

Dax's laughter mingled with hers. The deep rumble surrounded her, resembling a cocoon, keeping her happiness close. Joy spread inside her.

They moved their arms up and down creating the wings while continuing to chuckle. Stopping her movement, she took a deep breath of the cold night air. This was what it was like to be living in the moment. To be alive. This was what her mother wanted for her, and she'd never found it until now.

This was what her mother needed. Not a slow

death, but hope. Even if the hope was slight.

The experimental treatment would cause extreme pain, but if her mom came through successfully on the other side, she'd live. Like a beautiful butterfly emerging from a cocoon, her mom could go on to live life the way she wanted. Gratitude at the realization flushed through her, making her stronger. Dax had given her this gift. With his sunny smile and easygoing disposition, he'd helped her realize the serious choice she had to make.

With natural grace, he got carefully to his feet, trying not to ruin their combined creation. He held out his gloved hand for her, his expression sober for once, as if understanding this moment meant something. The cold air in her lungs exhaled, and she felt woozy. She placed her hand in his, and let him pull her to a standing position. She studied their artistic creation.

Two angels, one taller than the other, with their wings brushing tips. A wing-like sensation fluttered inside her chest. The profound angel images were a visual message. Peace filled her.

She'd agree to the experimental treatment for her mom.

Continuing to hold hands, they strolled toward the pub, both silent. Her head was filled with her mother's advice to have fun and live. She'd struggled to discover the best way to do that with her job, her invention, and her personality. She'd never realized how the concept could be so simple.

As simple as snow angels.

Once inside the restaurant, she sat on the opposite side of a booth from Dax. Excited trembles traversed across her skin. She couldn't believe she was having dinner with him. They'd hung out a few times. He'd introduced her to Quinn and the dance studio. They worked together. She'd kissed him and now he'd almost kissed her. Maybe it was the atmosphere of the private booth, or the sparkling wine they were drinking, or the personal conversation, but tonight seemed special. Maybe it was the moment of contentment they'd shared outside. Something had shifted between them.

"...and the guy falls flat on his face." Dax slammed his palm on the table to emphasize the end of the funny story. His nearly-empty plate jumped on the table and clattered.

Giggles bubbled out of her. It felt good to let go of her thoughts about her mom's illness now that her decision was made, and to forget about the stress of finding a backer for her prototype.

"It's nice to hear you laugh." The sincerity in his voice matched the interest in his gaze.

Her skin tingled. She'd always been tingly around him, which was one of the reasons she'd avoided social situations with the ski patrollers. At work, she was in her element. Socially, she was out of her depth, and his overwhelming presence made her awkward. He didn't have the false charm Andrew had used to put her at ease and catch her off guard. Plus, she was wary of becoming close to any patrollers, because they could find out about her family.

"I laugh." She needed to defend herself.

"Not very often." He angled his chin and studied her. "Or at least, not around me. Why is that?"

Her cheeks heated, and she dipped her head. "I don't know." Except she did. She rustled in her purse to find a distraction, and pulled out the notebook she always carried. Talking about work would get them on a more familiar path. A less stressful path. "I've started a list of new safety equipment we should consider."

Her own invention would be a great purchase for the patrollers. The Henderson Advanced Avalanche Warning Trigger, or HAAWT, could save lives, if they were patrolling and got caught in an avalanche. Too bad it wasn't anywhere near ready. She had a single prototype, and no funding to go forward with production.

He snatched the notebook out of her hands. "You're so serious all the time."

Her stomach clenched, panic slashing through her midsection. He couldn't see her notes about her invention. She snatched the book back. "You're never serious."

Hurt flashed across his face. His gaze narrowed and he contemplated her. "You know what you need?"

"A new dinner companion."

His chuckle at her joke brightened inside her. She'd made him laugh. The only other people she made laugh were her mom and brothers.

He jerked his head down, as if he'd made a decision. "You need fun lessons."

As if a drift of snow knocked her off balance, insult and shock plowed her under. "What are fun lessons?"

"Fun lessons are me exposing you to different kinds of fun." His lips spread into a silly grin.

She didn't move, skepticism hardening her muscles. What exactly was he referring to? Something dangerous or something sexual? Which could be equally dangerous. "All kinds of fun? Sounds risky and time consuming."

He pounded a fist to his broad chest. His green eyes lit with mischief. "It will be a hardship for me." His self-sacrificing expression conflicted with the tease in his tone.

She didn't agree to the deal, or even believe she needed fun lessons. She was curious, however. "What will I have to pay for these fun lessons?" She didn't think he'd ask for money. He didn't know she had money.

Leaning across the table, his gaze captured hers. His eyes darkened, swirling with an unrecognizable emotion. His piney scent surrounded her, tugging her forward. Her mind flew back to their almost-kiss. Her heart beat a little faster. Would he want a kiss? Another romp in the snow? A romp in bed?

Curiosity spiked her anxiety, causing her pulse to race in an uneven pattern. She didn't do casual sex. She'd only slept with Andrew, and that hadn't been anything terribly exciting.

The air between them thickened. Tension sparked off their skin. Sexual tension.

Was he thinking of a similar type of payment?

"O'Donnell!" Bode's voice boomed.

Lexi jerked back in her seat.

Making his way toward the booth, he didn't seem to be able to walk a straight line. She wiped off her warm palms.

"Check this out." Another patroller, Aiden, scootched into her side of the booth, crowding her. He took her unused spoon and placed a peanut in it. Slamming his fist on the end of the spoon, the peanut flew in the air. He nudged her aside and opened his mouth to catch the flying peanut. "Ta-da!"

Trying not to wrinkle her nose, she fake-smiled and moved closer to the wall. If this was the kind of fun Dax was referring to, she wanted none of it. She liked Bode and Aiden. They were good members of the ski patrol team. Some of their shenanigans were questionable.

"Whoa!" Bode puckered his big mouth and leered. "Are you guys on a date?"

Dax's face paled. "No. Not a date."

The emphatic denial caused her head to spin. Was the idea of a date with her so repugnant?

Aiden gaped, his red hair flipping to the side. "Lexi?"

The guy clearly didn't understand why Dax would want to be with her. And obviously, neither did Dax. She wanted to sink under the booth and disappear.

"Yes, Lexi." His defensive tone made it seem as if she needed defending.

So the guys' insults had been real and not imagined. Hurt cascaded through her, even knowing she'd never made the effort to be friends.

"Hey there." She tried not to sound stiff.

Aiden put his long arm around her shoulders. "Lexi never parties with us."

Her body stiffened, and she wanted to escape his cloying scent of beer and smoke. The stench was overpowering, pouring off his body. What had they been up to before coming to the pub?

"She's too good for us." Bode used an exaggerated-and-slurred, snotty tone.

Her hurt multiplied, hitting her while she was down. She tried to keep the smile on her face. Is that what the ski patrollers thought of her? Is that why they rarely invited her out?

Dax elbowed his friend and the jerk winced. "She is too good for you."

His defense of her brought a bit of the earlier spark back. Wait. His words repeated in her mind. Did he think she was too good for him, too? Had she given the wrong impression? She wasn't overly-social out of a sense of self-preservation.

"We're looking for a place to party." Aiden took Dax's beer and drank. "You know the ski patrol dormitory doesn't allow heavy partying."

Bode's square head nodded.

Dax shifted in his seat, appearing uncomfortable. Did he normally enjoy their company when he was out partying? Was he like these guys? Maybe she should've gone to the wild patroller parties and seen him in his element. Her torch for him might've been snuffed.

"You don't need a private place to party." Dax kept shifting his attention between her and Aiden. "I'm sure this place will pick up later."

Aiden pumped his fist in the air. "Hey, Lexi doesn't live in the ski patrol dorms." He swiveled in the booth to pin her down with his stare.

She bit her lower lip.

"Where do you live, Lexi?" Bode leaned toward her, his abundant muscles bulging against his sweater.

Swallowing her panic, she scrambled to think of a good answer. She couldn't say the Croft Mansion. They'd recognize the name, if not the place. In the area surrounding the main streets of Castle Ridge there were a lot of large homes, some lived in permanently, and some vacation homes of the rich and famous.

"Yeah, where do you live?" Dax's eyebrows gathered together. Obviously, he'd never given her home a second thought. Probably because he never thought about her.

Her shoulders slumped lower. She might as well be invisible.

"You're dating her, and you don't know where she lives?" Standing, Bode stuck out his hips in a humping action. "You're not getting anything from her yet?"

Flames swooshed up her body, heating her from the inside out. She couldn't believe how openly they shared intimate details. Mortification and panic baked inside her from the flames. Knowing Bode was a loudmouthed jerk didn't help. If Dax acted like this, even if only hanging out with the guys, she would never have sex with him because she didn't want to be discussed.

Her ex-fiancé had held similar discussions. Discussions she'd overheard, comparing one girl to another. One asset to another. She'd learned she didn't stack up, except for in one category.

"Shut up, Bode." Dax's expression darkened. His mouth flattened, and his gaze narrowed at his friend. He punched his arm.

"Ouch." Bode slapped back. "So much for being my role model."

Boys fighting added a new layer of low to the evening.

Aiden snuggled closer to her. "If you're not with Dax, then—"

"I have a boyfriend." In a panic, she shoved the guy away.

She shouldn't have lied, but she didn't want this guy hitting on her. She didn't want his hands on her.

"Leave her alone, guys." Dax's brow furrowed, resembling dark clouds. "You heard her, she has a boyfriend."

She'd have to think about his expression later. Right now, she needed to get away from the three of them. "I need to meet him, my boyfriend." She put the notebook in her bag and grabbed her coat, and tried to get out of the booth. "Now."

Aiden didn't get the hint.

"Let her out, dude." Dax reached across the table and slapped his friend's arm.

Aiden stood and she slipped out. "Thanks for dinner."

And Dax let her leave. Humiliated and scorned, she shuffled out of the pub, feeling less than womanly. A crack formed in her heart. He must not have thought the night special, because he let her go as easily as removing a temporary tattoo.

Dax was bored of checking off serial numbers with Lexi. They'd been standing in the cramped and cold storage area for an hour. The metal shelves were filled with scratched and dented skis, smelly boots, dirty hanging ropes, stacked safety packs. Who cared if they had one hundred ropes or more? It was mid-season. Patrollers were using equipment. "Wouldn't this be better to do in the summer?"

Lexi paused in the act of shifting first aid kits. She'd been bent over most of the time, and he couldn't help but notice her rounded butt and strong thighs. The room grew hot. He'd known she was good-looking when they'd hung out together as work friends, but she'd always worn an invisible *no trespassing* sign.

Until the first kiss. Then, he'd started paying attention, and liking what he saw.

So had his friends. Anger punched through him at their antics. Bode and Aiden had been a-holes last night. First, barging in on the non-date, then hitting on Lexi. Dax had wanted to ask both of them to step outside, even though it wasn't his place to fight for her honor. She had a boyfriend.

"Doesn't matter. This is what we were told to do." In a stiff, angry voice, she read out another number. She'd barely spoken to him today.

He checked off the number. He'd rather be checking her off or out. Her strong scent pulled him closer, a nicer smell than the mold of the storage room. His conscience caught and snagged. He had to remember Croft.

"How was the date last night?" The question came out surly. He didn't want to really know how she spent her time with Croft, and yet there'd been a need to know. Focusing on her boyfriend would be better than focusing on her perfectly shaped breasts.

"*We* didn't have a date. It was dinner, which was rudely interrupted by your friends." She sounded so prim and proper, and for some reason, Dax wanted to change her tone to wild and wicked.

The challenge ticked in his mind.

"Sorry about Aiden and Bode." Dax had been really sorry. He hadn't wanted the non-date to end. "I meant afterwards. Your date with the rich-as-Midas Croft."

"Oh, that date." She fidgeted with a couple of items on the shelf. Her short, non-polished, perfectly-manicured nails scratched against the metal. "Fine." She read off another number.

Checking off the number on the sheet, Dax shook his head, trying to get rid of this silly attraction. He wouldn't want his girlfriend telling another guy their date was only fine. He'd want grander adjectives. "You'd think a guy with big bucks could make a date better than fine."

Facing him, she scowled. "It's not about money."

Knowing they'd be working in the dirty storage room she wore street clothes, designer jeans that hugged her hips and a fuzzy sweater. Her clothes were expensive. She didn't live at the ski patrol dormitory. She drove a nice car.

"Tell me it's not about money, when your outfit probably cost hundreds of dollars." He scraped by. His parents had been solid middle class, and helped him and his siblings through college. After that, they were each on their own.

"Relationships should never be about money." Her gaze flashed a warning. Had others accused her of being a gold digger?

"You really love the guy?" The question scraped out of his throat. He shouldn't ask questions he didn't want to hear the answers to. With Lexi he couldn't help himself. Interest and lust combined in an irresistible combination. It was a moth to flame—she was the flame, and by asking these questions he was going to get burned.

She shifted and focused on the concrete floor. "I do."

Two simple words that stabbed him.

"Already rehearsing your wedding vows?" His natural sarcasm choked him, because he didn't want to be funny. He didn't want to see her hurt. "Don't count on it with a guy like Croft."

Huffing, she read another number.

"That's not on the spreadsheet."

"Are you sure? I thought I got all the numbers down." She tucked a pigtail behind her ear and he wanted to pull on it to yank her closer.

The innocent hair, the angelic face, the perfect breasts, the long legs and rounded ass, fused into the sublime. The small storage room started to steam. He needed to keep his mind on the task, not on her closeness. She was in love with another guy. He moved to the other side of the table. "You made the spreadsheets?"

She nodded. "I used Chuck's old information and created something we could put on a computer and update yearly."

She'd put a lot of work into their task, while he

hadn't done anything. Typical. "How long did this take?"

"Not long." She truly meant it hadn't taken her long. It would've taken him hours, possibly an entire day.

His siblings were brilliant and accomplished. Reed's symphony career had started right out of college. After the crippling accident, he'd turned his life around to become a remodeler and landlord. Isabel had conquered culinary school and become one of the head chefs at Castle Ridge Lodge. They both had passion.

Dax had nothing. He loved sports and being outdoors. He loved working with people. Being a paramedic was the next logical step. He'd always wanted to make a career out of it, working with firefighters and mountain rescue personnel. He'd had no one to push him forward and back him up. He wasn't ever going to be a doctor or a lawyer or a CEO.

Not wanting to think about his small, worthless goals, he focused back on their conversation. "When did you make the spreadsheets?"

"Last night after dinner."

The protector in him, and only of her, became alert. His muscles tightened. "Did Croft stand you up for your date?" She must've lied about the date being fine.

She tripped on her high-heeled black boots. "No. No. Ryder and I met for a drink. We both wanted to get home early."

Where was home? He wanted to know. He was curious about Lexi. Curious about everything. Where she lived, who she spent her time with, what she did for fun, why she'd been in the hospital twice in the past week. The questions swirled around in his head, making him dizzy. The biggest question dropped in his gut. Why did he want to know all of these things?

"That's how you spend your evenings? Creating spreadsheets?" At least she was being productive. He spent his free nights boozing and flirting.

The fun, partying lost some of its appeal. The glimmer fell away from the fun, exposing a desperation a lot of his friends seemed to have. As if they had to prove they were having the best time.

The realization sizzled through him. His entire life concept tilted and shifted. Having fun and living life fully was important, but staying home and having a quiet evening could satisfy. Couldn't it?

She shrugged and went back to the equipment.

He should've been more insistent on asking her to the ski patrollers' parties. While some of the shine of the parties had suddenly become tarnished, she hadn't experienced them yet. "I'm failing in my fun lessons for you."

Her hand slid off the metal shelf and she swiveled toward him. She bit her bottom lip. "I don't need lessons. I'm perfectly content."

Content wasn't the right description. There was a sadness around her eyes he hated to see.

"To spend your nights working on spreadsheets? Boring." Moving closer, he grabbed hold of her pointy chin. The soft skin was silk against his rough hands. He wanted to see her expression as he teased, see the way her blue gaze softened or dilated based on her reaction.

"I do other things." She jerked her chin out of his grip.

Pinching his fingers together, he tried to hold on to the sensation of her skin. He stayed where he stood, close enough to feel the heat from her body. He was tempted by her warmth. "Like what?"

"Things." She stepped back and bumped into the shelf. Her cheeks colored red.

He was making her flustered, and she was so damn cute. Inventory was getting interesting. "Like?"

"Um, spreadsheets and um...family, and safety invent—" She clamped her lips together.

He felt as if she pinched him. She didn't want to share.

She avoided his gaze, appearing guilty. "It shouldn't matter to you how I spend my nights."

Nights.

The single word shimmied in his head. He'd love to spend nights with her. His cock throbbed, picturing them in bed together. Her strong legs wrapped around his waist. Her fiery-red hair spread across his pillow. He squeezed his eyes tight, trying to stop the picture. She had a boyfriend. He had no right to be thinking of her in that way. And yet, he couldn't help himself. "You're right."

Her body leaned against the shelf, as if she needed to hold herself up.

He focused on the spreadsheet in his hand, trying to take his mind out of the bedroom. Her bedroom. "I wish I could create spreadsheets or be organized." If he got accepted, he'd have to figure out a way to get organized with classes, training, and work. "You should see my room at the ski patrol dorm."

"Messy?"

"My room resembles an avalanche running through it." He wondered what her bedroom was like, and her bed, and what she wore in it. Designer nightgowns or flannel? Both turned him on. "Where do you live?"

Her gaze shifted. "Outside of town." She snatched the clipboard out of his hand. "If I set this form up on my tablet, would you be able to mark it down there?"

Her quick change of subject piqued his interest. He didn't understand why she didn't want to talk about where she lived.

He put one hand on his belly and the other at his head and scratched, doing a poor imitation of a caveman. "Me caveman. Me write on rock."

Her giggle bubbled out of her in a happy glow. The glow shined on him and he chuckled, too. He loved her laugh, and wanted to hear it more often. Boyfriend or not, he planned to continue with the fun lessons.

"Glad to see you two are having fun." Chuck stepped into the room wearing a disapproving expression. "How's the paramedic school application coming, Dax?"

He froze. He'd wanted as few people as possible to know.

Lexi's laughter died. Her mouth dropped open. "What? You're applying?"

Without telling me, was implied. He heard it in her voice.

She probably believed he wasn't smart enough to get in or complete the training. After all, she didn't think he knew how to use a computer tablet.

"It's coming." He'd asked his boss for a reference, and to describe his current ski patrol and EMT position function.

"Good." Chuck gave them a final look before leaving them to get back to work.

Dax's shoulders sagged at his boss' final glance. Chuck must know he was attracted to Lexi. He'd warned him about her and now he'd probably keep a close watch on both of them. Which would be a good thing, because Dax wouldn't step across the line.

"Why didn't you tell me?" Lexi punched him on the arm.

The pain brought him back to reality. He hadn't told her, because he didn't want her to know. He didn't want to be teased if he failed to get in, or dropped out because the course was too difficult. "Don't know."

"I'm a paramedic. I can help you."

He knew what type of help he wanted from her, and it wasn't safety related.

"I know!" Her eyes grew large, and she grinned. "In exchange for fun lessons, I'll help you get organized for paramedic training and help you study."

His mind hazed. She'd gone in the opposite direction of his desire. "Why would you ever want to help someone study?"

"That's what friends are for."

Except maybe he didn't want to be so friendly anymore. Maybe he wanted to be more than friendly. And that was dangerous.

Chapter Five

Laughter shattered through the thin walls of Dax's tiny bedroom in the ski patrol dorm. The dormitory-style housing was one of the perks of being a ski patrol member. If you called living with fifty other people, sharing bathrooms, common rooms, and a kitchen a perk.

He covered his ears and skimmed the same page of the book he'd been studying for the millionth time. The laughter called to him. He wanted to enjoy the evening with a beer and his buddies. But if he wanted to get into the EMT-to-Paramedic transition program, he had to pass the entrance test. He'd been an EMT six years, and a ski patrol member since he'd been seventeen, minus his college years. His experience should count for something. Passing this test would mean he could skip the first semester of classes and enter the program at the end of the month.

Thrusting his immediate desire to have fun aside, he turned the book's page. Studying wasn't his thing. Sitting still wasn't easy. He wasn't brilliant like his siblings. He flipped the pen around in his hand and watched it twirl. Distractions were easy to find.

He'd promised himself he'd become a paramedic, and he refused to give up easily.

The door to his room pushed open, slamming against the edge of the tiny, scratched wooden desk. Dax jumped.

"Dude! There's a party on the other side of this wall." Bode slouched against the desk and handed him a beer.

Dax tossed the pencil at the book, wishing he could stab his friend, instead. "Yeah, I hear." How could he not?

"Reading?" His friend gaped at the book. "You're reading?"

He slammed the book closed, not wanting his friend to see what he was studying. "I do know how, you know."

Bode's forehead scrunched and he angled his head. "Why would you want to?"

Dax didn't. He hated reading and studying and tests. His fingers itched to toss the still-blank notecards across the room. Then, Lexi's serious expression while working on the man on the side of the mountain, flashed. The dead man lying on the cold snow pierced through his mind. Dax had to do this.

Didn't mean he wanted everyone else knowing. They wouldn't support him. "Leave me alone." He pushed against the door and his friend stumbled.

"Chill, dude." Bode's chuckle lingered, as he stepped out the door.

Even Dax's friends didn't believe he was smart.

Setting down the beer, he took another sip of his cold coffee, trying to re-focus. He was doing this for himself and for others. Becoming a paramedic was something he should've done a long time ago.

The hard, wooden desk chair dug into his butt. He glanced at the narrow twin bed, knowing if he tried to study there he'd fall asleep. His eyelids already drooped.

Focus.

He went back to studying the EMT manual. First aid response, assessment of injury protocol, drug reactions, radio procedure.

A familiar love song took him out of his studying. Phoebe's ring. He should've changed the ring tone right after she'd left. Or blocked her. His already-tired muscles sagged. Why would she be calling? He really didn't have time or patience for drama. She meant nothing to him, and to prove it, he answered. "Dax O'Donnell Fan Club. President speaking."

"I want to be your *vice* president." Phoebe's throaty voice and sexual banter used to set his skin on fire. Now, her voice sizzled out.

"What do you want?" In the past, he would've been praying to hear his name. He leaned back in the chair, balancing on the back two legs.

"Do I always want something when I call?" She sounded peeved he didn't immediately jump.

"Pretty much." He waited for her to get on with her selfish request. The awkward silence wasn't filled with sexual tension. And he didn't miss it.

"I miss you," she husked.

He processed the words. In the past, his cock

would've strained against his pants. He would've run to meet her. Gripping the pencil, he snapped the slim wood. He refused to go through an emotional rollercoaster again. He was done, and he didn't have time for her games.

That's all it had been between them. It took him a while to realize the difference. What had he been thinking when he'd hooked up with her? He hadn't been thinking with his brain, he'd been thinking with his cock.

Lexi didn't play games. She was straightforward, and honest. She didn't act like a sex kitten, and that turned him on even more.

"You only think you miss me because you're lonely." Keeping his tone even, he didn't want to be cruel.

The biggest lesson he'd learned in his yo-yo relationship with Phoebe. When she'd lived in Castle Ridge she enjoyed having him around because he was the fun guy and could always make her laugh. That got old. He didn't always want to be a clown. Sometimes, he needed to be cheered up. Sometimes he wanted to be serious.

Like now. Lexi's serious smile flashed in his head. She was always serious. They were complete opposites, and could appreciate each other, help each other. He let the four legs of his chair drop to the ground.

"I really miss you. I need you." The plea in Phoebe's voice didn't twist his stomach.

In the past, he'd believed her. He'd drive all night to get to Utah, and when he arrived, she'd be fine. She'd only wanted him for her amusement. Their relationship had been built on availability and proximity. Now they weren't around each other anymore, he didn't miss or need her.

He firmed his muscles and his stance. "You chose to move." So why should he be paying for her loneliness? Gas, hotels, taking her out for meals.

"I didn't realize how different everything would be."

He picked up the pencil pieces and flung them into the trash. "Different state. Different resort. Different ski patrol team." He couldn't help adding the last point. "Different boss."

He wasn't bitter anymore. She'd met her new boss at a ski industry show in Denver, and they'd had a fling. He'd offered her a job while they'd been in bed together.

"It was a promotion." Her shrill voice hurt his ears.

Promotion to mistress. He stopped himself from saying it. Her boss was married, and had dumped her right after she'd arrived at the new job. "Yeah, right."

"Dax." She chastised him with her tone.

"Stop, Phoebe." He gripped the phone tight, tired of being her go-to guy. "You moved and we broke up. That was your decision." Blowing out a calming breath, he realized the hurt was gone. The yearning was gone. The love, if it ever had been love, was gone. "This toxic, back-and-forth relationship is done. That's *my* decision."

"Thank you, Mrs. Barrington." Ryder winked at the older woman. "Everything was delicious, like you."

Lexi silently giggled. Ryder had been practicing his flirtatious ways with the housekeeper and cook since he was a teenager. The dining room hadn't changed over the years. Same elegant chandelier, same long, polished wood table, same Queen Ann-style chairs.

The woman blushed and tugged at her short, gray hair. "Your charm doesn't work with me, Mr. Ryder."

"Just Ryder." He glanced at Jackson's disapproving expression. "I'm not the formal one in this family."

She stacked their three empty plates from the dinner table. The woman was always moving, reminding Lexi of Dax's similar trait.

"How's your daughter doing in Barcelona?" Jackson's polite question had the woman's eyes lighting up. He wore the suit he'd worn to work, with the tie untied and dangling around his neck.

"Her interior design apprenticeship is complete." Mrs. Barrington beamed with pride and excitement. "Emory will be coming home soon."

The girl was around the same age as Lexi. Emory had gone to college in New York, and taken an apprenticeship with a famous interior designer in Spain. She'd only come home for short breaks.

"I bet *you're* looking forward to that." Ryder tried to keep a straight face.

Lexi swatted him. The girl had been awkward and shy in high school, and the three of them rarely saw her.

"I can't wait." Mrs. Barrington picked up the plates and started to stride out of the room, taking the wonderful smell of steak and roasted potatoes with her.

"The meal was wonderful," Lexi called to the housekeeper's back. "Sorry we were late."

Jackson was late. She had been here on time, like always.

"Couldn't be helped." Jackson's clipped voice told her he understood she was apologizing for him. "What business did you want to discuss?"

He zeroed in, as if he didn't understand how she could possibly have any business to discuss. She bristled. They'd already talked about her mom's health during dinner and agreed on the final experimental treatment plan, so he knew this was a completely separate item.

Taking a sip of red wine, she tucked in her abdomen, fluttering with nerves. Her invention wasn't going to be a Croft product. It was going to a Lexi Henderson idea. She didn't want the family name to influence investors. She did need business advice and contacts.

She glanced at Ryder for encouragement, and when he nodded, she began. "We all understand the danger of avalanches." A jagged pain shot through her lungs, thinking of her dad's death. "One of the biggest concerns is being buried under the snow and suffocating."

"If this is about donating to the ski patrol fund, we always do." With a bored expression, Jackson took out his phone and started swiping. His perfectly-coiffed hair didn't have a strand out of place.

Ryder nodded for her to go on. He was a skier, and he believed in her idea.

She pulled back her shoulders. "There are float

devices that help avalanche victims stay on top of the snow, except many times the skier isn't aware of how bad the avalanche is soon enough. The skier triggers the device too late." She squeezed her sweaty hands together. "I've mentioned how it would be great to have an advanced warning system, and automatic deployment of the float devices."

Jackson continued to type on his phone. "A scientist or engineer could develop the idea."

"No!" Her heart walloped. "It's my idea."

She did not want Jackson handing the idea off to one of his nameless developers, which was why she hadn't given him details. Even now, she held back information. She'd been an engineering major in college, and had been working on her invention for a couple of years. Sketches to CAD drawings to actual production of a prototype.

At his raised eyebrows, she rocked back, trying to appear less defensive. "The invention will be able to sense an avalanche by movement on the ground before the skier does. It will automatically trigger a float device."

"It sounds very theoretical." His skepticism dimmed her hopes.

"Give her a chance," Ryder butted in.

"I've built the prototype. I've tested it in a lab." She'd spent hours at one of their production facilities, using the equipment. She'd kept the process secret.

"I don't have time for this." Jackson never had time. He was always at meetings, or working at his desk. Talk about someone who needed fun lessons. "What're you asking me for? Money?"

Her body went rigid at the attack. Did he believe she always wanted money? Besides living at home, she was self-sufficient. Only lived at home so she could be close to her mother. She paid for her car and insurance. Paid for her clothes. Paid for her minimal social activities.

Guess he was used to always being asked for money, which was sad.

Determination surged through her rigid bones. She didn't want the Croft money or the Croft name. "I need contact information for people who might be interested in investing in my product."

"Not a good idea."

"I only want contact names and numbers."

"Using my name for influence." He set his cloth napkin on the table, giving her a signal he was done. "I pay people to come up with ideas and engineer them. People with advanced degrees and lots of experience."

Her body grew smaller with each word he spoke. She sank into the formal-dining-room chair. Jackson was not her father. He wasn't anybody's father. She might not have experience, but she had an engineering degree. She had a life-saving idea. She owned the patent.

He pushed his chair back and stood. "I'm surprised you're here, Ryder. No partying tonight?"

His mouth broke into a grin. "What a grand idea. One of us has to have a social life."

Shaking his head, her older brother put his phone to his ear while he walked out of the formal dining room, stomping on her hope for leads.

Ryder's grin slipped and he lowered his head, probably feeling as belittled. "Sorry, Lexi. I think it's great. If I'd said as much, Jackson would've thought less of the idea." He stood and tossed the cloth napkin on the table. "Time to do as the always-right big brother said, and find myself a party."

Poor Ryder. His older brother treated him like he couldn't accomplish anything. He acted as if it didn't bother him. She could tell it did. The reason he played the part of a worthless playboy. What was the point of working hard when your older brother had the entire company under control?

Her phone buzzed, and she noted Dax's name on the screen. Her pulse jumped, and she answered.

"I'm not interrupting your spreadsheet development, am I?" His teasing tone started a smile on her face.

"No, we just finished dinner."

"We?"

Shoot. He already thought Ryder was her boyfriend. She didn't want to give the impression they were inseparable. She'd used the imaginary boyfriend to put off his friends and to make Dax believe she wasn't thinking about the kiss, even though she was. "Me and my brothers."

"I didn't even know you had brothers." Dax didn't know her very well.

Which was her fault, for keeping her family a secret. After the way Jackson acted tonight, keeping them secret was a good idea. "Overbearing, overprotective brothers."

Dax's laughter chimed. "I've got one of those, myself. And an older sister."

"I know." She practically knew everything about Dax. She'd been watching him for a while.

"Why were you at Isabel and Michael's engagement party? I didn't realize you were friends."

"We're not. Ryder…" Her brother was working with Vivienne Tucker, who was Michael Marstrand's new agent. Except, she didn't want to talk about Ryder.

"Oh, Ryder was invited, and you were his plus one." Dax's disapproval was obvious even though it wasn't his business.

Her pulse raced faster. Maybe he was bothered by her having a boyfriend. "What's up?"

"I was thinking…"

About me?

"…you should play broomball with a bunch of my friends."

"Tonight?" It was ten o'clock, and she had work to do on the presentation she was putting together for investors. With or without Jackson's help, she was going to move forward. She'd research outdoor-equipment manufacturers and cold-call them, not using the Croft name.

"No, I'm studying tonight." Dax sounded proud. "Entrance exam tomorrow."

"Good for you."

"Too bad there's a party raging outside my bedroom."

The ski patrol dormitory was built similar to a college residence hall. Room after room, with thin walls between them. A lounge area and kitchen in the center. Her older brother had nixed the idea of her living there. Plus, she wanted to be close to her mom.

"Did you want to study here?" She slapped her hand over her mouth. The offer slipped out before she'd thought it through. She did not want him seeing the mansion she lived in.

"Thanks, but I can wear earbuds to block the sound. It's the temptation I'm worried about." His proud tone filled with doubt.

"Oh, you want to go and play with your little friends." She mixed teasing with scorn, hoping to encourage him to stick to the plan.

He laughed, making her smile. "Study tonight. Party tomorrow night."

She nibbled at her lower lip. Would he take his own advice and resist the party?

Chapter Six

Lexi stepped gingerly onto the ice rink wearing gym shoes, not skates. Her muscles tensed at the slippery surface. She gripped the top of the boards surrounding the rink and clung for life. Broomball. What a stupid game. No ice skates, so players slipped more. The only padding she wore was around her knees. The green bib penny she'd slipped on over her sweater matched Dax's and the other players on her team.

The other players slid on the ice, laughing and pushing each other, yet managing to stay on their feet. They were a combination of ski patrollers, and Dax's high school friends. She recognized the ski patrollers, but not the other people. Greetings, high fives, and teasing comments passed between those wearing blue and green jerseys. Even though this was a competition, they were friendly to each other.

Except her. She didn't know any of them socially. Hadn't gone to the local high school. Didn't socialize with the ski patrollers. What had she gotten herself into?

"Do you want a helmet, Lexi?" Dax slid to a stop at her side with confidence, obviously experienced at this game.

Dax wasn't wearing a helmet. Neither was anyone in the group of ski patrollers standing near the goal. In fact, none of the players wore a helmet. Indecision toppled in her veins. She wanted to say yes.

"No." Already the unknown, she didn't want to stand out even more. A risk. She tugged down on her knit cap, hoping it provided protection. "How did you do on the entrance exam today?" She'd been anxious for him all day, hoping he stuck to his plan to study and not party.

"I filled in all the tiny circles." Which told her nothing.

"I hope you didn't fill in *all* the circles." Teasing, she hoped he didn't pick every single option choice, because he would for sure have failed.

He handed her a stick with a plastic triangle on the end. "Here's your broom."

This broom wasn't for sweeping. She held it up and put another tease in her voice. "Broom?"

She'd heard of broomball, understood the basic concept. She'd never seen a game.

He shrugged. "I think in the old days, players actually used real brooms. Nowadays, we have this." He made a sweeping motion with the triangle. "The game is similar to hockey. You use your broom to sweep or push the ball toward your opponent's goal."

Nodding, she noted the size of the other players. Some were quite big. Gigantic, really. Her knees trembled. "Is there checking?" *Like in hockey?*

"Legally?" He chortled. "No. But there will be elbowing." He wrapped both hands around her upper arm, and tugged her away from the boards. Her gym shoes slid easily on the ice. Not a good sign.

"Some of us tend to get a little competitive." His mischievous-boy grin made her forget she was slipping on ice. Her trembling knees stopped for a second, and she wasn't afraid. If he'd smile again, she'd do whatever risk-taking activity he wanted. Her body went loosey-goosey, and she lost her balance. He grabbed her around the waist, and his piney scent made her knees weaker. "Maybe I should sit on the bench."

"No. You're going to be a forward." He dragged her closer to the opponent's goal. "Less running and less chance of getting knocked down."

She softened at his protective action. Or was she positioned there because he thought she couldn't play? Pursing her lips, she was here to conquer, not hide from her fears. This was the perfect opportunity to get to know Dax better, while not being worried about him hitting on her because he thought she had a boyfriend. She was taking a calculated risk. His fun lessons and her goal of being less cautious coincided. "Okaaaay."

Going slowly across the ice, he guided her into position. "You stay in the area between the goal and the post. Try to stay open from the other team's defenders. If someone passes the ball, try to score, or pass it to another player who's open and can score."

"I know how to play normal hockey." Sarcasm snuck out in her words. She didn't enjoy being treated like a kindergartener.

He placed a hand on both of her shoulders and slid in close. His green eyes had tiny black flecks that became more pronounced, the closer he tilted. "Good." The single word pitched sexy.

Licking her lips, she tried to breathe. Was he going to kiss her? Wanting a kiss, she leaned toward him, their mouths only an inch apart. "Good."

A sexy whistle interrupted their stare. "Dax brought a date!"

Her head dropped, more disappointed than embarrassed.

Dax's eyes widened. He slid back and scrutinized her, his buddies, her again. "I told you, it's not a date."

Hurt cracked her skin. Stiffening her lips, she took a step back. He'd denied several times that tonight and the pub night were a date. She shouldn't want a kiss from a man who wouldn't even consider dating her. Of course, he believed she had a boyfriend. Maybe he was being honorable.

Giving her one last look, he ran to his position, dropping down to his knees to slide into place. "Let's get this game going!"

Showoff.

A whistle blew, and everyone ran. She froze, resembling the ice beneath her feet. What should she do?

In the possession of the green team, a pack ran-slid toward her. The group surrounded the orange ball, trying to move it forward. The blue jerseys hurried. They slapped their brooms, trying to take control of the ball.

The ball rolled forward, toward her. Nerves spiked.

The guy leading the pack of blue stood taller and broader than everyone. He was huge. She probably came to his chest. He charged forward, trying to steal the ball from Bode, who was on her team.

Her gaze widened as big as the ball. Her muscles tightened in a fight-or-flight response. She didn't want Bode to pass the ball to her. She didn't want to get creamed.

Bode hit the ball. It cruised toward her.

All the air leaked out of her lungs. Choosing flight, she ran toward the boards, getting out of the way.

The big guy reached in with his broom, and easily stole the ball. Momentum changed. Bode sent her a disgusted scowl. Her body sagged. She had been open, and should've tried to get the ball.

The action went to the other end of the rink. Dax was in the thick of it. His blond head stuck out from the others. A cheer went up from the blue team. They scored.

Dax and an unknown woman faced off in the center. Dax won and swept the ball forward, passing it to Bode. He carried it down toward the goal. Bode glared at her, sending her spirits low. He kept heading toward the net. He shot. The ball was blocked by a defender.

The action continued. First one way, then the other. When the play came toward her, she tried to pretend to be in the action by running on the sides. The green team never passed to her again. The blue team ignored her, not even bothering to defend, because she was no threat.

The players laughed and joked. They pushed and

elbowed. Bode grabbed an opponent's arms and swung her around in a circle. The woman chuckled. Everyone was having fun. Too bad she wasn't included. Aloneness swirled in her belly, digging a deep and lonely hole. Her fault. She stayed closed-off at work, and shouldn't have avoided the ball during the very first play. Her team didn't trust her and she understood why. She was a chicken.

The score was tied, and the clock was running out.

"Lexi!"

She snapped out of her haze.

Dax had the ball and was half running-half sliding. He was being chased by a group of blue-jerseys only a few feet behind him. His arm went back with the broom and swung forward. The broom connected with the ball.

The ball missiled forward.

Toward her.

Her stomach muscles clenched and nausea stirred in her midsection. The other team knew she was useless. She was totally open.

"Get it, Lexi!" Dax tripped and fell to the ice.

She lunged forward as if she could save him. She couldn't.

The ball rolled and slid and rolled, as if in slow motion. She understood how fast it was actually traveling forward. She did the math in her head.

She tightened her grip on the broom, and pushed the plastic triangle onto the ice. Dax had passed her the ball. She had to receive it, and then somehow move the ball toward the goal. For him.

For herself.

To prove she could handle the game and the risk.

The ball hit her broom. Success! The round orange bounced off the triangle and sped back toward the approaching defenders. She couldn't lose the ball after Dax's perfect pass. Making a move to recover, she slipped, lost her balance, and almost fell.

The really tall guy's fierce expression had her shaking in her shoes. The woman who'd been swung around by Bode leaned forward in her run with an expression of grit and steel.

Lexi reached the ball and looked to pass. There was no one. The shaking went from her cold feet to her legs, slowing her pace. She hadn't planned to keep the ball, just retrieve and pass. She didn't want the other team crashing into her while they tried to steal the ball.

She sought out Dax, hoping he'd save her, or tell her what to do. He'd recovered from his fall and was running forward, nowhere near close enough. He waved at her. "Go, go, go!"

Her spine hardened. She couldn't let him down. Sweeping the broom, she pushed the ball forward toward the net. Not too far so it got out of control. She hoped someone from her team would catch up so they could take the ball.

She hit the ball again, and chased after it. She did it again. A small smile snuck on her face. She was actually playing. She hit it a third time.

"Shoot! Shoot!" Dax yelled from behind.

Air caught in her throat. What if she missed?

"Shoot!"

Glancing around, she noted none of her teammates

were nearby. The giant guy was getting closer and closer. If someone didn't take a shot now, he'd steal the ball. There were no other options. She had to take a chance and try to score.

With adrenaline coursing through her bloodstream, she lifted her arm and swept forward with all her strength. The broom came down and missed completely.

The ball sat in the exact same position.

Her head dropped with her spirits. She'd taken a chance and failed.

"Shoot again!" Dax shouted. He was almost beside her now.

His encouragement spurred her on. She had nothing to lose. Except bodily injury. The defenders, including the giant, were nearly on top of her.

Gulp.

She was right in front of the net. The goalie was out of the net. The risk of her missing was slim. Taking a deep breath, she raised her arm back with the broom and swept forward. The triangle brushed the ball.

She held her breath. The ball trickled forward.

And went in.

Her mouth dropped open. Disbelief collided with reality, as shock created a mix of laughter and tears. In jubilation, she jumped in the air.

Dax slid into her, wrapping his arms around her in a celebratory hug. He placed his palms on either side of her face and tugged her toward him. His lips aimed for her forehead.

No, no, no. She wasn't going to accept a celebratory kiss on the forehead. She'd take another risk. Lifting her head at the last second, she let his lips land on her mouth.

When their lips touched, there was a larger celebration within her body. Adrenaline rushed. Sparks flashed. Heat fired. Her mouth melted against his, moved, welcomed. His lips stiffened for a second, probably surprised. Then, he responded with an urgency she'd never experienced. He seemed to want to conquer her, and she loved being conquered.

His mouth attacked, plundering and sending cascades of shivers across her skin. Her lips made a counterattack, each of them taking and giving at the same time. It was as if they'd been thirsty for the taste of each other for a long time, and had finally gotten a sip.

Team members surrounded them, patting her on the head and shoulders. Their kiss was interrupted when players wrapped both of them in a group hug. She was enveloped in the warmth of the group. And while frustrated from the interrupted kiss the bright feeling of belonging made up for the loss.

"Not a date, my ass," someone whispered in the pack.

Before she could react, the group started chanting and jumping. Her body tussled in the mosh pit. The force of their celebration had the group toppling. She was going to hit the ice hard.

"Uh-oh."

Falling, Dax kept his arms around her and shifted her body, cushioning her from the fall. Instead of landing on ice, she landed on his hard body.

And he felt good. He held her against his carved

chest. His strong arms tried to protect her backside, as others fell on top of them. Their legs tangled. Their private parts pressed and mingled. Even with layers of clothes between them, a flame ignited inside her. Ignited a more serious yearning.

The rest of the team dog-piled around them. Everyone was laughing and screaming with happiness.

And she was part of it. Her spirits soared. She was part of the team. Part of their success and celebration. Part of Dax's life.

Dax hadn't meant to kiss Lexi. He'd aimed for her forehead. A celebration, not a sexual move. She'd lifted her head, and when their lips made contact he'd lost control. Her mouth had shaped to his in perfection. Her heat had warmed him all the way to his cold feet.

Earlier, he'd denied this was a date because she had a boyfriend. He had to remember that, too. No matter his own emotions. He didn't make moves on another guy's woman. So not cool.

His gaze skimmed the ice rink's snack-counter-turned-bar-at-night. The two teams talked and joked, expressing no hard feelings about the game. Music played on the stereo system, and a couple of the women danced by a table.

Lexi sat on the other side of the bar, sipping beer out of a bottle using the same lips he'd kissed, giggling at something Bode said. She was loosening up already.

Dax loved her rarely-heard laugh. The way it snuck

out of her mouth. He enjoyed the laugh more when he'd been the reason for the melodic reaction. He enjoyed making her laugh.

Grabbing his beer, he scooted between her and Bode, taking in her rich scent. "Have fun tonight?"

"I did." Her smile started off slow, and bloomed with brightness.

He imagined that's how she'd orgasm. Slow, and then shooting off and alighting his world with an intense fire. He already felt the heat. He needed to stop thinking of her in that way, but for some reason, he couldn't turn those thoughts off.

She pointed with the beer bottle. No wine tonight. "I didn't even know this ice rink had a bar."

"Only open at night."

"I've never been to the ice rink at night." Her expression grew soft. "Just for lessons after school."

He perked up. "You grew up here?"

"From middle school on." Finally, she was talking about herself.

"I don't remember you from high school."

Castle Ridge High School had been medium-sized, with students coming from Castle Ridge, neighboring small towns, and the residents in the mountains. He hadn't known everyone at school, but he would've recognized them.

The muscles in her face tightened. "I went to private school."

"Why?" The local high school had a good reputation.

She clamped her mouth shut and her gaze narrowed, studying him. She seemed afraid to share personal details, which made him want to dig deeper.

"My older brother insisted I go where he went to school."

"You mentioned your brothers on the phone." He was learning so much about Lexi, and he wanted to know more. He yearned to know everything about her. His gut clenched, because interest about her meant interest *in* her.

And she had a boyfriend. He couldn't forget that. He'd only just been burned by Phoebe.

"Two of them." Lexi flared her eyebrows, appearing to force herself to act casual, and then settled the red brows into a line of guilt.

"Two brothers?" He pushed, which wasn't his usual way.

She waved the beer in front of her face. "How long have you known the people who played?"

The swift change in subject verified his earlier suspicion that she was trying to hide something. Curiosity edged higher, but he'd go along with it for now. There were too many other things he wanted to learn about her. "Many since grammar school. Growing up here, you tend to hang out with the same people…"

Her eyes saddened into a cloudy blue.

Gripping his beer tighter, he fought the urge to hug her. "You didn't, though."

She shrugged and avoided his gaze. "Private-school kids live across long distances, so it makes it difficult to get together after school or on weekends."

"What did you do with your free time?" He couldn't imagine not walking to the ice cream parlor after school, or playing in the park.

Her cheeks turned pink. "This and that."

He didn't want to embarrass her. He wanted to figure out what ticked inside her head. As a friend only, to help him be successful at fun lessons. "What kind of this and that?"

"Reading. Science kits. Dorky stuff." Her cheeks went a deeper shade of pink. "So how did your entrance exam really go?"

Another change of topic.

He'd avoided her question earlier with a joke. His normal modus operandi. She seemed to really want to know.

"Good, I think." Doubts jittered in his midsection. He'd never been a great test taker.

She squeezed his shoulder in a reassuring touch. Her touch lit something he couldn't define inside of him. "I'm sure you did great. You're good at what you do."

The compliment obliterated most of his jitters. She believed in him, giving him a burst of confidence. Most of his ski patroller friends didn't. "Thanks."

The noise of the crowd got louder. Cheers and jeers. Bode stripped off his shirt and pants. A girl from the opposing team tossed off her sweater. A flying sweatshirt hit Lexi on the head.

"What's going on?" She twisted on her stool to watch.

"Snow strip challenge." He didn't want to worry about his test, or think about what his interest in a taken-Lexi meant. The snow strip challenge provided the perfect distraction. "Woo-hoo!" He unbuttoned his shirt and tugged it off.

"What're you doing?" She sounded cute and prudish, and he wanted to help her take off her clothes.

But he'd convinced her to play broomball, not strip. "Cooling down." Because the split-second thought of undressing her caused his skin to scorch. He unbuttoned his jeans and wrestled them off his hips. "Come on." He took her hand, and tried to pull her off the stool.

She resisted. "I'm not going to—"

"You don't have to. Just watch."

Playing the game had unlocked her fun side. Drinking beer had her fitting in with his friends and becoming more sociable. But stripping in front of strangers would be pushing her too much.

He led her outside, where people were jumping practically naked into a pile of snow at the edge of the parking lot.

They were screaming and laughing and rolling around.

He pulled off his socks and tossed them at her. Giving her a salute, he jumped into the snow.

Her chuckle followed him, keeping his almost-naked body warm.

Lexi untangled rope in the small storage room of the ski patrol headquarters. Dax was late again. He'd probably caught a cold after jumping in the snow naked last night. She shivered, not thinking about the cold snow, but of his hot body. His broad shoulders and thin waist. His carved abs and flat stomach. His tight butt and muscular thighs. His manly…package.

Fever flushed her face, and she waved the inventory paper in front of her. She'd fiddled with the hem of her sweater, considering joining in on the fun and jumping in the snow. But by the time she got her nerve, the broomball players were getting out and warming up with a shot of alcohol.

Dax had tugged her back in the bar and thrown his clothes on, before downing a fiery shot. His large Adam's apple had moved up and down, and an urge to kiss down his neck had overtaken her. She'd downed a shot, too, to stop the urge. Either she needed to stop thinking those kind of thoughts about Dax, or she needed to make a move.

Her fanciful thoughts froze, when she heard him greeting others in the main room. Trying to appear busy when he entered, she tossed the ropes on the scarred table, before pulling a new bunch from the crowded shelves on the wall.

"How was last night on the fun scale?" Dax slouched against the doorframe, beaming.

The small room was lined with filled shelves. A wooden table centered the room. With the door open, fresh air infiltrated from the front of the office area, clearing out some of the moldy smell.

"Fun. Stupid, but really fun." She'd been happy she hadn't ended up with a hangover, never having done shots.

"Broomball isn't stupid." His eyes blazed with intensity and he spread his legs in a defensive pose, looking like an adorable boy defending his game. "It's the *poor* man's ice hockey."

The emphasized *poor* rubbed against her bruised emotions about wealth versus poverty. "Not the broomball. Jumping in the snow without your clothes on. You could get sick." She'd worried about him last night, even while she'd ogled.

"I'm a fit and manly specimen." He thumped his chest with his fist in a he-man imitation.

She giggled. He had a great sense of humor. And her attraction grew the more she learned about him. She wanted to continue the teasing atmosphere. "Well, most men are stupid." She held her breath, waiting to see if he'd be insulted or understand she was joking.

His laughter filled the cramped storage room, and she slanted against the wall of shelves, letting the vibration weave through her. The loud guffaw followed by a deep rumble. She'd done that. She'd made him laugh. She wasn't known for her jokes or comedic talents. Fear had always paralyzed her witty tongue, except around her family.

"We definitely can be." He faked a fall toward her, and grasped the shelf behind her head. "What's on the safety agenda for today?"

He was so close, his fresh, pine scent surrounded her, as did his arms. She tried to ignore the heat igniting between them. "We're checking ropes for frays and age."

"Stimulating." His voice dropped low and husky in her ear.

A nervous chortle escaped her dry throat. He was so close. His tongue could flick the sensitive skin by her ear. "It's important. Any rope older than five years needs to be thrown away."

"That's ageism." He whispered across her skin.

Quivering, she laughed again. This time, the laugh was breathless.

"I love your laugh." He stared at her, as if memorizing her face.

The stare burrowed deep, like he was digging into the depths of her soul. An answering tug had her leaning forward. She'd love to reveal all, except she had secrets and needed to be independent from her family connections. Nervous, she giggled, imitating a teenager and not a sophisticated adult. Warmth flushed through her. She bit her lip, knowing the women he dated were sexy and composed.

"Chuck is going to wonder if we're working or playing, with the laughter." She hated being the no-fun gal, but they had work to get done, and with Dax so close, she couldn't think straight.

"Okay, ropes." Tilting slightly away, he pulled a rope off the shelf and twisted it around his strong fist. "Anything over five years old goes in the trash."

"And you need to check for frays or damage." She pressed against the shelf, trying to create space. "I have a spreadsheet here to keep track."

"Of course, you do."

She ached before she saw the glint of a tease in his eyes. Everything in her chest lightened. "Once we figure out how many ropes are serviceable, we can decide how many to order."

He tossed a rope into the trash. "Such a waste to throw the oldies but goodies away." He picked up another rope and grabbed her arm. He wrapped one end around her wrist and tied a quick knot. "I could think of some fun things to do with these."

"What would that be?" Her voice came out huskier than intended.

Unless someone walked past the open storage room door, they couldn't see her and Dax. It was a thrilling gamble.

He wiggled his eyebrows and grabbed her other hand. The spreadsheet fluttered to the ground. Going torturously slow, he wrapped the rope around her wrist. The soft nylon slid across her sensitive skin, sending shivers down her arm. The entire time, his gaze captured hers. The emerald green turned dark, sensual. Heat pooled to her center.

Using the rope, he tugged her against his hard body. Her core brushed his manhood and a throb spiraled through her body. She stiffened and nerves swooshed in her stomach. Need combatted with common sense. They were at work and she knew they shouldn't be doing this now.

She pulled her hand. "I need my hand."

I need you.

Her own thought shocked her, as if gripping a live wire. She'd lusted after Dax. In the last few days, her attraction had grown to wanting him. But needing him?

"You're so cute when you blush." He slowly, painstakingly slid the rope off one wrist and her skin felt branded.

Letting her arm drop, she wanted to stroke his hair on the way down. She didn't. She wasn't bold. "Well, um, you might be into that kind of thing. I'm not." She sounded like a total prude, even though every sexual nerve shivered. "What I mean is…"

He took her free hand, unfolded her fingers, and kissed her palm. "I was only teasing."

Sprinkles of lust showered from her palm. She fisted her hand, wanting to keep the feeling, his touch, alive. He'd left her hanging by a…rope.

"The idea is tempting, though." He stepped back, continuing to contemplate her. "With the right woman."

Her heart stuttered, and her knees went weak. He'd never used ropes during lovemaking. The idea became more attractive. To do something original with Dax. Something he'd never done with any other woman. Her stuttering heart flew in her chest, trying to escape her ribcage.

Was he hinting she was the right woman?

Chapter Seven

Dax's entire body felt alive. His blood sung and his skin tingled. Heat flared off Lexi and singed him. He wanted to grab hold of her luscious hair and bend her to his will. A kiss wouldn't be enough. Except he wouldn't steal a kiss. Because he wasn't hitting on her. She had a boyfriend, and this friendly banter was only part of the fun lessons. Part of his charm routine.

But...what if she needed more than fun lessons? What if she needed him?

Her slightly open lips were plump and rosy. Her high cheekbones stained red. Her blue orbs had darkened and swirled with what appeared to be excitement. She was becoming less rigid. Maybe too much.

Why would she react to him if she loved someone else? Maybe Croft wasn't the right guy for her. Dax understood her needs, knew she needed to venture out and have fun. Maybe *he* was the right guy.

His cell phone rang, interrupting his perusal of the wanton woman in front of him.

Not recognizing the number, he answered absently, his sex disappointed, his conscience relieved. He didn't know how much longer he could resist Lexi.

"Wanted to call and let you know you've been accepted into the EMT-to-Paramedic Transition Program."

The words didn't register. "What?" He had to get his mind off Lexi.

"You've been accepted, O'Donnell." Paul's congratulatory voice came over the line.

Dax's muscles tensed and his stomach dropped. This time he understood, and couldn't believe. Excitement burned his throat. He. Couldn't. Believe. It. Paralysis zapped his body. Many of the things he'd studied hadn't been on the entrance test. He'd thought he'd messed up. Disbelief and fear banged in his brain. What if he screwed up?

"O'Donnell?"

He shook himself out of his blizzard of uncertainty. "I'm here." He squeezed the phone harder. "Thank you. Thanks for calling." He hoped he'd still be thanking him in a few weeks. "Thanks for everything."

The program director droned on about the acceptance letter with the details to come. The schedule, the start date, the books and homework.

He couldn't breathe. He couldn't think. He couldn't process. He mumbled another thanks before hanging up. His hand fell from his ear, holding the phone.

"Everything okay, Dax?" Lexi's soft tone centered him, helping him to take in oxygen.

"Yeah, um, yes." He wiped his hands on his jeans trying to get a hold of his mind. "I've been accepted to the EMT-to-Paramedic Transition Program."

"That's wonderful." She hugged him, and her scent surrounded him, bringing more clarity.

He'd been accepted. The program believed in him. Lexi believed in him.

He clung to her tighter, not wanting to let her go. "Is it?"

She leaned back. He kept his arms around her waist, unwilling to let her move away. Her expression narrowed, analyzing him. "Yes. Why wouldn't it be?"

She looked at him. Really looked at him. He hadn't had that type of perusal in a while. His siblings were wrapped up in their lives and expected him not to have any cares. Because that was his persona. His parents were in their own happy bubble in Florida. He didn't want to pop that. His friends weren't all that deep.

Unable to take her knowing perusal, he dropped his arms from around her and stepped back. She frowned, a disappointed-in-him frown.

He hated being the reason for her expression. He missed her warmth and confidence. She was always confident, in herself and in him, when it came to work things. Socially, he was the confident one.

She believed in him and challenged him to try. He needed to at least explain a few of his doubts.

"What if I can't keep up? The homework and studying. The training." He ran shaky fingers through his messy hair. The depth of the commitment hit hard.

"You're going to do fine." She tugged at the hem of her sweater.

"Plus, there's my job on ski patrol." He felt as if he

were skiing in deep powder. "If I had money, I could quit and focus on becoming a paramedic."

Her lips puckered in sourness before she cleared her expression. "You're a quick learner, and you already have a ton of experience for the training." She punched him on the arm. "Even if you don't like hospitals."

The powder got deeper, covering his head. His fear of hospitals punched in his gut. It was her knowledge of the fear that backhanded him on the cheek. "How did you know?"

"When you took your sister-in-law Quinn skiing, and she twisted her ankle and ended up in Emergency."

That's right. Lexi had stopped by to check on Quinn and he'd been there, too. The noises and smells had reminded him of his grandfather's illness. He'd been an impressionable middle-schooler when the old man had gotten sick. The family had visited daily, and he'd seen his grandfather's deterioration. He remembered the tests and treatments being painful, and wondered if the hospital and doctors were helping or hurting the family's patriarch.

When the old man had died, Dax's confidence in his intelligence had died with him. As the third child, his grandfather had been his champion, always believing in him, supporting him and his dreams.

"And when I saw you at the hospital the other day, you were so pale you could've used a doctor."

A green arrow spiked through his chest. The day he'd seen her in Ryder's arms. The spike charred his lungs. She had no right to ask intrusive questions when she had another lover. "Why were you and your *boyfriend*," Dax emphasized the title, "at the hospital?"

Her eyes liquefied into blue pools. She wrung her hands. "My mom is sick."

His anger cooled. He shouldn't have asked in accusation form. "I'm sorry, Lexi." He put his arm loosely around her shoulders in a friendly, comforting gesture. *That was all.*

She blinked and her lips stiffened into a line, obviously trying to pull herself together and not show worry. "Well, the doctors are doing everything they can."

He noticed every little change about her. Her expression, her mood, the lilt of her voice. Never before had he noted every single detail and inflection about anyone. He wished he knew what to say to make her feel better. He hated that he didn't know how to deal with illness and hospitals.

Her lips jerked into a short smile. "We should celebrate your acceptance."

Letting out a relieved breath, he was glad he didn't need to talk about her mom's illness, because he was ill-equipped for this kind of conversation. Better to distract with fun. "I know just the thing."

Cold air seeped between Lexi's facemask and goggles. Snow sprayed to her shoulders, as she took a turn around a large mogul. Swooshing through the deep, backcountry snow, she was overwhelmed at the majesty surrounding her. Besides the occasional ski patrol training session, she never ventured off-resort.

She skied above the tree line near the high peaks and sharp crags. Off-resort. Solitude.

Except for Dax skiing below her. Talk about majestic.

He skied with grace and power and confidence. His hips danced back and forth in black ski pants. His shoulders moved with his hips, a fluid rhythm of motion. Making love with him would be amazing.

Her knee flared, and she lost her balance for a second. She'd been keeping up with him. On groomed slopes, or even powder-filled trails, she'd be his equal. Here, on unmarked paths and unknown territory, she picked a more cautious route, going out wider and looping back around.

Dax went straight downhill.

Thrills trailed her spine and electrified her limbs. She hadn't skied out-of-bounds since she'd been a kid. The thrills short-circuited. Her eyes burned, thinking of her dad. They were skiing in avalanche country. No controlled explosions or patrols. Risks. Lots of risks. Her muscles stiffened, and she almost wiped out.

Pull yourself together. Don't think about Dad.

Dax swooshed to a stop above the tree line. "That was epic."

Her skis chattered to a stop beside him. "Yeah."

With her gaze darting around, she checked for moving snow, crusty crevices, and small balls signaling the beginning of an avalanche. The high crags loomed. The snow appeared to be a dusting. She knew differently. The crevices held feet of powdery whiteness. What could potentially set it loose?

In the tiny storage room, he'd asked her to

celebrate his acceptance into the paramedic program with him with a friendly-ski-not-a-date. The way he'd phrased the invitation had melted any resistance. She'd wanted to go with him, to celebrate with him, to be with him. And she'd been willing to face one of her biggest fears.

He lifted his goggles off his face. "You okay?" Real concern softened his tone, and brought down his excitement level.

She didn't want to be the one to take away his fun. "Awesome." Forcing enthusiasm, she normally didn't use the term. Here, it seemed justified. She was tired of always being overly-cautious, tired of being afraid.

"Ready for a break?" He winked.

Again, she surveyed the area. Her tummy twisted, thinking of the possible awful scenarios. The longer they stayed in backcountry, the higher the risk. "Here?"

"Brought a snack along." He wiggled similar to an excited kid, and she couldn't stop a small smile.

But, the twisting tightened into a knot. She glanced at the blue sky and down toward the tree line. "Um, this isn't the safest place."

He skimmed the area. "In my expert avalanche opinion, this area hasn't seen an avalanche before, we haven't had any new snow to destabilize the slabs, and the snow cornice is small."

His knowledge didn't assure her. "Still."

"Do you think I want to take the chance of getting buried in an avalanche again?" He rubbed her shoulder trying to encourage. "Come on. This boulder is toward the side. We'll be fine."

Even through the heavy layers of clothing, she felt his touch to her bones. She wanted to stay with him. "We could go back to base."

"What fun is that?" He whipped off his backpack.

Fun.

There was that word again. He didn't think she was fun. He was trying to teach her fun. She wanted to show him she could be fun. "Okay. A short break."

He dug his poles in the ground and snapped off his skis, placing them in a position where they wouldn't slide down the steep slope. She did the same. He took out a red vinyl blanket and laid it on a flattish boulder.

Setting out the cheese, bread, and bota bag, he settled himself on one side of the rock, completely at home. "Take a seat."

A radiance lit inside, as if she sat in a single sun streak. He'd prepared a slopeside picnic for the two of them. She had to calm down. He was an expert, and believed they were safe.

She scanned around one more time, letting the majestic view settle her nerves. "It's beautiful here."

Beautiful wasn't even an apt word. The wind rustled the trees below, playing natural music. The green of their needles stood out from the white snow. The bluebird sky made it the perfect day. Or was it the company?

He took out two plastic wine glasses, and poured the wine. He handed a glass to her. "Cheers."

"To you." She raised her glass and clinked against his. "To your acceptance."

The reason she was out celebrating with him. He'd gotten the good news, and this was how he chose to celebrate after shift. She was happy she'd been around to experience this with him. Glad he hadn't asked his friends.

His gaze darkened before he flashed a grin. "Take a sip."

Feeling decadent for drinking wine in the middle of the day, she took a sniff, noting the bouquet. They were off duty, and she didn't need to drive anywhere. She swirled the wine around in her mouth, and swallowed. "Good."

He peered with rapt fascination. "Are you a wine connoisseur?"

"Why do you ask?"

"The way you swirled your glass and took a small sip, tasting properly." He over-exaggerated her actions.

Chuckling at his demonstration, she took a big swallow of the wine. Living with the Croft family had taught her how to taste and appreciate good wine. "I'm not a wine snob."

He broke off a piece of bread and handed it to her, practically hand-feeding her, making her feel even more decadent. "Try the cheese."

She shoved a piece of Brie in her mouth, and followed it up by biting the bread. She didn't want him to think she was uppity. "Good." She purposely talked while she chewed.

His chortle mingled with the breeze, lessening her worries and lifting her spirits. The dramatic scenery, the food and wine, and the company relaxed her in a way she hadn't experienced in a long time.

She reclined against the rock, trying to appreciate

the moment. Appreciate the change in herself. Appreciate being alive. "The skiing is amazing out here."

"Don't you ever ski off-resort?"

The sun dimmed. "No." *Not anymore.*

"Ever?" He stretched out on the rock beside her. His arm brushed hers and she wanted to take hold of his hand, laying so close. "Why?"

He seemed to want to get to know the real her, why she was cautious and not social. Not fun.

There was that descriptor again.

Uncomfortable, she took another sip of wine and swirled the liquid around, hoping it would give her courage. Anxiety brushed inside her stomach, making her heave. It was time for him to know why. She wanted him to understand. "I was caught in an avalanche once."

He lifted his head and tilted on his side to study her. His initial jerk of surprise settled into a concerned expression. Tiny lines formed on his forehead, and his lips flattened. "When? What happened?"

"I was ten." The sun moved behind a cloud, similar to how her life had been lived in a shadow since her father's death. Like the clouds, she'd tried to cushion herself from life. She remembered the turbulent snow, the roaring, the complete and utter silence when the avalanche stopped. Panic had gripped her. She couldn't see anything or find her dad. A renewed panic, one gripping her heart with an iron fist, returned. She forced out the tale. "I was skiing in the backcountry with my dad."

With his glove on, Dax took hold of her hand and squeezed, sensing the terrible end of the story.

She clung to his hand and fought the lump in her throat, fought the tears, fought the memory. "My dad died." Died a few feet from where she'd been rescued.

Dax tugged her into his arms and held her tight. He stroked her cheek, communicating his empathy. "That's why you're so cautious."

The finger caressing her cheek sent fireworks through her body, rejuvenating and warming. The extra heat brought comfort. Even though her dad had died years ago, the sadness flowed through her bloodstream. With Dax's compassion and his touch, he lessened the pain.

She believed he understood her now. Her cautious nature, her solitude. She could be honest with him. "The reason why I was so scared when you were buried in the snow. I couldn't lose you." Sucking down cold air, she waited for his rejection. She couldn't believe she'd confessed her emotions. Well, not outright.

When he felt nothing but sorrow for her. Sorrow for the loss of her father and sorrow for her no-fun attitude.

Biting on her lower lip, she added, "You know, as a friend."

His body stiffened while holding her. She should've left the statement alone. Adding the friend part probably told him the exact opposite. That she had more than friend feelings for him. Worry chafed. She'd ruined the mood of their fun day, and wanted to shift it back.

He still didn't say anything, so she decided to make the mood lighter. "What makes you so reckless?"

The question shook Dax out of his cocoon. He was thinking about her *couldn't lose you* statement, because that's how he felt about her. He didn't want to lose her, even though she wasn't his to hold. She was only a friend. Which she'd made perfectly clear. Except he didn't want to be only friends. He wanted more. His turn to be cautious.

"Me? Reckless?" Using an are-you-kidding voice, he removed his arm from around her to get away from temptation. He didn't want to do something stupid and lose her as a friend.

He lived life to the fullest. Why wouldn't anyone? When his grandfather had been sick the man would complain about how he'd wished he'd climbed Mt. Everest, or swam with sharks, or kissed a pretty girl he'd met on a beach. Regrets. Dax didn't want to die with regrets.

When his parents were busy running his brother to piano lessons or his sister to cooking class, he'd done something crazy to get their attention. Being the third kid in a multi-talented, double-income family was tough. An idiot stunt and a trip to Emergency usually focused their sights on him.

Lexi leaned up on her elbow to watch him. Her red coat was halfway unzipped. "You blow up avalanches for a living." She flicked snow at him.

She made it seem as if his job was stupid, making him bristle. "To keep other skiers safe."

Flicking more snow at him, she giggled. "You ski off-bounds by yourself all the time."

Her laughter made fun of him, and his hackles rose. "I'm safe."

Her eyebrows arched and she gave him a challenging glance.

"Usually."

She flicked more snow at him, this time hitting him in the face. "You jump practically naked into the snow."

"All my friends were doing it." After he spoke, he waited for the typical response. *If your friends jumped off a bridge, would you?* His parents' admonishment from his past streaked in his mind.

"I heard at summer camp you jumped off a cliff into a lake. You were the only one." Not the exact jumping off a bridge response, though close.

"Where did you hear about that?" The question came out in an angry rumble. His past escapades were going to define him forever.

She blushed and ducked her head. "Doesn't matter. It's true."

He sat up and wrapped his arms around his folded knees. Rocking back and forth, he controlled his temper. "I'm not a complete moron."

Which is obviously what she thought. And here, he'd imagined she'd believed in him. Believed he could succeed at paramedic training.

"I take precautions. I knew how deep the lake was, because I'd been swimming there since I was a kid." He didn't want her thinking he was an idiot. "And the day of the avalanche, I checked the weather, the slope rating, and did stability tests." He shifted his body and lay down beside her, ready to end this picnic-interrogation. "Whenever you ski on- or off-piste, you take a risk. What fun would life be, if you didn't take a chance now and again?"

He contemplated her eyes. The dusky blue swirled with uncertainty and interest. He could think of other risks he'd enjoy taking. Like right now. With her.

Her tongue darted out and moistened her lips. Her mouth opened slightly and her gaze softened with passion. She must sense this connection between them.

No risk. No reward.

He leaned into her and pressed his mouth to hers. Slowly, he moved his lips in a teasing-testing action, waiting for rejection. When she didn't push him away, he used his tongue to tempt her mouth open and dove inside. She tasted as good as he remembered. Better. The wine and cheese complemented her natural taste. His tongue tangled with hers, and they began a complicated dance. Sparks ignited between them, electrifying every place they touched. His body heated and he pressed against her.

She arched toward him. "Dax." She murmured his name against his lips.

The way she said his name was a prod. His cock hardened, and he wanted to get naked on the side of the mountain in the frigid temperatures. Which was crazy. "We should stop."

And continue in a bed.

Anger kicked in his gut. He'd acted like a madman. Even knowing the avalanche risk was low, he'd lost all sense of priority. *Always be aware of your surroundings* was a standard backcountry saying. He wouldn't risk Lexi's life by taking additional chances, even if he risked his own.

He gave her a quick kiss. "Our lips might freeze together."

Her smile glowed, warming whatever doubts he'd had about the kiss. Her eyes flashed with something he hoped wasn't guilt. Something about the situation was off. This was super-cautious and super-sincere Lexi. Yet, she didn't act like she had a boyfriend.

He jumped to his feet to get away from her magnetic attraction. He couldn't control himself around her. She tied his priorities and his ethics in complicated knots. "And I forgot about your boyfriend." Acid leaked into his tone. "Guess you forgot about Croft, too."

She gaped resembling a scared rabbit. "It was only a kiss."

Is that what she thought?

Because for Dax, the kiss had been monumental. A turning point in his needs and affection. He wanted her. Had lost himself in her heat. Forgotten where they were, and the fact she had a boyfriend.

Was she playing with his affections? He'd had enough of that with his ex. A lark in her risk-taking adventure? One risk he wasn't willing to take.

Chapter Eight

"Here's the online class syllabus, and the physical in-classroom schedule." Paul, the program director, handed Dax a bunch of papers.

What should've been weightless was lead in his hands. What had he gotten himself into? Boring school. Sitting inside a classroom instead of being on the mountain. Homework instead of partying.

He knew he wasn't dumb. He'd just never been as smart as his siblings, so he hadn't bothered to apply himself.

Paul bent his blond head while he searched in a drawer. He added another sheet of paper to the pile. "This is the training schedule for working with the paramedic teams out of the hospital."

Dax's stomach swirled thinking about the time he'd be spending in the hospital. Bringing patients to Emergency, the various follow-up work, the reports. All things he'd need to do while physically being in the hospital house of horrors.

Once he was a full paramedic on the ski patrol

team, things would be different. There'd still be trips to Emergency, but he wouldn't be at the hospital for hours at a time like while in training.

Patting him on the back, Paul sent him a sunny smile. "We're looking forward to having someone of your caliber on the team, O'Donnell."

Dax snorted. The program director didn't know about his hospital phobia, or his fear of boredom in classes. But he'd love being in charge on the mountain, carrying the right equipment, saving a life. This was his motivation for the program. Get through the training, and he'd be back on the mountain full-time.

Managing a thanks, he stumbled out of the small, cramped office and into the hallway filled with empty gurneys and nursing carts. The smell of rubbing alcohol and cleaning solution overcame his senses. He tried to balance his fears with his wants. Ever since he'd been a kid, he wanted to be a paramedic. He wanted to save lives. He knew he'd hate the training, and the time spent in classes, and the hospital. It would be worth it.

He still remembered when a fire had broken out at his grammar school, and the paramedics had saved his teacher's life. He remembered how hard the paramedics had worked on her after the teacher had saved his and other kids' lives. Combining this desire with his love of the outdoors and skiing was the perfect pair.

An older man lay on a gurney further down the hall, near the Emergency room. The man clasped a little boy's hand who stood by the top of the gurney.

Two adults conversed with a doctor nearby. Melancholy flowed through Dax's veins. The image of the boy and old man reminded him of the time he spent by his grandfather's side, praying the man's life would be spared, that he'd have more time to hear the old man's stories and feel his love.

Halting, he observed. His stomach squirmed with nausea, worse than he'd felt in a long time. Because of the man, or the paperwork in his hand? Even if he could handle the classes, and the homework, and the training, could he handle the hospital?

"Dax?" Lexi's sweet voice floated toward him.

She pulled him out of his funk, righted his stomach, righted his world. Which threw him into a different kind of tailspin. He didn't know what to do about her. Another thing he wanted, but had no right to have. He straightened from the wall, keeping his hand braced for support.

The last time he'd seen her was a perfunctory goodbye after they'd come off the mountain. Guilt about their shared kiss had put him in a foul mood. If anything, she should feel more guilty than him. She had a boyfriend.

The big question: What was he going to do about that? About her?

"Are you okay?" Walking up to him, she placed her delicate hand on his shoulder, and rubbed.

The sensation spiraled against his skin. He pulled himself together, not wanting her to witness his weakness. "Awesome."

"You don't look awesome." She didn't look great, herself. Her eyes were rimmed in red, and her pale skin colored in an unhealthy glow. She wore tight leggings with an oversized sweatshirt. He'd never seen her less put together.

To take the focus off himself, he asked, "What're you doing here?"

"I need to talk to Paul."

Sensing her upset, Dax put an arm around her shoulders, and realized how right it felt. She fit with him. "What's up?"

She bit her shaky lower lip, and seemed to be deciding what to tell him. "I need to schedule time off."

The sick feeling in his stomach returned. "Why? Where are you going? What's wrong?"

"My mom."

The sickness subsided. That's right. Her mom had been sick. Lexi was okay.

"She...she's going to be starting an experimental treatment." She tripped on her words.

Experimental meant serious.

"I'm sorry." He searched for something more to say. Inadequacy stomped on his midsection. Another reason to hate hospitals. He never knew what to say around the sick or the people worried about the sick. "That must be terribly expensive."

Her eyebrows rose so high they almost hit her hairline. Her mouth dropped open, and she stared at him like he was an idiot.

Because he was an idiot. He didn't need to remind her how expensive treatments were going to be, how chances of success were low, how he was a complete imbecile. He slapped his palm to his forward.

"I'm sorry. I'm sure everything will go fine." He sounded stilted, his insecurities displayed in his tone.

"Thanks." Her sad smile ripped him apart. "I gotta go."

With slow grace, she pivoted from him and marched into the program director's office. She walked as if headed toward a firing squad. Here, he'd been feeling sorry for himself when she was going through so much more. So much worse.

He was a heel.

Escaping out of the hospital, he took a deep breath of cold, mountain air and choked when he saw Ryder standing near the exit.

Croft wore torn designer jeans, a nice ski sweater, and matching jacket. His longish-hair was loose around his shoulders. He must've been with Lexi at the hospital.

Coldness traveled through Dax's body, chilling the warmth of her presence away. "What're you doing here, Croft?"

Ryder's surprised expression probably came from Dax's surly question. "O'Donnell, right?"

"Yeah." He felt small beside the wealthy and mighty Croft. The guy wasn't even sure of his name.

"Rude, much?" Putting him in his place, Croft slapped his tailored gloves in one hand.

Dax had been rude. So sue him. He didn't like the guy. Croft was a billionaire playboy who was playing with Lexi's affections. Or was it the other way around? If Lexi liked Croft, why did she kiss Dax with complete abandon?

His heart dropped. He'd seen them both at the

hospital together. Lexi's mom needed expensive medical treatments. Croft was rich. Dax had never been good at math, but the equation started coming together.

The thought tasted bitter on his tongue. She didn't appear to be a gold digger. And yet, what else would explain her reaction to Dax when she dated another?

He had to know. "Why are you at the hospital?"

Croft peered down his superior nose. "I was visiting my mom." His what's-it-to-you tone put Dax in his place.

He'd created this entire unreal scenario of Lexi and Croft in his head. "Sorry, man. I thought..." He couldn't tell him what he thought. "Never mind."

"You're the patroller hanging out with Lexi." Croft seemed more protective than jealous.

That couldn't be right. If Lexi was Dax's girl, he'd worry about her—especially after the kisses they'd shared.

"We're friends." The truth clobbered him, and he wavered on his feet. He wanted to be more than friends. He wanted more than her body and more than a few stolen kisses. He wanted to date, to have a relationship, to be together.

Croft contemplated him. "Good. She's got a lot going on right now between her mother and searching for investors."

Investors? To help fund her mother's medical treatments? If Dax had the type of money this guy did, he'd pay for whatever Lexi's mom needed. He thought of his empty wallet which left a bigger hole in his chest.

Dax didn't need to appear more stupid. He nodded, pretending he knew exactly what Croft was talking about, pretending he knew Lexi more than he actually did, pretending it didn't bother him.

But it did.

Lexi twirled her finger around the condensation on the outside of the glass. Sitting in a booth in the corner, she watched the crowd at the bar at Castle Ridge Lodge, while conversation flowed around. Reed O'Donnell sat at the upright piano, fiddling on the keys, combining notes in unique patterns. His wife sat beside him on the bench, looking adoringly at him. Ex-professional skier Luke Logan stood at the bar with a couple of ski patrollers. Including Dax.

He'd invited her to go out with the ski patrollers as part of her fun lessons, and then ignored her. This fun lesson wasn't so fun.

Dax slanted away from the group to smile at a slim blonde who squeezed in next to him. The woman whispered something in his ear, and his smile grew larger.

Lexi choked on her sparkling water, and set the glass back on the table a little too firmly. The clattering brought the attention of the three female patrollers in the booth.

"Maybe you need something stronger." Heather passed her a full glass. "Especially the way you've been following Dax with your eyes."

Her cheeks warmed and she sank farther into the booth. "Have not."

"Don't blame you." Heather shifted to leer in his direction. "He's nice to ogle."

His jeans hugged a nice ass. His shoulders filled out the ski sweater he wore, and she imagined running her hands across his bare pecs. His hair was tied back in a short ponytail.

"He is not." Lexi crossed her arms, wanting to yank on his hair and drag him out of the bar and away from the woman.

The other two patrollers in the booth tuned into the conversation. Both of their expressions showed disbelief at the statement. The three women laughed.

Lexi wiggled in her seat, wishing she could disappear. They saw through her lie.

Cindy, the woman sitting beside her, tapped her finger on the wood tabletop. "You can't deny his good looks."

"And incredible body." The third girl said it as if she'd experienced his body intimately.

Heat turned to ice in Lexi's veins. She didn't enjoy these women ogling him.

"You know that's Dax's standard operating procedure." Heather's understanding voice tried to comfort. "Flirting is part of his charm."

Knowing this, and watching him flirt with other women, hurt even though it shouldn't. Lexi and Dax were not dating. They'd only shared a couple of incredible kisses she couldn't forget. He believed she had a boyfriend, and after tonight, she wanted him to continue believing. Having a boyfriend was similar to having protection from him making moves. Moves she knew she couldn't resist. She didn't want to be similar to the other women in his life.

Been there, done that.

Andrew had roaming eyes and roaming hands. He didn't have the relaxed charm Dax possessed, though. For Dax, it was part of his personality, a niceness to everyone around him. Andrew had used his cold charm like a snake, mesmerizing his victim and going in for the kill.

Dax's gaze moved from the blonde beside him to a new couple entering the room. At least he wasn't picking up on the woman.

The owner of the lodge, Parker Williamson, and Shey Webber, a woman who'd gone to the same private school as Lexi, walked into the center of the bar, arm in arm. The couple didn't fit together, appearing awkward.

"Lexi!" Shey stopped at their booth. "How are you?"

Surprised, Lexi stared at the woman with the cascading chestnut hair. She'd barely spoken to any upperclassmen in high school. "Um, good."

"How's your brother Ry—"

"He's good." She jumped to standing, in case she needed to cover Shey's mouth. Lexi didn't want anyone to learn the truth about her, especially overhearing it in the bar. She wasn't ready for all the patrollers to know her background. "What're you doing at Castle Ridge Lodge?"

Castle Ridge Resort was a main competitor to the Webber family's controlling interest in another local ski resort. To find Shey on the arm of Parker was similar to a fox and a hound. They were competitors, not partners.

"Excuse us." The ski patrollers got out of the booth and made their way to the bar for a refill.

Lexi relaxed. The last thing she needed was her coworkers learning her real last name and spilling to Dax. Losing her cloak of invisibility might happen at some point. She wanted to be ready for, and control the exposure.

"Parker and I had business to discuss." Shey gave him a short, professional smile. She wore a business suit with high designer pumps. "Parker Williamson, this is Lexi Croft."

Her breath caught and her pulse raced. "Henderson." She glanced around to see if anyone was listening. The Croft family did most of their business in Denver. Her brothers and mom weren't recognizable on sight. "I go by Henderson."

"Oh." Shey's dark eyebrows arched in a confused expression. "Tell your brother I said hi."

After agreeing, Lexi slumped back into her seat and the couple moved away. She let her forehead hit the table of the booth, uncaring what the other ski patrollers thought of her pathetic action. Her cover had almost been blown. Her plan was to keep her identity secret until she had secured financing for her project.

"Was that Shey Webber you were talking to?" Dax picked *that* reason to pay attention to Lexi.

She smashed her lips together and slowly lifted her head, not wanting to have a discussion about the rich, beautiful woman. "Yes."

"How do you know her?" He inclined his lanky body against the booth seat, his hip jutting close to her head.

Confusion about her damned attraction braided with her anger at being ignored. "We went to school together."

"Scootch." Giving her a gentle push, he shifted in beside her in the booth. His push shot instantaneous fire through her. This uncontrollable attraction was going to get her in trouble. She moved, not wanting to have additional contact with him. "Where did you go to school?"

High school was over. He didn't need to know about her past. Although he wasn't interested in her past, he was interested in Shey.

"Highlands."

"Wow!" His eyeballs practically fell out of his sockets. "Expensive school."

"I was on scholarship." Which was true. An academic scholarship she'd earned, and not because of the Croft money. The Crofts might've insisted she attend Highlands, but she'd wanted to make her own way.

Joining the family in middle school had been difficult. She hadn't been raised in the lap of luxury, and never wanted to forget her father and her roots. Her father had taught her to work hard and achieve her own dreams. She wanted to live by his lesson, not accept handouts.

Dax leaned out of the booth. He must be ogling Shey.

Lexi's ribs closed in on her heart. This was ridiculous. "Stop staring. It's rude. Do you like her?"

"She's beautiful." He said it casually, not passionately. "And she's rich. What's not to like?"

Lexi fisted her hands, trying to control the urge to punch him. How could she have fallen for a guy similar to her ex-fiancé? "Don't be an idiot."

He wheeled back around to face her, getting in her space. "Like you're being an idiot over Ryder Croft." Dax's fierce expression ripped into her, shredding through her lungs.

He didn't know what he was talking about, and that was her fault because she'd kept the truth from him. Still, how dare he accuse her of liking Ryder because he was rich?

A dark, foul mood thundered in her head. She remembered the petty and hurtful gossip when her mom had married Stephen Croft. The way the other mothers at Highlands had treated her mom, as if she was beneath them. The way the girls at school had dissed her, because she hadn't been born wealthy. The way the boys had wanted to know her because of her new last name.

Lexi was being smart not to tell people her full name. "I'm not being an idiot."

Dax's lips pursed in a disapproving shape. His gaze narrowed. "Is Croft paying for your mom's experimental treatments?"

As if she'd been slashed and burned, Lexi sank to the bottom of the booth seat. Her bones couldn't hold her body upright because of shock. She'd kept the secret for fear of exactly what he was insinuating about her. "Why would you ask such a thing?"

Of course, the Crofts were paying for her mom's treatments. Her mom was a Croft.

"Because experimental treatments are expensive, and Croft is rich." Dax sneered. His lips twisted together in an ugly line. His green eyes narrowed to tiny, green slits. "You're giving me a hard time for appreciating Shey Webber and her money, but aren't you using Ryder for the exact same reason?"

Freezing, she let each of the hurtful words prick her skin. She hated using the Croft money. Using the name Henderson was one way for her to stay independent. Having a job while developing her product was another. She'd worked hard her entire life. In school. In college. As a ski patroller. On her invention.

Her bones hardened and she sat up straight. She was tired of being judged, which was why she kept her identity secret. She was tired of being used, that's why she told no one about her wealth. If it hadn't been for her mom, she would've moved to another ski town outside of Colorado.

Anger powered through, making her actions jerky and uncontrolled. Grabbing hold of his sweater, she fisted the material in her hands. "Don't you dare judge me based on things you haven't got a clue about."

No clue, because she hadn't told him. Out of fear. Her ex-fiancé's words taunted. *Marry Lexi, use her Croft name to get a high-profile position, invest her money, and dump her in the backwoods of Colorado where she grew up. Never the wiser I was acting the single man in New York.*

Dax placed a hand over her fist and leaned closer,

bringing her back to the present. "If you love Croft, why do you react every time I'm near?"

His quiet tone and caress had her hands un-fisting. She'd acted a maniac. None of this was his fault, except for being interested in other women. And why shouldn't he be? He believed she had a significant other. She let go of his sweater.

Dax refused to let her hand slip from his, possibly afraid she'd run. She tensed, waiting to see what would happen next.

He flattened her palm against his chest, and she felt his heart beating fast. "Why do your eyes go soft when I get close, as if you want to kiss me?"

Her eyes were probably going soft right now. Her entire body went soft. She wanted to *deny, deny, deny* out of fear. She knew the truth was in her expression, and he'd recognized the attraction. She'd been caught in one of many lies, and she wanted to confess.

He tilted his face towards her. His mouth was only an inch away. So tempting. His big, emerald eyes sharpened, trying to pry the truth from her.

"Why, every time we kiss, do you respond with unrestrained desire?"

The question hung in the slight bit of space. Threads of tension wove between them, pulling them closer and closer. She sucked in a sharp breath, right before his mouth locked on hers in a hard, punishing kiss.

His lips attacked hers, as if through assault he could pull the truth from her. And he did.

She responded with an attack of her own, proving his observation true. Threading her hands through his hair, she tugged him closer. She couldn't help responding with passion. Wanting his mouth on hers, wanting his hands on her, wanting his body on her.

He ran his hand up her side and stopped under her arm. She pushed her breasts out, wanting him to make the move, wanting his palm upon one of her most intimate spots. He obliged, cupping her breast through her sweater, using the booth wall as protection from others' glances.

Tingles traveled from her breast, making them ache for his hand to be touching her skin, not her sweater. She arched into him.

Conversation from around them seeped into her consciousness. Glasses clinked. They were in a middle of a crowded bar with people they knew. Her muscles tensed. What was she thinking? Her hand went from clutching his chest to pushing him away. "Stop."

Dax's lips stiffened. He took his hand off her breast and sat back. Swiping his hand across his mouth, his expression turned nasty. "Do you kiss your boyfriend Ryder that way?"

Oxygen seeped out of her lungs. She should tell him the truth. She didn't cheat on people, unlike her ex. But she needed to be sure she could trust him. "Why would it matter to you? You're only kissing me because I'm here."

Dax was a flirt. He'd dated plenty of women, and she'd watched. He wanted to meet Shey Webber. Did he really care about her more than any other woman?

His mouth settled into a stubborn line. "Do you have feelings for Croft?"

"Of course I do. He's..." She bit her lip, unsure

what to say. After Dax's comments about Shey, Lexi wasn't sure how much information to trust him with. If she told him who Ryder was, she'd give up her secret. "He's important in my life."

A compromise.

"Ha!" Dax pointed a sharp finger. "Do you love him?" His green gaze bored into her with intense interest.

Her abs tightened, trying to control her churning emotions. Confusion, fear, insecurity combined in a cocktail more potent than anything they served at the bar. He had no right to question who she kissed and who she loved. They weren't dating, only having fun lessons. She'd had enough of Dax and his accusations about dating Ryder for money. That didn't justify him checking out Shey.

Lexi would tell Dax the truth to put him in his place. "Of course, I love Ryder. He's my—"

A love song blurted from Dax's pocket. His expression morphed from interested to angry, his lips flattening in a red line. Without apology, he slipped the phone out and answered. "What's up, Phoebe?"

Lexi's emotional cocktail had her head spinning. Shots of fury and insult added to the mix, sending flames down her throat. His ex-girlfriend's phone call was more important than their current discussion, proving how important she was to him. Good thing she hadn't told him the truth.

She'd watched his relationship with Phoebe develop. They'd been on ski patrol together. Phoebe had a love-'em-and-leave-'em reputation, and yet she was the only woman he'd ever had a serious relationship with.

The on-again-off-again romance had been awkward between them from the start. Each trying to prove who was more fun and more flirty. It had been a game or a competition.

One Lexi had watched warily from the sidelines.

Using her anger, she shoved on Dax's shoulder, so he'd let her out of the booth. She didn't plan to sit here and listen to his conversation with his ex-girlfriend, or current girlfriend, or whatever the heck Phoebe was to him.

He stood and Lexi slipped between him and the table. Shooting him a final glare, she stalked toward the bar.

When Phoebe moved to Utah, the relationship should've been over. Obviously, it wasn't. Lexi had heard rumors of Dax visiting the woman. The fact they were talking on the phone gave credence to the gossip.

Her heart cracked. So where did that leave her?

She'd been about to tell Dax the truth about her brother, because she thought he'd been acting jealous. She'd been wrong. How could he be jealous when he was still in love with another woman?

Chapter Nine

Dax never should've answered the call from Phoebe. He'd answered because he didn't want to hear Lexi's declaration of love for Ryder Croft. The man had everything. Good looks, great skier, money, and Lexi.

The green shooting through Dax's bloodstream had changed him into a rude monster, and he'd answered the call. Now, he regretted it. He wanted Lexi with a desire he'd never experienced, and was at a loss on how to handle his attraction. If she kissed him with such passion, how did she kiss someone she loved? The fantasy made him hot, almost as hot as he'd been during their explosive kiss in the booth.

Phoebe droned on about her loneliness. He barely listened.

"I'm sorry you're having a difficult time in Utah. You chose to move." He didn't want to be mean. Unfortunately, they'd had this conversation several times. He needed to apologize to Lexi for answering the phone mid-conversation. He'd just been so angry at her confession of love for Croft, and he didn't want to hear her go on about the guy's virtues.

She was currently talking to Heather and Cindy, and it appeared she was saying goodbye. Lexi's long, red hair was tied up in a ponytail, but there was nothing childish about her. She wore a fluffy sweater and jeans, not succumbing to the pressure to dress sexy for a night at the bar. There was nothing fake or phony, either. She was real and honest. What you saw, was who she was. No pretense.

Except when it came to her relationship with her boyfriend. He'd sensed it before, something wasn't right.

"Come for a visit." The invitation didn't tempt.

"No, I can't come for a visit. I'm busy."

Phoebe continued to complain, and he couldn't get a word in. That word being goodbye.

Zipping up her heavy winter coat, Lexi stopped at Shey Webber's table, who was currently sitting alone. They chatted for a few moments, and Lexi pulled out a notebook from her bag and showed a page to the other woman.

Shey indicated the chair, and Lexi set the notebook on the table, unbuttoned her coat, and took a seat.

Phew. He'd be able to apologize, and hopefully continue their conversation. Time to prove to her she should give the two of them a shot. A quiver trembled through him. A shot at what? He knew Lexi wouldn't want a fling. Surprisingly, neither did he. So, what did he want?

"Listen, Phoebe. I've got to go."

"You can't hang up on me." Had he ever realized

how whiny his ex-girlfriend's begging was? "I need to see you."

He kept his gaze on Lexi at the table, as the two women chatted. Shey's expression became more intense, and she nodded a few times, then handed Lexi a business card.

Interesting.

Parker Williamson returned to the table. Seeming flustered, Lexi stood to vacate the man's seat. The two women shook hands, as if it was a business meeting. Turning, Lexi re-buttoned her coat, and put on her hat and gloves. She headed for the door.

An urgency pressed into his gut. He didn't want her leaving, furious at him. The way she'd shoved him to get out of the booth, and the final glare had lanced through him. "I really have to go, Phoebe."

Lexi hit the exit and rounded the corner, passing the lodge's front desk.

"Listen, I got into the paramedic program and I'm going to be busy with school, training, and work." He was tired of Phoebe's needy personality. Always wanting attention.

Unlike Lexi, who didn't want to draw attention to herself. She resembled an unopened gift, tempting and waiting to be unwrapped.

"You can skip a few days. No big deal." Phoebe didn't care about his future. She only cared about herself. Again, he questioned his thinking when it came to her. Sleeping together and dating were one thing, how had he gotten involved in a relationship, with her?

Everything had kind of been assumed. Going home

together after a couple of wild parties, planning to meet after work, hanging out on their days off. Neither of them had asked to be in the relationship.

"I can't. I've gotta go. Bye." He hung up for the final time, unwilling to answer her calls again, and hurried around the corner by the front desk.

Lexi was gone.

With slumped shoulders, he ran outside. The cold air hit his exposed skin. He glanced left and right, not seeing her or her car. She probably didn't want to talk to him after he'd taken the call from his ex. Which he understood. Giving her time might be best. He wondered if Shey could answer a few of his questions.

Going back to the bar, he hurried to her table and took a seat. "Hi, I'm Dax O'Donnell. Friend of Lexi's." He rushed the greeting wanting to get right to the point. This desperation to learn about her was a disease running through his veins. A fevered disease with the only cure spending time with her.

"Lexi already left." The woman was beautiful, with shiny, shoulder-length brown hair.

Too bad he couldn't get his mind off of fiery-red hair and angry, blue-ice eyes.

"Yeah, I saw." He leaned forward as if a co-conspirator. "How do you know Lexi?"

"I went to school with her and her brothers."

Nodding, he pretended he knew about the Henderson boys. "At Highlands."

"Yes." Shey tapped her manicured fingers on the table. "Can I help you with something?"

Which worked with his agenda fine. Despite what Lexi believed, he wasn't interested in her rich friend.

"Lexi and I are on ski patrol together at Castle Ridge Resort."

"Oh." A cautiousness glinted in the woman's gaze. "If you're looking for a position with Webber Resorts, you'd have to talk to human resources."

"No." He searched for the right words to dig for information without letting on how little he knew. "I'm happy where I'm at. Lexi and I are working on the safety committee together."

"Do you see her very often?"

"Almost every day." Or at least he'd like to.

"She forgot this notebook." Shey pointed to the blue, spiral-bound notebook. "And I'm going out of town tomorrow."

"I'll give it back to her." He reached for the notebook.

She slapped her hand on his. "Can I trust you?"

"Trust me?" It was just a notebook. The same one Lexi had taken out at the pub the other night to talk about inventory.

"It's important to her. She'll need it to prepare for the meeting with my father to discuss financing."

Confusion swirled in his mind. He tried not to show his confusion on his expression. Croft had said something similar outside the hospital. Did she need financing to pay for her mother's treatments? Or was this something else, entirely? Dax had accused Lexi of using Croft for his money. The confusion settled in his belly, and he began to sweat.

"Right. The financing." He pretended he knew. He didn't. Instead of things becoming clearer, Lexi became a bigger puzzle.

"So, you know about the HAAWT?"

The temperature in some tropical paradise?

He had no clue. He wanted to find out. "Of course. We've discussed the *hot* several times."

"You'll give the notebook to her tomorrow?" She lifted her hand off the spiral-bound book. "I've got to go. Nice meeting you, Dax."

Waving absently, he flipped through the pages of Lexi's notebook, not thinking about her privacy because it was just scribbles and doodles. He'd probably find information about their safety committee.

Instead, he found pages of notes and sketches. Mostly of ski boots, and ski boots attached to skis, and one of those backpacks with an avalanche flotation device. He went back to the beginning and started reading the notes. Specifications and math equations. Items scratched out and rewritten. He didn't understand most of it. One thing he did understand was, Lexi was smart. His jaw dropped. And not ordinary-smart, but super-intelligent.

So far above his level, he couldn't even comprehend.

He rubbed the pages together with his fingers, knowing he shouldn't continue reading. Positive she'd want this notebook back and unread. Except the needing-to-know-Lexi fever scorched his skin. He opened the book to the first page. In big letters, she'd spelled out: HAAWT.

"Hot?"

He knew she was smart enough to spell the word correctly. His attention caught on the small words scribbled below.

Henderson Advanced Avalanche Warning Trigger.

An avalanche triggered in his brain. "Whaaat?"

He dropped the notebook onto the table. Between the notes, equations, and sketches he'd skimmed, he understood what she proposed. Maybe he wasn't so stupid after all.

That's what the initials stood for. Lexi was developing an avalanche safety device, and from reading through the rest of the notes, her idea was incredible. A device that could've kept him above the snow when he'd been caught in an avalanche.

This invention had the potential to save lives. And make Lexi millions of dollars.

"Where could it be?" Lexi's tummy tumbled. She tore everything out of her bag, and tossed the items on the dining room table. "I had it last night." She rummaged through the empty bag, hoping it had slipped to the bottom. "I showed Shey, so I could get her dad's personal number." She turned the bag upside down, knowing her notebook couldn't be in there. "What if someone finds it?"

"Finds what?" Jackson checked his emails as he drank his morning coffee. He wore a blue, pinstriped suit. His everyday attire.

"As if you care." Her breaths came in ragged puffs. She tossed the bag onto the gleaming dining room table. The fine leather skittered across the shiny wood surface. "My notebook is missing. It has my equations and sketches."

"Maybe it's a sign."

She narrowed her gaze, wanting him in her sights. "You don't believe in signs." Her brother didn't believe in much of anything, except money and business. "Or fate. Or love."

The bottom line was his first and only love. He took calculated risks after researching every possible angle. He didn't do things spur of the moment, and he wasn't a dreamer. He didn't believe in her idea.

She remembered a younger, more carefree Jackson. Before his dad died and he'd left college a semester early. That Jackson had believed in her, had taken risks, had lived.

She might not take risks in her personal life, but with her invention she'd gambled, and she planned to see the Henderson Advanced Avalanche Warning Trigger to production. If she could find the notebook…

"I believe in being honest to the people I care about." He set down his phone for a nanosecond to patronize. "You have no experience with product development."

"Neither did Steve Jobs."

"You should be worrying about Mother." Jackson set his cup on the small china plate a little too hard. The clattering caused her to jerk. "The doctor should be getting the experimental biologic any day now."

Pain surrounded her swollen heart. Her mom would be starting the treatments soon. The day after making snow angels with Dax she'd gone to the hospital and told her mom to go forward. The angels had been a sign.

Mom would be in the hospital for weeks. Lexi's

fingers shook, and she gripped the edge of the table. "I'm going today after work."

The business card was in the notebook. She'd wanted to call Shey's dad first thing this morning and set up an appointment. Lexi wanted her mom to see her invention come to fruition. A jagged pang spiked through her lungs at the idea of living without her mom.

"If I thought you had a chance to succeed, I'd back your little idea." Jackson's bland expression proved he didn't mean it. He wouldn't take a risk on the HAAWT.

Forgetting her notebook, she fisted her hands at her sides. "Little?"

"You have no experience, no capability of producing the product, no way of testing it successfully."

Each of his insults slashed at her pride, and ballooned her anger and determination.

Her little idea had a successful prototype test in a lab. Now, she needed to find the best way to attach the device to a ski or snowboard, and possibly find someone willing to take a big risk to provide real-world test results.

She held onto her temper. Yelling at Jackson would only make him act more superior. "My device will save people's lives." She had to believe in herself. In her product.

"I know you're thinking about your father. He's been gone a long time. It's time to let it go." Her brother stood and patted her head.

The pat initiated boiling in her blood. She wanted to slug him. She wasn't a little girl to be patted on the head and sent to play with her dolls. Or in her case, a chemistry set. She had a great idea and had developed it. She just needed investors to get it to market.

"Yes, it is about my father. It's also about the hundreds of other people who die in avalanches every year." Her heart slammed against her ribcage, thinking about Dax's near miss. "If I can stop one death, my invention will be worth it."

"Go see Mom today."

Wanting to defy him, she spit out, "I told you, I was going after work." She planned to spend time with Mom, especially now the treatment was going to start. That's why she'd asked for the leave of absence from the paramedic part of ski patrol.

Jackson answered a call on his way out of the dining room. He never, ever left the virtual office in his mind. "Have you analyzed the possible merger financial data?"

Shaking her head, she tuned out his phone call and their discussion. He'd refused to rationally discuss her ideas from the very beginning, so she'd developed her prototype without him and without Croft funding. He didn't think her device was worth the risk.

She did. This was one risk she knew was worth making. She'd continue taking gambles to get funding. She'd contact George Webber, and anyone else who might be able to help her. She didn't want Croft funding. Only the name Henderson would be on her invention.

Her phone buzzed on the table and she answered.

"Hey, gorgeous." Her ex-fiancé's voice crawled over the line.

Cringing, she couldn't believe she once thought he

sounded sexy. Or the nickname was cute, when it meant he couldn't be bothered remembering her name, because he had too many other women in his life. "What do you want, Andrew?"

Maybe she should give him a nickname: Gold digger.

"I was meeting with some investors from the ski industry, and I thought of you." His words sent cold shivers down her spine.

The day she'd broken up with him for the final time stuck in her head. She'd been trying on wedding dresses, and Jackson had stopped in. For her older brother to visit a bridal shop, there must've been a major emergency. She hadn't realized at the time the emergency was her life and her relationship. Mid-twirl, he'd blurted out how Andrew had approached him about financing a risky scheme in South America. When Jackson said no, Andrew had threatened to break off the engagement.

She'd flopped onto the ground, with the fluffy folds of white surrounding her. Numb, she'd asked her brother to clarify. Jackson couldn't mean what she thought he'd meant.

He repeated himself, while standing her back on her feet. "I thought you should know what kind of man you're marrying." Her brother hadn't said anything more. He'd pulled her into a hug and let her cry.

Up to that point, every bad incident with Andrew had torn off a small piece of her heart. He'd apologized about comments and gossip, he'd been sorry about cheating, he'd proposed with a five-carat diamond ring. She'd loved him so much, had been blinded by his false charm, she'd stitched the pieces of her heart back together and continued moving forward with the wedding.

But using her to get a deal with her family had been the final black mark.

Why was he calling her now?

"I don't think of you, Andrew." She didn't have time to circle around an issue. "What do you want?"

"I remember talking about an invention you came up with in college for ski safety equipment, and a couple of ski equipment companies are looking for new product development ideas."

She never should've shared her invention with him. Not when it had barely been a glimmer of a thought. Looking back, he'd never believed in her, either. The HAAWT had started out as a class project. The professor had wanted her to contact companies and sell the invention. Andrew had dismissed the idea, saying she'd be too busy being his fiancée. Very nineteen-fifties of him. The first sign making her uneasy.

And yet, he'd been the first man to show any interest in her, and she'd bent to his will. She'd been young, infatuated, and totally inexperienced.

"I hope you didn't blab my invention to a bunch of people." She didn't want others with more financing or the backing of a ski manufacturer to steal the idea and get it into production first. She'd patented the design. That wouldn't stop others from coming up with something similar.

"I'm a finance guy. I know how to keep confidential information."

Quietly, she snorted. "Why would they tell a finance guy they were looking to develop new products?"

"Because they know I hear things. They know I live part-time in Denver, and part-time in New York. I have connections there. They know about Croft Industries."

"I'm not Croft Industries." One of their major fighting points. "My idea does not belong to Croft Industries." Her chest squeezed. Because her brother didn't believe in her. "And it's more than an idea. I've got a prototype."

"Fantastic, sugar."

"Lexi." If he couldn't get her name right, she should hang up.

"Lexi." He emphasized her name. "Would you be interested in pitching the idea to one or two of my investors?"

Her mind calculated. This is exactly what she needed. It was as if fate was stepping in. Andrew might provide the connections she needed to make her project happen. She might not get an appointment for months with Shey's father, or the other contacts she'd made. Jackson's patronizing opinion made Lexi more determined to succeed. And to make her dream happen while her mother lived… "Yes."

"Great. Let's set up a date."

Misgiving sent up a flashing warning sign. "A date?"

"A meeting. I'll be in Castle Ridge in a week."

The misgivings settled in a lump in her stomach. Andrew had been persistent every time she'd broken things off. When she'd caught him cheating, he blamed his friends and alcohol. When she'd confronted him about Jackson's story, Andrew had at first denied. When she'd shown him the presentation as proof, he'd confessed about the pressure he was under to succeed. He'd blamed her for his issues.

But it had been two years. Two years where he'd been working in New York. Two years for him to make business contacts and learn about production and financing. Two years for him to get over their breakup. To mature.

"I thought you said I'd be meeting with investors."

"I need to understand how your idea works. The type of manufacturing facilities you'd need. That type of thing." He spoke slowly, as if explaining to an idiot, when he knew she'd been *summa cum laude*. "Then, I can pick what companies I believe would be the best suited. Call this a pre-meeting."

She reined in her concern. This would be good. He already knew the basics of her invention. She'd patented the idea, so he couldn't steal it and sell it as his own. She could use his contacts in the world of finance as he'd used her last name to get his first big job. She knew how to handle him now.

Setting up a time and place, she disconnected. Now, she really needed to find her notebook.

"Think." She tapped her phone against her forehead.

The phone buzzed again, and she recognized Dax's number. Her pulse jumped. Her reaction to him was so much stronger than it ever had been for Andrew, because her feelings were stronger. In college, she'd been a geeky science girl, and when someone as charming and popular as Andrew had paid attention to her, she'd swooned.

Things were different now. She'd taken the ski patrol job to understand exactly what was needed for her invention. She'd lived at home to be close to her mom and to spend all her money on development of the prototype. She'd matured and grown, and knew her own mind.

"Looking for something?" Dax's teasing tone had become endearingly familiar.

She processed his words and gave a start, wondering if he could read her mind. That would be bad. "Yes. I am."

"It's your lucky day, because I have it."

Tension stretched through her body. "My notebook? You have my notebook?"

"Blue with a spiral."

Her body slumped onto a dining room chair. "Oh, my gosh. Thank you! Where did you find it?"

"Shey Webber had it. She gave the notebook to me."

Relief mode halted and vaulted into jealousy. He'd been with Shey. Lexi felt similar to a bouncing ball, the way he went back and forth between her, Phoebe, and now Shey.

"How badly do you want the notebook back?" His teasing held an edge.

"Quit joking, Dax." She had other things to worry about than petty jealousy. She had no right to be jealous. Biting her bottom lip, she hoped he hadn't opened the book. "The notebook is mine."

"Do you want the notebook enough that you'd go on a date with me?" The edge sliced through her.

"A date?" Her brow furrowed and her head hurt. "Why would you want to go on a date with me?" Lexi couldn't stop the question. Especially since he'd been with Shey.

The woman had glamour, prestige, and wealth. She was nice, too.

"Because you intrigue me, Lexi." His voice deepened into a sensual tug. "With your cautious nature and your ingenious invention."

The first part of his declaration caused her knees to tremble. *She intrigued him?* A thrill slowly moved from her quaking knees and up her spine. Then, her head pounded. He'd read her notebook. He'd seen her secret notes and product details. He probably thought she was ridiculous, like Jackson.

She forced a laugh, trying to make everything seem less important. She needed the notes and drawings to put together her presentation for potential investors. If Dax didn't realize how critical the notes and drawings were, maybe he'd let the issue drop. "Those are silly sketches."

"Doesn't look silly to me. Looks lifesaving."

She caught her breath. He understood her designs and appreciated them. The thrill started again, this time in her head and in her heart. Could he possibly believe in her idea? "Dax. I want the notebook back."

"And I'll give it to you." His obliging tone didn't convince. "Meet me at the apartments above Quinn's dance studio."

The thrills clogged Lexi's throat, and she couldn't breathe. She wasn't sure if she should run, or get a Brazilian wax. What kind of date did he have planned?

Chapter Ten

Lexi forced her feet up the narrow set of stairs leading to the apartments above the dance studio. She'd dressed in professional, black pants and a rounded-collar blouse, topping it off with a soft, gray sweater. Picking what to wear had been an issue, and she'd spent an hour trying on various outfits. She didn't know what to expect from this cloak-and-dagger date.

Dax would never hurt her physically; emotionally, he already had. Not that he knew how she felt about him. How she'd always felt about him. Although between the fun lessons and the kisses he could probably figure out exactly what was going on with her emotions. She was attracted to him.

And more…

Her pulse raced, trying to catch up with her heart. Except this wasn't the time to be thinking about the L word. This wasn't a fun lesson. It was a blackmail date. He held her notebook hostage.

The door on the right was open. Even though Castle Ridge was a safe town, she'd been trained to always lock her doors. Smells of garlic wafted from the apartment. Music filtered down the steps. Reaching the top, she wiped her sweaty hands on her pants. Raising her hand to knock, she stopped.

Dax stood in the kitchen, stirring a large pot. Focused on his task, she had time to really study him. His usually messy blond hair appeared to have been styled. His eyes crinkled, concentrating on whatever he cooked. He wore a gray sweater closely matching her own, and a collared shirt underneath. He'd taken time to dress nice.

For her?

She gasped, and her insides went mushy. This is how it would be to come home to this guy every night. *Whoa.* She couldn't jump that far ahead of herself.

He lifted his head and spotted her. His gaze softened, and a smile lit his face. "Lexi. Come in."

He seemed happy to see her, which caused her insides to twist. She didn't know what to expect. "Hi."

The small kitchen table had been set with candles, and two place settings close together. A vase with flowers sat in the middle of the table. The seduction scene caused the twisting to knot.

"Let me take your coat." He set the spoon on the counter and sauntered toward her.

Not a threatening move, and yet her feet poised to run. She wasn't sure if she wanted to take her coat off. "Where's my notebook?"

"You'll get it back." He placed his hands on her shoulders and she jumped, showing how nervous she was about the evening. She didn't know what to expect, and she liked to know details in advance. "Take off your coat. Have dinner."

"Dinner?"

He hung the coat in the small front closet. "The price to get your notebook back is a date."

What else did he think he'd be taking off of her tonight?

The knot in her stomach tightened, one end pulling with jealousy, and the other end with desire. Conflicted, she didn't know what she wanted. A fling with Dax, or to escape emotionally unscarred. "Why would you want a date with me, when you were with Shey Webber last night?"

His eyebrows arched and he studied her, as if she were a scientific experiment. "You say that like I had sex with her."

"Did you?" She didn't want to know the truth. Better to stay oblivious. And yet, the need to know burned.

"We talked." He poured red wine into two glasses, and held one out. He focused, studying her more. "About you, mostly."

Taking the glass, she twirled away from his contemplation. Had Shey mentioned her money? "Why would you talk about me? I'm not very interesting." Or too interesting. Between her wealth and her invention, Lexi had kept secrets from Dax.

"You're interesting. Especially to me." He grabbed her free hand and spun her back to face him. Lifting her hand to his mouth, he stared the entire time. He pressed his lips to her skin.

Her hand sizzled. Heat rose in her cheeks. The stare

was more unnerving than the kiss. And yet, on the phone he'd said she intrigued him. "Ridiculous."

She avoided his glance, her gaze skimming the apartment. There were books on the coffee table, and clothes in the closet. The kitchen counters had cereal boxes and fruit. Things not needed for a seduction dinner. She didn't spot her notebook. Should she demand her notebook and leave? Sucking in a short breath, she decided she was going to take a chance. Not with Dax pushing her, but because she wanted to see what developed.

She took a sip of wine before trying to make conversation. "I thought Reed and Quinn lived in a house on Pearl Street."

"They do." Dax's smug smirk showed he meant to be ambiguous.

"Who lives here?"

"I do." He spoke with pride.

Nodding, she peered around again, being more observant this time. Besides the paramedic training books, she didn't notice anything stamping the place with his personality. "When did you move in?"

"A couple of days ago." He moved to the kitchen, and lifted the cover to check whatever was simmering on the stove. "I needed quiet if I'm going to study."

She smiled, glad he was taking the paramedic program seriously. "Smart decision."

He put the cover back on the pot, and moved to the couch. "Sit down. I'm not going to bite." He patted the seat beside him. "Yet."

"You must be hungry." Her laugh caught in her throat. "When's dinner?"

"The food can wait." He patted the couch again with a faster action. "We should talk."

Folding her leg beneath her, she sat. Not too close. She had too many questions. "Why did you ask me here?"

His expression grew serious. "It wasn't to seduce you."

Disappointment dropped into the center of her nerves, scattering them in different directions. He'd rather seduce Shey or Phoebe, or any of the other women he was flirting with last night. If he didn't want to seduce her, why did he blackmail her into a date?

"You're disappointed." A teasing grin appeared around his lips.

The jerk.

"Why the secrecy?"

"I figured you'd appreciate the private location since you're *dating* Croft." Dax didn't appear jealous, more like he was digging for information. The way he said dating made it seem he knew it was a lie.

Anxiety ruffled her skin and she shivered. She didn't want to be considered a two-timer. She'd been on the back end of that with her fiancé. Time to confess part of the truth. "I'm not dating Ryder. We never were."

Dax beamed, lighting up his face and eyes. The green color sparkled like emeralds. "I guessed from something Shey said."

"What did she say?" Lexi's muscles tensed. If the woman told her Ryder was her brother she'd die from embarrassment.

"You and Ryder had known each other since you were kids. Your families were close."

She froze, waiting for him to reveal the fact she was a big, fat liar, thinking of denials and explanations in her head.

Dax took the glass of wine from her and set it on the coffee table. Taking hold of her hand, he rubbed his thumb across her skin. "I know you were trying to tell me something about Ryder the other night before we were rudely interrupted."

The quivers Dax's thumb incited stopped. "By Phoebe."

He gripped her hand tighter. "Phoebe and I are done."

"I've heard that before."

His lips pursed together and his gaze focused in an earnest expression. "We truly are over. I don't know what I ever saw in her, especially now I truly see you." His velvety tone caused her heart to melt.

She leaned closer, her resistance fading. "What do you see?"

"I see a quiet beauty." He ran a finger from her chin, across her cheek, to her temple.

His stroke sparked, kindling passion.

He tapped at her temple. "I see an intelligent woman and I appreciate her intellect."

Talk about the way to a smart woman's heart. Andrew had hated when she'd shown how smart she was in front of his friends. She'd always hidden her intelligence, for fear of being out of reach. With Andrew, her brothers, her few friends at school.

"I see a woman who hides behind her efficiency and her lists."

Warmth lit inside her, ignited by his observations. He really did see her for who she truly was. Not because of her money. He liked how she was smart, and he seemed impressed with the HAAWT. He liked her cautious nature, and yet pushed her to be more adventurous. He was good for her. She tilted toward him wanting his caress, his kiss.

"To be clear." He tugged the hand he still held, and she fell against him. Already warm from his words, her body flamed on contact. "You are not dating Ryder, and I'm not seeing Phoebe. So it was okay we kissed before, and it's okay if we do this now."

Dax's mouth came down on hers in a featherlight kiss. And another and another. His touch invoked heat and need and want. She responded, trying to deepen the kiss. He sipped, as if she was a delicate flower, making her feel precious and special. Moaning with need, she opened the seam of her mouth, wanting more than chaste kisses. The fire inside her conflagrated with lust.

Finally, his tongue took the invitation, diving inside. He tasted of spicy pasta sauce, and she wanted to eat him up. She tangled her tongue with his, expressing her desire. They'd established they were both free to kiss and whatever else they decided. Her center throbbed. They were in his apartment. Just the two of them. They could do whatever they wanted. And she wanted. She ran her hands through his hair and trailed her fingers down his neck. She was acting reckless.

Kissing the corner of her mouth, he pulled back. "I do need to know one other thing."

She didn't want to talk. Giving him a pout, she asked, "What?"

"What's your relationship with Jackson Croft?"

She tensed, and her hands stopped their path of discovery. Dax must've found out the truth. Why else would he be asking about her older brother? "Why?"

He pulled out her notebook from beneath the cushions of the couch. "I found his name and number in your book, and wondered why."

"You shouldn't have gone through my notebook." Yanking the book from his hands, she checked to make sure the pages and loose notes were inside. How could she forget her purpose for being here? How could she forget that the notebook had all the details about her invention, her baby?

His chin went down. His eyes watched her, appearing contrite. "I told you, you intrigue me. I want to get to know all of you. The real you."

His words pumped her up, yet guilt poked holes in her happy balloon. If she confessed Jackson was her brother, she and Dax would end up in a deeper conversation, possibly heated, and that would totally ruin the mood. Plus, by reading her notebook, her personal property, how could she completely trust Dax? Now wasn't the time to tell him everything. She needed to keep things simple. "Jackson Croft was someone I was hoping to ask to invest in my—"

"In your HAAWT idea." There was real excitement in Dax's voice.

A familiar alarm rang in her head. She'd been so

protective over the years, for fear someone would steal her idea. She didn't have the protection of a large corporation with a team of lawyers. Just a patent. But Dax wouldn't steal from her. He was excited, and understood what she was trying to do because, similar to her, he'd almost died in an avalanche. "You looked through my notebook."

"Sorry. You're such an enigma, and I hoped the book would shed light on you."

"Why?" Completely baffled, she wasn't sure if she should be angry or scared. A tremble started at the base of her neck, and traveled down her spine. Scared. Because she was hiding something.

"I'm interested in learning everything about you." The open, honest eyes and serious mouth changed the tremble to a tingle.

"Why?"

His lips twitched, making her feel silly. "After that kiss, you don't understand?"

Her silliness faded, and something more grave, more profound, settled in her chest. She shook her head slowly.

His lips flattened. Grew more serious. It was as if he'd taken a leap and didn't know where he was going to land. "I like you, Lexi. Want to spend time with you. Get to know you." He took her hand and drew it to his chest. "And I'm hoping you feel the same."

His heart beat in tune with hers. Rapid and fluttery. Unsure. "I don't know what to say."

He dropped her hand. His expression fell. "It's not a huge commitment." His tone teased, and yet he also sounded disappointed. Was he expecting her to say no? "It's just dating."

"Just dating." Dazed, she repeated. "Dating you."

"That's right."

Everything inside her fit into place. She was willing to take a risk. A risk on Dax. "Okay. Yes."

He gave a wolfish grin. "The fun lessons might be ending, but the real fun has just begun."

Dax couldn't take the anticipation tingling across his skin any longer. Now that the air was cleared, he lunged for his prize. He took Lexi in his arms and held her close. His mouth pressed against hers, not in gentleness, staking his claim.

He wanted Lexi like he'd never wanted anyone before. The thought excited and scared him. He needed to take his time with this precious and skittish woman. Savor everything about their relationship. And make sure she wanted him as much as he wanted her. He'd laid everything on the line, taken a leap of faith about his emotions to win her trust. If she and Ryder had been more than family friends, if she'd been dating him, Dax's actions would be those of a total jerk. He'd decided asking her out was worth the risk. And definitely a challenge.

She sighed against his mouth, and the vibration echoed through his chest and speared his heart. Her flabbergasted expression when he'd stated he wanted to date her gave him pause. How could she not comprehend how beautiful and smart and interesting she was? Who had damaged her confidence in herself?

A rumble of anger shook the mood. He wanted to find the person who'd hurt her, and rough him up. But her body next to his was too enticing. Nothing was on pause now. His body came alive, as her hands tangled in his hair and across his back. She grabbed his butt. His cock hardened, and he pressed into her pliant body, groaning when he made contact at her core.

His hand grazed her breast and cupped the fullness. He wanted to feel her skin against his. Hold her naked in his arms. Just imagining their eventual joining made his head ring.

Ring, ring, ring.

Not his head. It was the kitchen timer. So caught up in their make-out session, he'd forgotten about the boiling water on the stovetop, and the garlic bread in the oven. And he *never* forgot his stomach.

Letting go of her, he gave her one last kiss before speaking. "Dinner is almost ready."

Her expression showed disappointment. He didn't want to stop, either. How was he going to take it slow with her, if they didn't stop now? At least none of their clothes had come off. Yet.

With reluctance, he forced himself to push away. Padding to the kitchen, he tossed in the linguine and checked on the garlic bread in the oven. The sauce had been simmering.

Just like him.

He'd been more than simmering. He'd been steaming hot.

He blew out a breath trying to cool himself down. "Hope you like pasta."

"I love pasta." She stretched on the couch, calling attention to her delectable shape under a preppy outfit.

"Good. Because I don't cook much else. My sister always brought home leftovers."

"Good leftovers, I bet." Lexi picked up both wine glasses and brought them to the table. She moved with grace and style, resembling a model or a debutante. "Thanks for this. It's lovely."

Her compliment slid against his heart. Phoebe always complained, and his other myriad dates he'd never cooked for. A ripple of unease went through him. "You haven't tasted it yet."

He joked when he was nervous. Cooking dinner for Lexi, being alone with her, dating her made him nervous.

Why?

Was it because she was so different than other women he dated? Was it because he generally cared about her? Was it because he was well on the way to falling for her?

Sitting at the small, second-hand table, Dax served. They enjoyed salad, garlic bread, pasta with a spicy marinara sauce, and good conversation. They talked about small town life, ski patrol, and college. Nothing consequential. And yet, every word she spoke seemed important.

They laughed, but not because he was trying to be funny. The laughter was natural and collective. He didn't need to impress or flirt to try and get in her pants. He enjoyed just being with her. A new sensation he didn't want to think about too hard.

"Do you enjoy living here?" She set her fork on the empty plate.

"I haven't been in the apartment long. I've never lived on my own before. It was about time." He stood, stacked the plates, and carried them to the kitchen counter. This was how an adult behaved, and he enjoyed the sensation. "Parent's house to college residence hall, to college apartment with friends, and back here to the ski patrol dormitory."

She picked up the pasta bowl and garlic bread, and followed behind. "Do you get lonely?"

Not if she'd keep him company. Amazing how a quiet evening with Lexi soothed the need to go out and be social. How he enjoyed time with her and her alone. Even when he dated Phoebe, they both wanted to go out and be with other people. That should've told him something about their relationship.

He made quick work of putting the leftovers away, and led Lexi to the living room. "The other patrollers at the dorm didn't understand when I needed to study, or if I was tired and needed to sleep."

Having women in his single room in a small, single bed was difficult, too. Not to mention the thin walls. In his own apartment, he could invite Lexi to stay for the night. Or his life.

He swallowed the thought. No way was he ready for that serious of a commitment. His life was in total upheaval. "Where do you live?"

She swirled around on the other side of the coffee table. Her wide-eyed expression showed panic. "Outside of town." She'd mentioned the generic location before.

Why was she evading his question? A tiny sliver of

concern threaded through him. He'd believed she was honest and open. "Where? An apartment or house? Do you live with a friend?"

She picked up one of his paramedic books and examined the spine. "I live in the family home."

She must not want him to know. Why? He wouldn't become a stalker.

"With your mom and brothers?" Maybe she was embarrassed to not have her own place.

Her stiff smile lifted the corners of her mouth for a second, and then she frowned. "Yes, my brothers. And my mom."

Sadness encased Lexi. She stood frozen in one spot. Her blue eyes dimmed.

"Maybe I can come with you to the hospital to visit your mom sometime." He took a shaky breath, unbelieving he'd made the suggestion. First, he hated hospitals, and second, meeting a woman's mother was practically being halfway to engaged.

Angling her chin, she skewered him with a glare. "Really?"

"I'd enjoy meeting your family." The words settled in his gut because it was true. He wanted to meet her mom and her brothers. He waved her to the couch. "I said I wanted to get to know you."

"But...but you don't like hospitals."

Her resistance had him wondering if she didn't want him to meet her family. She'd met his brother and sister. Was she embarrassed by him? He pushed away the idea, and reminded her he planned to do more with his life. "I've got to get over it, if I'm going to become a paramedic."

She continued to avoid him and the couch by walking around the room. "I can help you get organized for studying."

Another topic changer. She did that a lot.

He went with it, not wanting to rock their very new relationship boat. "What do you mean?"

"Do you have a desk?"

"No."

"We could buy a desk, a corkboard to pin your notes, a whiteboard for scheduling training and assignments due, notebooks." Her voice went faster with excitement.

His head spun. "Whoa." He held up his hands. "I don't have the money to go out and buy stuff." Plus, he didn't know how to use study and organization items. He was a winging-it type of guy. "Speaking of notebooks." He picked up her notebook, surprised she hadn't tucked it in her bag right away.

Hurrying over, she tried to grab the notebook from his hands. "I wish you hadn't read through it."

"I did and what you've described sounds amazing if it works." When he'd originally looked at the notes and drawings he couldn't believe her intelligence. He'd studied the pages last night and been blown away. Impressed. "I've got an idea—"

"Please give it back." She didn't give him a chance to speak.

Probably a good thing. She was too intelligent and his idea probably wasn't a good one. No point in embarrassing himself. Didn't mean he'd give the book right back to her. Standing, he held it above his head. "For a kiss."

She placed her hands on her hips and frowned, contemplating him. "You told me I'd get the notebook back if I agreed to this date."

His shoulders and arms dropped. He didn't want to force her into a relationship. "You're right." He handed the book back.

Grabbing the notebook, she pushed him onto the couch and joined him. "Now that I have *one* of the things I want..."

The titillation in her tone tingled across his skin.

She straddled his waist and came in for a kiss. Her mouth locked onto his as if she'd never let go.

And he didn't want her to.

Chapter Eleven

The doctor held the syringe in the air. "Are you ready?"

The seriousness of the doctor's tone started Lexi's knees quaking. This was the beginning of the treatment which would either cure Mom or kill her. "Are you sure, Mom?"

The family had agreed, and she'd signed the paperwork. She still could back out.

Lexi's throat went dry. The astringent scent burned her nose. The shaking progressed from her knees to her stomach, swirling the meager contents around. This was a huge decision. A huge moment. A huge risk.

Mom lay in the hospital bed with one machine beeping and another monitoring her heart. An IV bag hung from a pole and stuck in her mother's arm. Her pale face had a firm expression. She held Lexi's hand and squeezed. "I've got nothing to lose."

The blood drained from her head and pooled in her feet, making her toes numb. "Time." She refused to cry. She didn't want to upset her mother. "You could lose time."

"Are we moving forward?" The doctor's impatience lined with understanding. He understood the odds.

"Lexi?"

Staring at her mom, her pulse throbbed with extra force. She needed to be brave for her mother. The decision had been made. Lexi nodded.

"Yes." Her mother closed her eyes, her expression peaceful.

The doctor plunged the syringe into the PICC line in her mom's arm. The experimental treatment had begun.

Lexi cringed, imagining the powerful medication streaming through her own veins. Thinking about how she'd feel knowing she lay close to death. Feeling the cancer eating away from the inside, and hoping the invading drug would attack the cancer and not the body.

Her mom was at peace with the decision. Calm. While Lexi's nerves pinged and ponged, imagining one terrible scenario after another.

The doctor noted something on the chart, and gave last minute instructions about side effects. She found it hard to listen and comprehend.

Her mom squeezed her hand again, assuring her, when it should be the other way around. "If the treatment works I'll meet my grandkids someday."

She couldn't stop her lips twitching at the image of small, blond-haired children, with Dax's green eyes and reckless attitude. His kids would be a handful. Not that she was thinking about kids with Dax. Their make-out session had ended before children were even a possibility. "From Ryder or Jackson."

"I see the short smile and faraway gaze." Amusement underlined Mom's tone. "There's a new man in your life."

No wonder Lexi got away with nothing as a teen. Her mom could read her mind.

Deciding to be brave, she risked loving Dax and agreeing to her mom's treatment. In both cases, she needed to relax and enjoy every minute spent with her mom and every minute enjoying Dax. Worrying about what would happen in the future would be for later.

"We're not talking about me." She didn't want to talk about what was happening with Dax. She couldn't define it yet. "We're talking about you."

"I've lived a wonderful life." Her mom sounded upbeat, even though her smile fell. "Losing your father so early hit me hard."

Lexi's heart constricted, causing pain to radiate around her ribs. She couldn't forget the roar of the avalanche or her dad's last minutes. The way his hand had reached for hers before they'd lost contact. She stroked her mom's hand in empathy.

Mom's mouth lifted slightly, and a dreamy expression softened her face. "Marrying Stephen Croft gave me a second chance at love. And two wonderful sons."

Wonderful, but busy. Ryder had disappeared for a couple of days, and Jackson had gone to Denver on business.

Ever since her father's death, she'd lived a safe existence, afraid to venture out of her comfort zone.

She'd buried herself in books. When she'd lost her stepfather, she'd focused on studying and getting into the best college possible. Her eyes prickled. She couldn't lose her mom.

"I'd rather take a risk for a chance to live and see you and your brothers get old." Mom's voice cracked. Her mom embraced life with its pain and heartache.

Lexi didn't want her mom in extreme torture, and yet that's exactly what the doctor initiated. Extreme pain in a risky trade-off for life. She didn't want her mom to die, either. None of those things were in her hands. She had to be brave for her mom. Gathering her inner strength, she pushed the tears away. "We're going to fight this. And we're going to win."

"Where were you all night?" Bode grabbed Dax's ski helmet off the bench of the locker room. "Or should I say, *who* were you doing last night?"

Taking off his equipment, Aiden gave a sexy whistle. They'd gotten off shift, and were done for the day.

Dax didn't approve of Bode's suggestive tone, didn't enjoy how his friend talked about women and casual sex. Dax had never liked the talk, yet he never said anything, and probably should have. If he'd been with Lexi all night, he'd have punched Bode in the face for his slur.

Except Dax hadn't spent the night with Lexi. The way they combusted whenever they were near, he knew he could've convinced her to stay, except he didn't want to convince her. He wanted her to be sure.

He wanted to take things slow, which was odd, but Lexi deserved to be treated different, special.

He finished unbuckling his ski boots and placed them in his locker. "I'm in the process of moving out of the patrollers' dormitory. That's where I was last night."

Sleeping in his own bed, in his own place. Sleeping, cooking, paying rent. He was *adulting*.

Aiden dropped his poles, and they clattered to the ground. "Where?"

"Yes." Bode gave a fist pump. "Party place, people!"

"No." Dax wanted to toss his gloves at his friends. He didn't want to throw a party, he'd moved out to avoid their constant partying. "I moved out to get peace."

"Where to, dude?" Aiden slapped him on the back. Maybe he understood the reasoning.

"I moved to an apartment above Quinn's Social Dance Club on Main Street." Dax's brother had given him a deal on rent.

"Awesome. First party tonight." Bode lifted his hand for a high-five.

Dax didn't return the gesture. "No. No party. I've got paramedic training now, and I've got to study tonight." Surprisingly, saying no wasn't hard. He anticipated a quiet night at home.

His body tensed. Had he ever thought that before? Stripping off his ski pants, he shoved them in the locker, and changed into his paramedic training uniform. The blue pants were so different than the bright-orange of the ski patrol ski pants. Just like he was different. Changed.

He went to slam his locker shut.

Bode stopped him by putting his hand out and blocking the door. "Dude. You're getting too serious on us."

Aiden ran a hand through his bright-red hair. "Yeah, even when you were dating Phoebe you'd party with us. Both of you would."

"No partying. No Phoebe." Dax's spirits lifted. Maybe he'd invite Lexi over tonight for another make-out session. This time he might take things farther. More than his spirits lifted with the thought. He was happy being with Lexi, and he wanted to tell his friends. "I'm actually dating someone else."

"Noooo." Bode grabbed his chest and fell to the ground in an exaggerated fashion.

"That's why you're so solid about school and paramedic training." Aiden stuck out an accusing finger. "It's the girl."

Dax squirmed. Lexi had influenced him, but he wasn't becoming a paramedic for her. He was doing it for himself, and the promise he'd made when buried under the avalanche. He was doing it because of his dream from when he'd been a child.

"Does it matter why?" He slammed his locker shut, and grabbed his backpack.

Bode made whipping noises and Aiden's chuckle followed Dax out of the locker room and the ski patrol headquarters. He didn't care what his two buddies thought. The promise to become a paramedic had been made before Lexi's first kiss. It had been his decision. Not hers.

Arriving at the hospital ambulance base, Dax

clocked in for his first shift with the paramedics. His muscles contracted and tensed. Today was only a ride-along. Within months, this would be his real gig. Paramedic in an ambulance and on the slopes, dividing his time between the two.

He greeted the two men he'd be tagging along with, and they immediately put him to work restocking supplies on the rig. So much for adventure and excitement. Dax held the grumbles inside. He understood the work was necessary, didn't mean checking and filling up tubing, syringes, and sheets was fun. Curbing his energy, he learned to check each piece of equipment. At least a little more interesting of a task.

When the radio cackled, his adrenaline spiked. This was it. A real call.

Following the paramedics, he climbed in between them on the front bench of the ambulance. The sirens and lights went on, and he felt giddy. This shit was about to get real. He'd get a first-row seat on what paramedics did off the mountain.

The close quarters in the ambulance smothered some of his excitement. He was a professional, and had to behave like one. Snow had been falling steadily all day. On the mountain, the flakes added to the pleasure of the environment. On the road, the vehicle slipped on icy streets.

Within minutes, they arrived at the car accident at a highway intersection outside of town. Police had the area blocked and their sirens wailed, adding to the noise. The ambulance driver drove around the barricades and got close to the scene.

A gold minivan was flipped on its roof. His own stomach flipped. A small, red, two-door car's front end was smashed to the dashboard. A third vehicle, a utility truck, had minimal damage to the rear.

Dax wondered how the three vehicles had collided. That wasn't his job. His only job today was observation. Stay out of the way, watch, and learn.

The ambulance driver and other paramedic jumped out of the cab and headed toward the back of the ambulance shouting observations to each other. Dax followed and listened, while at the same time doing his own assessment. One driver in the red car. At least one in the truck. Multiple victims in the minivan.

The paramedics took out the most basic of equipment in what they called a tacklebox. The driver hurried toward the upside-down minivan. The second paramedic headed toward the smashed red car.

"O'Donnell," the second paramedic pointed at the utility truck. "Check on the truck driver."

"Right." Controlling his surprise, he hurried toward the white utility truck's driver's side. This wasn't really action, only assessment. Still, his adrenaline pulsed. He was doing *the* job.

The truck driver sat behind the wheel, not moving. His ashen face muscles were lax. He stared straight ahead in shock. No airbag had been released. No damage to the front end of the vehicle.

Dax knocked on the window. "Are you all right?"

The man didn't answer. Didn't move.

He grabbed the handle and tried to open the door. It was locked.

Pounding on the window, he shouted, "Open the door."

Still no response.

Okay, maybe not a simple triage and assessment. His EMT experience qualified him to administer first aid. Surveying, he noted the ambulance driver worked with the firefighters to remove two victims from the minivan. The second paramedic struggled to extricate the driver of the smashed red car. They were going to need more help.

He signaled one of the firefighters to jimmy the truck's door open. "Don't know what's wrong. He won't respond. I'll be right back."

Unable to do anything until the truck door was open, he grabbed the spine board from the ambulance and brought it to the red car. Not only was he doing the job, he was going to do the job well. "There are two people in the minivan, and I've got an unresponsive victim in the truck. Possibly shock. Should I call in a second ambulance?"

The second paramedic nodded. "Help me get this kid on the board. I did first aid for the lacerations to the head and chest. Not sure about the legs yet. Says he can't move."

Dax made the call and slipped on another set of gloves. Until this point, the adrenaline rush got him through the first-call nerves. He found he could hold his emotions in while focusing.

He got to his knees on the snowy ground by the front door of the red car. The kid's airbag had been cut away, and his shirt slashed open. He wore a collar the paramedic had put on for safety. The teen's lower legs were not visible, because the engine had smashed into the space where the gas pedal and brake were located. The stench of blood and gasoline turned in Dax's stomach. He forced the horror to the back of his mind. He'd seen bad accidents on the mountain; this was on another level.

"My legs! I'm going to be a professional skier. I need my legs," the kid screamed.

The teen's raw agony shot through Dax, as if he'd lost his own legs. He held back a shiver and helped get the kid on the board.

"I've got him. Go check on the truck." The second paramedic instructed.

The truck door was open. The man inside hadn't moved. He was breathing, which was a good sign.

Dax noted his ashen skin. Grabbing his mini-light on his equipment belt, he clicked it on and shined the light in his eyes. No response. He went through his EMT training for assessing the injury.

"Sir. Can you tell me your name?" He hoped the man could communicate verbally.

"Sal." The man slurred his words.

Dax didn't smell alcohol on the man. The slurring could be part of the shock.

Sirens from a second ambulance interrupted the exchange.

"Okay, Sal. Tell me what hurts."

"My conscience." The horrible joke slapped Dax.

He ignored the man's answer. It wasn't his job to assess fault. "Anything else hurting?"

The man didn't appear physically injured. No bumps or bruises or cuts.

"My fault. My fault." Sal placed his hands across the steering wheel and lowered his head. He broke down into tears, exhibiting emotional pain.

Dax sympathized, but he needed to be where his skills were necessary. He quickly explained the situation to a police officer who helped the man out of the car. "He'll need to go to the hospital for observation."

"O'Donnell. Need a hand." The ambulance driver called out from beside the minivan.

A woman lay on a spine board, wearing a collar. Her shirt had been cut away, and bandages were already wrapped around her midsection. A girl sat on the ground nearby.

The ambulance driver pointed his chin at the child. "Girl's arm is injured. You should know how to handle that."

Dax bristled, not sure if he'd been given an insult or compliment. Yes, he knew how to handle broken bones and sprains. He hadn't been playing or observing. He'd been *being* a paramedic.

Taking a small step, he approached the girl, who appeared to be about ten years old. "Hey, there." He slipped off his gloves and put on a new pair. "I'm Dax. What's your name?"

The girl's blue eyes widened, reminding him of Lexi. She probably looked similar when she'd been scared trapped in the avalanche. Stopping a shiver, he focused on his task.

"Can I take a look at your arm?"

The girl nodded, even as she wore a deer-in-headlights expression, and appeared ready to get up and run. He'd seen the expression many times at an accident scene in the mountains. Slow and confident was the best way to handle.

"I'm going to have to touch your arm. It might hurt a little." He took out another glove and blew air into it, similar to a balloon. "Can you hold my friend Five Fingers while I look at your arm?"

Her slight smile was a huge reward.

He started at the shoulder, using a gentle touch. "Does it hurt here?" He moved his fingers down her forearm knowing this wasn't the spot where it was broken, wanting her to get used to his hands. At the shake of her head, he grasped her elbow and moved to her forearm.

She flinched and grimaced. "Ah!"

"It's okay." He held both his hands up. "I'm going to get a sling for your arm. Can you hold your arm completely still while I run to the ambulance?" He dashed to the back of the rig for a sling and blanket, and dashed back. "Okay, we're going to put your arm in the sling, and they'll take an x-ray at the hospital."

Her lips pulled in, and she bit the lower one. "Does it hurt?"

"The x-ray? No." He wrapped the blue sling around her arm and tied the ends around her neck, making sure the arm was high enough. "It's like taking a picture."

"What about my mom?" Her voice wavered as she gaped at her mom, lying on the ground.

"She's going to go to the hospital, too." He wrapped a blanket around the girl.

"Are they going to take a picture of her arm?"

"I'm sure they will." *And a hell of a lot more.*

Based on the time spent with the mother, he knew her condition had to be bad.

The crews loaded the victims into the two ambulances. The first ambulance took the truck driver and the severely injured kid from the red car. His ambulance carried the mom and the girl.

Dax sat in the back, comforting the girl, while the other paramedic monitored the mom's more severe injuries. His adrenaline was spent, yet he couldn't help being amped by the event. The victims would survive. He'd helped the truck driver and the girl, physically and emotionally. Doing his job, actually doing more than he was supposed to as a trainee.

Something solid settled in his gut. A rightness. A knowingness.

Paramedic training was the right choice for him, and dating Lexi was the right choice. He could see his future, their future.

After shift, he tried to call Lexi to tell him about the day. He got no answer. Instead of leaving, he headed to the main reception area of the hospital, thinking he might catch her at her mom's room. The serene, blue walls of the reception area were very different from the sterile, white walls of the Emergency room. The furniture here was living-room quality, and arranged in cozy settings.

He tapped his knuckle on the main lobby's reception desk waiting his turn.

"May I help you?" The gray-haired woman asked.

"Can you tell me what room Mrs. Henderson is in?" He couldn't wait to tell Lexi about his shift.

The receptionist typed on her keyboard. "Do you have a first name?"

He didn't even know Lexi's mom's first name. He had so much to learn about her, and he was looking forward to it. "No."

"There's no one by the last name Henderson."

There was only one hospital in Castle Ridge, and he'd seen Lexi here several times. This had to be right.

His thoughts darkened, and his earlier happiness at saving a life died. Lexi was keeping secrets from him. She rarely talked about her family, and wouldn't say where she lived. He liked her because he thought she was real. But if she was so real, why did she keep her background so mysterious?

Chapter Twelve

"Did your mom remarry?" Dax's question took Lexi out of her concentration.

She tensed, sitting at the small kitchen table where they'd had their first date, and now doubled as his desk. She studied him, in his oversized blue sweatshirt and jeans. "Why do you ask?"

He'd called her in a panic earlier in the day after he'd gotten off his paramedic shift, asking if everything was okay, if she was okay, if her mom was okay. His concern had been sugar in her blood, sweetening her up and making her gooey for whatever he wanted. When he'd asked her to dinner, she couldn't say no.

"I tried to find your mom in the hospital today." He focused on her, making her nerves tingle, and not in a good way. "Trying to find you."

"My mom did remarry, so she has a different last name." The tingles tangled in her belly. She told the truth, yet she was leaving a significant portion out. Before he could ask further questions, she asked one of her own, knowing he'd want to go into detail. "So tell me again about how you helped with the accident victims."

"A training session became the real deal." His expression lit up and he went into specifics. The confidence in his expression made him even more handsome, showing a depth of character he didn't display around others.

Only her.

She warmed inside. "What a great experience."

"The little girl was so worried about her mom." His gaze deepened, expressing concern for the victims, making her heart flow with an intensified longing. "I should check on them at the hospital."

The naturally fun and flirtatious Dax was attractive, but this Dax, the assured and sympathetic Dax, drew her in like snow on the mountain.

He paused and took her hand. "I love how we can talk about this stuff and you understand."

The word love had her pulse dropping. Her mind knew he didn't mean he loved her. "It's great how serious you are."

His chin tilted up. "I am and I like it."

Warmth spread through her bloodstream. The lust she'd felt for the charming rake flowed deeper. He was deeper. And she wanted to demonstrate how much she appreciated this deeper, more complicated Dax. Steadying her nerves, she decided to be bold. Take a risk. Do something different.

"Me, too." She flicked her nail across his palm and trailed her finger up to his wrist. "This confident-serious Dax is a real turn-on." Her voice went husky.

His eyes rounded, and his mouth softened. He stared for several seconds, as if debating what to do. His lips lifted into a goofy grin. "You don't like the fun-loving Dax?"

The grin, normally so attractive, speared through her lungs. Rejection. By changing the mood, he'd pulled the chair from under her, and she floundered. She crossed her arms. "I like all sides of Dax."

"I like all sides of Lexi." He tugged her crossed arms apart and held both of her hands in his. "All sides."

His smooth words ignited sparks across her skin. Not a rejection, more of a delay. She didn't want a delay. She wanted to make a move, wanted him, wanted him to know she wanted him.

She leaned forward and kissed him on the left cheek. "I like this side." She kissed him on the right cheek. "And I like this side." She moved to center, targeting his mouth. "And I like—"

"I did say I had to study tonight." Words raced out of his mouth and crashed into her, knocking her flat.

She'd been rejected again. Maybe he didn't appreciate when the woman made the move.

"I'm so sorry, Lexi." He yanked on her arms, and tugged her from her chair to his. He pulled her onto his lap. His erection poked.

Heat blasted her. She sensed how his body reacted to hers. He certainly wasn't indifferent. "I don't understand." Not wanting to seem less experienced, she hated how she sounded hurt and confused even though she was both.

He gripped her chin and brought her head up. "I'd

love to kiss you and do a million other things with you. I know if we start I won't be able to stop."

A tremble struck deep inside her body. Not of fear, of desire. Of taking a risk and knowing it was right. She wanted to be with him, wanted to make love.

"I don't want you to stop." Even though she whispered, her declaration landed like a shout.

Desire swam in his eyes, changing the color to a deep moss. His nostrils flared. His mouth opened and he licked his lips. "Wow. I want you, too."

Holding her breath, she heard the *but* coming. She didn't know if she could take a third rejection in as many minutes.

"I would love to take you in my arms, and kiss you, and carry you to my bed." His sensual tone barreled through her, resembling a warm hurricane.

She still held her breath, waiting. Her head felt woozy. What if she fainted before he said yes? Or no?

"But..."

There it was. She let out her breath in a slow, steady flow, and braced herself.

"When we come together I want to make it special." He stroked his knuckles down her cheek. "Tonight, I'd feel rushed. I've got studying. You brought your prototype to work on."

The prototype was complete. It was the placement of the HAAWT on the equipment she struggled with. And the presentation. She dropped her head. He'd warned her how much studying he had to do, when she offered to bring dinner. "You're right."

Funny how tonight he'd been the one unwilling to take a risk. With her. Something twinged in her head.

Why was he being careful with her? Because while he might want her, did he want more than a few dates? Or did he care more about her than others? She smothered the short thrill. *Do not jump to conclusions.*

He lifted her chin and gave her a chaste kiss. "Your offer is very tempting." He wiggled in his seat to emphasize his condition.

She got the point and giggled, blowing away any insecurities. "So, you're saying this is *hard* for both of us."

He guffawed, making her feel as if she'd won a downhill slalom. She loved making him laugh, showing him her fun side existed.

"I should get off your lap." She moved back to her own chair.

His expression appeared pained. "Let's finish dessert, and then I really need to hit the books." He took a bite of the brownie she'd brought with the meal. "Let's talk about something non-sexual. Tell me about your brothers."

Her hand stopped halfway to her mouth. She didn't want to lie. "One is in business. I think the other brother is finding himself." If she'd mentioned Ryder was a ski coach and playboy, Dax would figure it out. "This is good." She took a big bite of brownie, hoping she wouldn't need to do much more talking.

"It's weird we've known each other for years, yet we don't really *know* each other."

Not that weird. She tended to keep to herself. Although she knew a ton about Dax because she'd watched him over the years. Knew his family, and had become friends with his new sister-in-law. She knew his parents moved to Florida, and he'd been on the ski patrol since he'd graduated from college. She knew he liked action films and red pandas, and hated hospitals. She could name every woman he'd dated.

Her thoughts tangled in the long list of names. Was she another on the list? "How many women have you had deep conversations with?"

"Good point." His cheeks reddened. "Do your brothers live in Castle Ridge?"

Her lips went numb, unsure what to say. She wanted to trust him. Her past held her back. "Yes."

"Where?"

"I told you, they live in the family home with me." She wanted to be the one woman Dax had in-depth conversations with, just not about her family. At least not yet.

"The family home." He used a staged, uppity voice. "You make it sound like a mansion."

She turned her choke into a cough. *Spot on.* Not compared to some of the other people who'd gone to school at Highlands. Needing a distraction, she pointed at the book on the table. "What kind of studying do you have to do tonight?"

"The clinical stuff is easy. Being an EMT, most of it I know. It's the academics. Chemistry and pharmacology. That's harder for me." He picked up their dessert plates and took them to the sink.

She liked a guy who picked up after himself. Her brothers had been spoiled with maids. Her ex-fiancé expected her to do it. "What was your major in college?"

"Environmental sciences."

Getting up, she took the dishtowel from him and grabbed a plate. She'd already been more of a distraction than he'd probably wanted. Encouraging him to move forward was her plan, not tempting him with other activities. "Let me do the dishes while you study."

With takeout, there weren't many dirty dishes.

He moved around the counter and patted the large bag she'd brought. "How big is the prototype? Looks as if you're moving in."

"I'm not moving in." Blushing, she finished the last dish and put away the plates in the cabinet. Not much in dishes or glasses in the kitchen. If she ever did move in, they'd have to buy a few more things. Startled, she fumbled a plate and caught it between shaking fingers. "I'm working on my project."

He grabbed his books and slouched on the couch.

Avoiding his glance in case he could figure out where her thoughts had flown, she set the large bag on the table. "You study at the kitchen table, or on the couch?" If she'd studied sitting on a comfy couch, she'd be asleep in minutes. "The lighting is terrible."

She'd brought dinner over, and her prototype to work on while he studied. He had to study, and she had to work on her presentation and practical applications. They'd be together, but each accomplishing something of their own.

"This is one hundred times better than at the ski patrol's dorm." He balanced the book on one knee, and a notebook on the other, trying to take notes resembling an awkward scale.

"We need to do something about your studying

conditions." She started to open the bag, and paused.

He'd seen her notes and drawings, not the actual prototype. Even her two brothers hadn't seen the prototype. Her stomach clenched. Studying her sketches was different than seeing the small plastic piece. He'd thought the idea amazing. Would he think the design worthy?

She took out the snow boot and a piece of a ski. She didn't work with the entire ski because of size, although at some point she'd have to run the HAAWT through real testing, under real conditions.

Next, she took out a padded box holding the device. This was it. The moment someone besides the scientists she'd collaborated with would see the actual prototype. Someone who was knowledgeable about skiing, and whose opinion she trusted. Because she did trust him. Trusted his opinion. She flipped the lid.

His jaw dropped. "Wow. It works?"

She straightened her shoulders. She was proud of her accomplishment, and believed in the device. "In labs."

The idea for the HAAWT had started in her college engineering lab. The original mechanism and drawings had been vetted by her professor. It was the practical application she'd struggled with for the last couple of years, spending her free time doing research, talking to expert seismographers, and working with 3D printing.

"I understood the basic concept from your notes, but how does it work?" Jumping to his bare feet, he peered into the box and studied the device. He looked like an eager student, excited to learn and tinker.

"Similar to an advanced earthquake warning, the device senses ground movement. Instead of alerting the wearer, it will send a signal to the airbags most backcountry skiers and boarders carry."

"Except me." His blush would've been adorable, if it weren't for such a grave subject. As if sensing her disapproval, he kissed her on the lips.

"I hope not anymore." Her worry about his reckless ways had increased since they'd begun dating. She didn't want to be the strict girlfriend, even though she wanted him to be careful. "The signal actually activates the airbag before a skier or boarder even knows an avalanche is occurring. Many times, the skier or boarder activates the airbag too late to help."

"More intuitive than the airbag packs that say they have intuitive deployment." Dax understood safety equipment, even if he didn't use it.

"Exactly."

"Once the airbags are deployed, the rider will float to the top of the avalanche." He made a waving gesture with his hand.

Smiling, she contemplated the device and him. She tapped her chin with her finger, trying to decide how much more to share. This was her baby. An idea borne out of what happened to her dad, something she'd designed in a college class, and something she'd slaved over the last couple of years, without her brothers' knowledge.

Dax understood the need and the basic mechanics. Plus, she wanted someone to confide in. Someone she trusted, and who'd understand.

"My issue is how to attach the device to the skier,

to ensure adequate ground contact for the sensors to work."

"May I?" He indicated the prototype.

Protective, almost maternal instincts tightened her muscles. It was one thing to show her baby off, but to let someone else handle it was something else entirely. Except Dax understood the prototype, he'd been caught in an avalanche, and regularly skied the backcountry. He might provide another perspective.

At her nod, he picked up the device and examined it closely. "It's small, so it won't add much weight to the gear."

"I was thinking of putting it directly on the ski, except that might interfere with performance."

He gave a silly leer. "And you know how we men don't want our *performance* to be inhibited."

"Dax." Giggling, she playfully slapped his arm, loving how he could tease and yet focus. She couldn't wait to see his performance in the bedroom. Focusing back on the project, she said, "The prototype is durable. I've tested it in weather control labs."

"Amazing." He whistled. "You've put a ton of time and money into the project."

"Now I need to get funding." She'd been making phone calls, and was working on a professional business presentation. "The problem is the investors want to see real-world results before investing."

"Who have you solicited?"

Her thoughts warmed at his interest. He believed in her invention, unlike Jackson. Dax understood the lifesaving capabilities. The warmth wrapped around her heart. He believed in her. "I'm trying to get an appointment with George Webber, Shey's father."

"They own resorts, not manufacturing facilities." Dax carefully placed her invention back in the padded box. His care proved he understood the time and attention she'd devoted to the HAAWT.

"They have money to invest, and have interests in the ski industry." She'd take any connection right now.

"Hmm." He scratched his chin, appearing scholarly, showing another facet.

All of his facets combined like a beautiful jewel. She kissed him on his strong chin. "Hmmm."

Not a thinking hum, a sexual hum strumming in her body.

"Let me think about other ski industry types."

"The thing is—" she couldn't help trailing a finger across his chest "—you can't divulge the project to lower-level people in a company."

"Are you saying I only know lower-level people?" His tone hardened, and his brow furrowed.

"No. No." Her finger stopped on his abs as she focused on the conversation, not his body. "I'm saying I need to be careful who I share my project with."

"You shared it with me."

Her lips twitched. "I trust you." She almost added a silly on the end.

"You do?" His surprise made her glad she hadn't called him silly.

How could he not think she trusted him? She was here, in his apartment. Alone. The word beat against her chest. Desire strummed through her veins. Need pulsed at her core.

"If I didn't trust you, I wouldn't be here showing

you my project." She pressed up against him, showing him her need. "I wouldn't be willing to do this." She wrapped her arms around his neck and kissed his lips. "I wouldn't be willing to share my body."

He wrapped his arms around her waist, pulling her in closer, tighter, more intimately. She melted against Dax, inhaling his piney scent. His strong arms stayed wrapped around her, keeping her near. His manhood pressed against the juncture of her thighs. The urge to get even closer, naked, more intimate charged through her. She'd already tried to tempt him and she truly did want him to do well on his test.

He'd said he wanted to wait, but could she?

Could Dax wait? He wanted Lexi badly. And she'd indicated enough times she wanted him. Her body pressed against his, igniting every single nerve ending. Her rich scent wove around him like a velvet chain, tying him to her.

He kissed the top of her head. A comforting peck, nothing more, trying to keep control of his libido.

She raised her face, her gaze searing into him, displaying her desire with her soft eyes, flushed cheeks, and slightly open mouth.

With a will of its own, his mouth moved toward her again. He kissed her forehead, his tongue laving the smooth skin there.

She smiled, her lips lifting, imitating a tempting seductress.

Magnetized, he kissed the tip of her nose, not willing to fall for the temptation of Lexi.

At the moment.

She moued her mouth, her tongue flicking out and licking first the top, and then the bottom lip.

His will abandoned him completely. He kissed her lips. Softly, gently. Showing he cared, yet not planning to take it farther.

She pressed her tongue against his mouth.

And he lost control. Sparks shot from her tongue and through his body, electrifying every nerve ending and energizing him. His body responded by tugging her against him, grinding his cock against her core, imitating what he really wanted to accomplish. His tongue dove deep in her mouth. He wanted to be as close as possible. Inside her any way he could.

He'd never felt this way about a woman. No control or finesse. This urgent need to possess, and yet cherish. To protect, and yet let her shine. To move slow, even though he wanted to go super-fast.

She untucked his shirt from his jeans, and ran her fingers under his shirt and up his back. The ecstasy spiraled across his skin. He wanted her hands on his body. Wanted to experience her skin pressed to his.

Just a touch.

Untucking her silky blouse, he played with the buttons at the neckline. She always wore such prim clothes. It made him wonder what was underneath. Like a curtain revealing a pageant. He undid the top button with tingling fingers revealing a sheer, sexy, black bra, plunging low in the center.

He sucked in a sharp breath. The reality was better than his imagination.

Rolling his thumb over the tip of the covered-in-black-lace breast, he appreciated every bump and nuance. His greedy hands wanted to squeeze the plumpness. He wanted to go slow and worship.

He slipped his hand beneath the black silk. She gasped.

The gasp made his knees weak. He held on to her to stop from collapsing to the ground.

"Lexi." Her name was a mantra. "Lexi, Lexi, Lexi." He couldn't stop, didn't want to stop. He *had* to stop. She said she trusted him, and he wanted to be worthy of her trust. He wanted her to be proud of him because he did well on his tests. "Lexi."

"Yes, Dax." Her lips moved against his, starting a new round of fireworks.

Fireworks he tried to put out. Her lips evoked an incredible response. What would happen once they truly came together?

"Lexi." His breathing was harsh. He couldn't believe he was stopping their passion. He wanted their coming together to be special, and he had to study. She'd understand. She had to understand. "I'm sorry to stop this." He spoke against her lips, his mouth trying to continue the kiss. "I really do need to study. Test tomorrow."

Her mouth stiffened against his. She took her hands away from underneath his shirt. She tried to step away. He wouldn't let her.

"I'm sorry. I..." She'd lost control, just as he had.

They'd both lost control, and that comforted him.

Breathing heavily, he gave her a chaste kiss. "Don't be sorry. I love how we both lose control." He kissed her again, unwilling to stay apart for seconds. "I'd love to take this to the next level, but…"

Her eyes closed. Her chest heaved, lifting her very enticing breasts. Opening her eyes, her expression appeared more calm, yet he saw the pulse moving at the base of her neck. "You have to study and I distracted you."

"And I loved the distraction." He let his arms slip from around her, before they yanked her closer to him again. "Any other time, it's an open invitation." He wiggled his eyebrows trying to add humor to the situation.

His friends would think it humorous. Dax O'Donnell turning a woman down so he could hit the books.

Her slight smile showed quivering lips. She'd been as excited. Studying was the right thing to do. She'd respect this more committed Dax.

"You're okay with working?" He wanted to be sure.

"Yes. You're right." She took her seat at the kitchen table and took out her laptop. "I should never have distracted you."

"You're always a distraction." He sat on the couch, trying to shift his enlarged cock to a more comfortable position. "A good distraction."

She settled into her work, comparing her notebook to whatever she was doing on the computer. He tried to focus on studying pharmacology. He couldn't help glancing in her direction every once in a while. She'd catch his glance and beam back.

He appreciated she could work in silence. That she didn't need to constantly chatter. Normally, if his date wasn't filling the dead air between them, he would believe silence meant boredom. With Lexi, he found it the exact opposite. Silence meant completeness.

After an hour, he stretched and closed his book. "Do you want coffee?"

She grinned and his insides went soft. "Love some."

Moving to the kitchen, he measured the grounds and filled the pot with water. Lexi continued to work. Her lined forehead proved her concentration. She used a small ruler to measure her device and took copious notes. Her fingers flew on the keys of her laptop.

"You look so science-y."

She chuckled and the warmth spread through him. "Is that a word?"

"It is now." He poured two cups and brought hers to the table.

She didn't even acknowledge him.

If any other woman had ignored him, he would've ended the date. Lexi was different than anyone he'd ever dated. She was smart and focused. Cautious and prickly. Trying to be more reckless. She'd made him laugh and desire, and really, really think about his life, his future.

Frowning, she yanked on her ponytail.

"What's wrong?" Did she believe he was smart enough to help?

"I need to get the investor presentation perfect." She yanked her ponytail again. "But if I don't know the best position to place the HAAWT, how can I sell it?"

"Can I see?" Setting down his mug, he took the chair beside her and waited. Would she trust him enough to show him, or even believe he was capable of an idea? "I am an avalanche expert."

"Getting caught in an avalanche does not make you an expert." Her teasing tone caught at his center. She swung her laptop to face him. "Here's the problem. Putting the device on the ski is too risky."

"I thought you wanted to start taking risks?" The tease came out before he could stop himself. She wanted to start taking risks, while he wanted to be taken seriously.

"Personally. Not with my invention." She picked up her mug and took a long sip, watching him study the diagram. "What do you think?"

His heart pounded. She believed he might have a decent thought, that he could add value to her design. He studied the schematic again and again. He had one idea. The pounding lurched to a sudden halt, and then raced ahead. What if she thought it was stupid?

He could present the idea as a joke, and if she hated it, he'd play it off as comic relief. That would be shorting himself. He knew he wasn't dumb, but the teasing from his brother and sister still echoed in his head.

Steadying his hands, he spewed, "What if you attached the HAAWT sensor to the bottom of the boot? It would be between the boot and ski, and yet have contact with the ground."

She stilled, her cup halfway to her mouth.

His breath shattered in his lungs. She hated the idea.

Slamming her cup on the table, she reeled toward him. Her gaze lit like a torchlight parade, flaring with some unknown emotion. "You are brilliant!"

She hugged him in celebration. She might've been celebrating the idea, he was celebrating himself. He wasn't as dumb as people thought. Lexi didn't think so. And now, neither did he.

Chapter Thirteen

Juggling the keys she'd borrowed from Quinn, Lexi struggled getting the small desk through the door of Dax's apartment. She'd seen it in a store and couldn't resist. Shopping most of the afternoon, she'd added a planner, whiteboard, and a cute desk lamp resembling a ski.

Last night, Dax had slouched on the couch in a dimly-lit corner of the room. She glanced at the couch and what they'd done to each other there. Her body tingled at the memory. She'd been so close to begging him to take her at that moment. The passion she'd experienced had been a mini-explosion. Talk about taking risks. The weird thing was it hadn't felt like a risk. It had felt right.

She positioned the desk by the small window, and set up the lamp. The lighting would be so much better for him to study here. Her brother believed she bought too many gifts for people. A tablet for a kid who was bored after breaking her leg skiing; a large decorative mirror she'd seen in an antique shop for

Quinn's dance studio; new scrubs for a nurse who spent extra time with Lexi's mother. She had the money, and she enjoyed spending on deserving people.

Dax was deserving. He was trying hard to be a success in his training. The right tools helped success.

She unwrapped the rolling desk chair with arms and placed it by the desk. Using the magical strips so she wouldn't ruin the paint, she hung the whiteboard and calendar by the side of the desk. She could teach him the best way to organize himself with color-coded markers and Post-it Notes. The planner she set in the center of the desk. She'd lived by her planner in college.

The door pushed open wider, and Dax stomped in, wearing his paramedic-blue pants and shirt. He stopped when he spotted her. His gaze took in the new furniture and accessories, his eyes widening.

She clapped her hands together. "Wait." Plugging in the ski lamp, she turned it on.

His sharp frown could've cut through her. His brows furrowed in an angry line.

Her happy clap died, and she bit her bottom lip. Maybe purchasing gifts this early wasn't the right thing to do. Her ex-fiancé had loved her gifts, but then again, that's all he'd loved about her. "What do you think?"

He moved into the room and ran his finger across the desk and chair.

She swallowed a lump. Had she been too presumptuous? "Dax?"

He picked up the planner, scanned it, and tossed the book back on the desk. "What did you do to *my* apartment?"

She fumbled for words. "Helping you. This is the perfect place for you to study."

He glared at the door and back at her. "How'd you get in?"

The lump stuck in her throat. He didn't want her there, didn't want her intruding on his life and his privacy. Didn't want her gifts. She'd thought after last night he'd welcome her help. She told him she trusted him, and she thought he'd trusted her, too.

It wasn't as if this was a big deal. She had the money. "I borrowed a key from Quinn."

That sounded bad. He probably thought she'd become a clingy and possessive girlfriend. Here she'd taken a risk, wanting to surprise him, and it wasn't paying off. Her stomach vaulted, ready to spill up lunch. It was too soon to buy expensive gifts, even though the cost meant nothing. What had she been thinking?

"Have you been in any other room?" He held his body tense, as if her answer was important.

"No. I wouldn't go peeking around." She wasn't spying. She was trying to help.

His body relaxed. He ran his fingers over the top of the desk. He picked up a marker and drew a line on the whiteboard. He sank into the cushy desk chair. "Where'd you get this stuff?"

"I bought it."

"Why?" He swiveled the chair around to face her. His expression wasn't as angry or tense, more in awe.

"Why would you buy this for me?" The wonder and amazement in his voice made her tension lessen.

Because she cared about him. Cared he had the proper tools to study. Cared about him being successful. Cared. Really and truly cared. Her infatuation had turned to liking, which had morphed again. To something deeper and more meaningful.

The thought thrilled and scared her. This was more than she'd felt about anyone before. Even her ex-fiancé.

"I got it for you to help you get organized." She wasn't about to admit the truth.

He ran a hand on the edge of the wood desk. "This is nice stuff."

"Not that nice." She hadn't bought Chippendale furniture.

"Nice for me." His original shock had changed to appreciation. "You shouldn't have done this."

"I wanted to." Not wanting to make it a big deal, she shrugged. "In exchange for the fun lessons."

"Thank you." He opened the planner again. She'd put in the times of his weekly classes using color-coded pens. He picked up the marker and twirled it around his fingers.

"Do you like everything? I can take it back or exchange something."

"I've slacked off in my fun lessons. You want fun?" His mouth picked up into slow, sensual smirk, soothing her misgivings and kindling her desire. He used the pen to draw a big smiley face on the whiteboard. "I'm going to give you fun."

He grabbed her and pulled her onto his lap where

she could feel his appreciation. A spiral of lust twirled inside her. He captured her mouth with his, while tickling her waist with his fingers.

"Stop." She pushed against his solid chest.

He angled his head. "Stop tickling or stop kissing?"

"Stop tickling."

Doing as requested, he focused his attention on her lips. Sucking at her mouth, he deepened the kiss, plundering and pampering at the same time, making her feel sensual and special.

"Thank you for the wonderful gift." He gave her a quick kiss. "Before this goes any further, I need to shower after my paramedic shift. I stink."

Staring at his chin, she kneaded the blue material of his uniform. She wanted to make sure she understood where this was going. "Are you ready to take this further?"

He tilted her chin up. "Are you?" His deep voice trembled through her.

Her confidence didn't tremble at all. She was sure. "Yes."

"Good." Lifting her up, he stood and set her on her feet. "Because I had a surprise planned for you, too." He sounded like a little boy with a big secret.

Happiness rocketed through her bloodstream, and she soared.

"Stay here while I shower." He headed toward the bathroom door opposite the kitchen. "Don't peek in the bedroom."

"Talk about a tease." She wanted to barrel past him, and fling open the bedroom door. She loved surprises.

He stopped outside the bathroom, and cocked a sexy hip. "Don't even think about it. Promise."

Her shoulders slumped, knowing her expression must be transparent. "I promise."

"There's Champagne in the fridge." His smile struck at her knees and she gripped the new desk. "Go ahead and open it. I'll only be a few minutes."

After he disappeared behind the bathroom door, she went to the kitchen and opened the Champagne. She filled two glasses and took a sip. She could wait a few minutes to see the surprise. Couldn't she?

Nerves tingled in her tummy and anticipation slid down her spine. Their fiery kisses had ignited her sensual side. She'd been turned on for days, wanting Dax more with every kiss they shared and every moment together. Now, it appeared her fantasies were about to come true. She and Dax were going to make love.

She heard the shower go on.

Tapping her foot on the tiled kitchen floor, she timed it with her quick heartbeats as she imagined him in the shower. Naked body, water sluicing over his chest and legs. Excitement combined with anxiety, creating this jittery need for action. Why should she wait any longer for what she wanted? Dax had only been waiting on her for days, she'd been waiting for him for years. She'd been taking it slow. Too slow.

It was time for her to ramp up the pace, to do something crazy, to take another risk.

Her heart thudded and silenced. No time for second thoughts. Then, her heart raced ahead. She was going to take what she wanted. She picked Dax's glass off the counter and boldly walked down the hall. As promised, she didn't go in the bedroom. Instead, she set the glasses on a shelf and stripped off her jeans, top, and undergarments leaving them in a pile on the hallway floor.

She clutched her arm around her middle and studied her naked form. How did she compare to the other women Dax had slept with? She'd only slept with Andrew, and he wasn't an athlete. From her discovery caresses, Dax's body appeared to be all lean muscle. Her body shook. She couldn't wait to have his body wrapped around hers, inside hers.

Her shaky hand gripped the bathroom door handle. The shower was still running. She imagined the water droplets running off his hair and onto his wide shoulders, and down his back to his fabulous butt. Licking her lips, she opened the door, grabbed the glasses, and sashayed inside the bathroom.

The steamed glass door of the shower hid portions of Dax's lanky form. He had his head tilted back, rinsing his hair and displaying his strong jaw and muscular neck. Small, soapy bubbles clung to his carved pecs and slid down his defined abs.

Just like she wanted to do.

Without any clothes, she should've been cold. She wasn't. Her body steamed.

"Here's your Champagne." Getting his attention, she held out the glass.

He turned his startled face toward her. His gaze flashed surprise and delight. His emerald eyes twinkled, and he smiled. "What're you doing?"

She slid open the glass shower door and stepped

inside. "Delivering your Champagne." She took in the full length of him. His strong calves and muscular thighs. His penis grew bigger as she stared. "Personally."

His gaze traveled her naked form, and she froze. *Oh, hell.* She'd done this wrong, similar to buying the desk. She'd acted rash. It was too soon for her to be bold. And yet, he'd wanted her to do exactly that. To take a risk.

His eyes softened with appreciation and desire, making her knees flimsy. She handed him the glass and he downed the bubbly liquid in one swift swallow.

"I'd rather drink you." He set the glass on the window ledge and pulled her against his body.

Her skin slid against his wet body, and every nerve ending smoldered. She wanted him. Here and now.

His lips took hers in possession and control. He tasted of Champagne and she felt drunk on his kiss. She responded, holding her own glass. Their tongues clashed and twisted, raising the sexual tension between them, each mimicking the final act of love.

He took the Champagne glass out of her hand and set it on the ledge next to his. A matched set. Pushing her up against the wet, tiled wall, he rubbed his body against hers, creating a hot friction. If they weren't standing under a running shower, she thought they'd catch fire.

"I want to taste you." His eyes gleamed and connected with hers. "All of you."

The words drilled into her. Her core dampened. Her body went weak. "Yes, yes."

She wanted to be tasted and teased and titillated.

His mouth trailed kisses down her chin and neck. Streaks of delight shot across her skin. His head went lower, his tongue circling her breast. The swirls created delicious sensations in her midsection. His hand squeezed her breast, making it tender and aching for more attention.

She jutted out her breast. His tongue brushed the nipple and didn't stop. She ached and arched farther. His tongue circled the nipple, sending vibrations of desire through her. His mouth settled around the nipple and sucked.

Her core contracted and she moaned her pleasure. "More." Her boldness shocked her. She'd never before spoken of her longings.

His other hand grabbed her other breast. His thumb and forefinger pinched the nipple. Her knees buckled. If it wasn't for the wall, she would've slid into the tub.

While his lips rained kisses on her breasts, his hand moved farther south. His clever fingers found the swollen nub between her legs. Streaks of white light careened from her core at his slight caress. Her body trembled.

His finger moved back and forth against her clit, creating a tension that grew tighter and tighter. She closed her eyes and melted against the tile. He continued his ministrations and her mind dazed. She didn't know which way was up or down.

Until he went down.

His mouth trailed kisses from her breast, across her abdomen, and to her inner thigh. Each kiss imprinted on her skin. Heat flared from the spot and steamed toward her apex. She felt wet and wanton. "Oh, Dax."

He lifted her leg and placed her foot on the edge of the tub. The position seemed reckless and lustful. And vulnerable.

Her body went rigid. "Stop."

"What? Why?" He gaped at her from his suppliant position on his knees.

Torridity scorched her body, and not the desirous kind. No one had done this to her before. "What if…what if you don't like my taste?"

His wolfish grin made her embarrassment disappear. This was her Dax. The one she'd been attracted to forever.

"I'm going to love how you taste. I already do." He held up the finger that had been massaging her most private part and stuck it in his mouth, then popped it out. "Lovely. May I continue?"

Tiny explosions went off in her head and her core. If he could make her sensible mind agree, she had nothing to lose. "Yes."

"You'd like some more?" The tease in his tone didn't match the lust in his gaze.

"Pleeeeease!" She hadn't finished the word before his tongue laved at her clit.

His tongue sucked and circled. Her breathing grew heavy. Sensation after sensation, wave after wave. She was being stretched tight from her core to the sky. Her sight darkened and she saw stars in that sky. She reached for it and exploded. The stars shattered.

Her body bucked against him. "Dax, Dax, Dax." She couldn't stop saying his name.

"You're beautiful, Lexi." He kissed her in her most sensitive spot before raising his head. "You are beautiful."

She felt beautiful and loved and relaxed. And she'd completely lost control.

Which was good and bad.

She'd thoroughly enjoyed herself, yet she'd come into the shower for a purpose, and he'd taken control.

"We should dry off." He grabbed the knob.

"No." She grabbed his hand. "I'm not done with you."

One of his eyebrows arched in a tease. "You sure sounded as if you were done."

She couldn't stop the small grin, remembering her pleasure. "I'm not done with *you*." Grabbing the bar of soap, she swished it around in her hands.

"Feeling dirty?" His brow arched again—a sure sign of a tease.

"Oh, I'm feeling dirty." She set the soap down and took his penis in her hands.

The member twitched and grew. She moved her hands up and down, squeezing and massaging and teasing the top. Loving the smoothness, she lavished attention on him. It was his turn to experience ecstasy.

"Lexi." He threw his head back. His entire body went taut. "I can't. I can't…"

"You can." Her hands continued to move up and down, and up and down. He was getting more and more excited. Larger and larger. His body bent like a tree in the wind. He placed one hand on the tiled wall the other slapped onto her shoulder. His fingers dug into her skin with his increasing tension.

His body tightened and rocked and trembled. He moaned her name.

Not only was she feeling dirty, but powerful and back in control.

After Dax recovered from his *shower*, he got both of them dry and threw on a pair of shorts. He gave Lexi his robe to throw around her delectable body. Her brash action of joining him in the shower had shocked him.

He wasn't disappointed. He'd just had other plans for the evening.

He hadn't been mad about her invading his space, or the gift of the desk and organizational items. Shocked, yes. No one outside his family had ever given him such thoughtful gifts. Gifts that showed her support, and told him she believed in him.

He'd been upset because he'd bought new silk sheets and put them on his bed, roses he'd planned to peel off the petals and throw on the bedroom floor, Champagne for them to drink, and a large box of condoms. He'd wanted to surprise her, and his plan had been turned similar to a Rippey flip.

"More Champagne?" He held up the bottle.

"Are you trying to get me drunk and have your way with me?" She held up her glass, as if willing to let that happen.

"I think you had your way with me." Pouring, he sank onto the couch. "You exhausted me."

"In a good way, I hope." She snuggled into him, and she felt so right.

"Definitely." He regarded the desk and organizational items. The gift had been thoughtful. The ski lamp looked similar to an expensive furniture designer's creation he'd seen at a ski show. "I love the lamp."

"It suits you." She snuggled in closer.

He relished holding her in his arms. Loved the sensation of her warm breath against his skin, her scent surrounding him. He wanted to make real love to her, yet he wanted to give her recovery time. "I've been thinking about the HAAWT."

"And?" Her eyes stayed closed, demonstrating she was comfortable with the discussion and his involvement.

Something fluttered in his ribcage. She was comfortable with him and he with her. Their opposites complemented each other. They fit. Except for in one area. She was a brainiac, and he was not. Doubts invaded his mind. He'd been smart enough to help the victims of the accident, he'd graduated college, he could handle a little brainstorming for her invention. "I want to tinker with the prototype and its placement. Can I come to your place tomorrow?"

Her eyes flew open and she sat up straight. "Why don't I bring it here? It will be easier."

She didn't shoot him down. She was willing to listen to his idea. She didn't think he was dumb.

Nodding absently because his body was happy and satisfied, he pulled her back against him. It didn't matter where he looked at the device. Something picked at his brain, though. Something concerning and unsteady. She'd maneuvered him out of coming to her place, of learning where she lived. He thought they were growing so close. Why did she not want to share all of her life with him?

Stretching in bed a few hours later, Dax reached for Lexi beside him. They'd snuggled and napped on the couch until he'd carried her to bed. Once cuddling together, he hadn't been able to sleep, thinking about her body and her avoidance. For some reason, she didn't want him to know where she lived, and yet she said she trusted him.

Her long, red hair spread over the pillow, and the urge to run his finger through the curly strands caused his fingers to itch. His new silk sheets were tucked around her naked body. What did it matter where she lived? As long as she felt at home with him.

He couldn't wait any longer.

Slowly rolling back the sheet, he slipped out of bed naked, and padded to the kitchen. The cold floor chilled his feet. He wanted their first real time to be right. Because she was right.

The rightness settled around him like a warm blanket. Or her warm body.

If he even stayed the night at a woman's place, he tried to get out early. Not wanting to deal with the awkward morning-after. Today, he was finally in his own place, and he didn't want Lexi to leave. He wanted to make love with her tonight, and hold her until the morning.

He poured two fresh glasses of Champagne. Tiptoeing back to the bedroom, he set the glasses down, and picked several of the roses out of the vase. Their rich, fragrant smell reminded him of Lexi's sumptuous scent. He plucked the petals, and tossed them on the bed. Keeping one rose petal in his hand, he got back into bed and spooned against her back. Rubbing the rose petal between thumb and forefinger, he held it by her nose. The smooth texture was similar to her skin.

Her eyelids fluttered. Rosy cheeks blossomed against her white skin. She was beautiful.

Her red lips bloomed. "What is that wonderful smell?"

Definitely didn't wake up cranky, even after only a short nap.

He kissed her bare shoulder, getting another taste of her skin. "Me."

"Roses." She opened her blue eyes and grabbed his hand. "You plucked the roses?"

Continuing his path to her neck, his lips suckled her skin. "Part of my seduction plan for this evening."

Her lips lifted into a sexy grin. "You didn't need a seduction plan."

Nuzzling at her ear, he thought about what they'd done to each other in the shower. Technically, they hadn't had sex, and yet, he'd been completely satisfied with the outcome. Cuddling on the couch had been a bonus. He choked on his thoughts. He wasn't a cuddler. At least, he never had been before.

Using the petal, he rubbed it down her neck, her collarbone and over a nipple. "Then, my seduction plan for now." He pressed his swollen cock between her buttocks.

"With your wake-up greeting, you don't need a plan." She flung her hand out and grabbed his hip.

Her fingers scratched against his skin, causing streaks of lightning to sizzle in his body.

"I need you." The desperation in his tone didn't upset him, it was freeing.

He moved the rose petal to her other nipple and skimmed her stomach. The silk-on-silk caused friction and heat in his fingers. He moved lower, finding her nub. Rubbing the petal against her clit, he imagined what the sensation must feel like.

She gasped.

Must feel pretty good. He couldn't stop his smug smile.

Abandoning the petal, his fingers found the moist spot between her legs, the place he'd tasted in the shower. He remembered and craved to be inside the hot, tight place. His hand moved in a rhythmic motion, and her body responded, moving back and forth. Her movement stroked his cock between her butt cheeks, making him harder.

"You're so wet. So ready." He whispered in her ear.

Her body hummed. She moved to an internal beat. "I'm ready."

He was so ready. Ready faster than ever. His cock moved between her buttocks imitating the final act. This time he needed to be inside her. "Are you ready for me?"

"Yesss," she purred.

Her purr sent spirals of lust up his spine. If he didn't get inside her soon, he'd embarrass himself.

Stretching his hand to the nightstand, he opened the drawer and took out a foil packet. When shopping, he'd studied the options, picking something he thought she'd enjoy. Another exception. While he'd always wanted to pleasure his partners, he'd bought condoms based on practicality.

He flipped her to her back and straddled her waist. Ripping open the foil, he took out the condom.

"Hurry." Her flushed skin and bright gaze told him she was near the edge.

"You put it on." He knew he'd be dragging out the action, and he wanted to.

Slow. With Lexi, he wanted slow and perfect.

With shaky fingers, she slid the condom on his tip. Her simple touch sent a swoosh of excitement through his system. Her hands rolled the condom down his penis, performing an intimate massage. "You're so big."

He grew bigger, and his breath came in shallow gasps. So much for slow. "I thought you wanted to hurry."

Her lips twisted into a tease. "I enjoy watching you suffer."

"There are paybacks." If he thought of ways to make her suffer sexually he'd lose control and wouldn't get what he wanted.

She tugged the condom on the rest of the way. "Promises, promises." She laughed and he realized she was fun in bed.

Why did he ever think she needed fun lessons? "Please put me out of my misery."

She removed her hands from his cock and placed them on his ass, encouraging their connection. He placed himself in position and paused at her entrance, gathering strength for this momentous occasion. He was going to make love with Lexi Henderson. A girl he never knew he wanted, until he couldn't live without her.

His heart clutched—in a good way, and he entered her, pushing into the tight, hot space. Moving slowly, he wished there didn't need to be a barrier between them. That it could be his cock experiencing her innermost secrets, not rubber to interfere with the friction.

But there was friction. Static, electric, flaming friction.

"Oh, Dax!" Her calling his name in pleasure had him moving faster.

Slow would have to be for another time. Right now, he needed to reach the point of no return. To reach his final destination, not before her, but with her.

She moaned. The moan vibrated in his ears, and had a direct line to his cock. Her body moved in time with his. He couldn't control himself any longer. An avalanche rocked inside his body. He didn't need her HAAWT to know the signs. The avalanche rumbled and roared. And so did he.

"Lexi!" He called out as he came.

Her body rocked with her own passion.

"Lexi." Whispering, he collapsed against and rolled to his side, taking her with him.

Her body quivered with aftershocks.

"Lexi." Still joined, he held her close, never wanting to let go. Wanting to spend every minute of the day and night with her, because she was home.

Chapter Fourteen

Lexi watched Dax use a thin wire to tie her prototype to his boot. She appreciated how his nimble fingers worked carefully with the item she'd spent years developing. She appreciated his nimble fingers in other ways, too.

Her body heated, remembering last night's activities, and how his large hands had held her, caressed her, made love to her. Glancing around, she waved at her hot face. Hot because she was wearing a ski outfit of simple, tight, black pants and purple jacket. Plus, a matching ski sweater underneath. Not from the memories.

Yeah, right.

The ski patrol locker room was empty. They'd passed a few patrollers sitting around the table in the lounge, drinking coffee and discussing the resort runs. Hopefully, they wouldn't intrude. Biting her bottom lip, she couldn't help but worry about the device. It had never been tested in the real world. The HAAWT was her baby, and Dax planned to take it out for a spin.

"That should do it." Straightening, he lifted the boot and showed her how it was connected. He'd really gotten involved and believed in her project, causing her affection to grow. "The HAAWT is ready for a real-life test."

Nerves pulled tight against her chest. His announcement sounded so official and final. "Shh! I don't want the world to know—"

"You and Dax are dating?" Aiden swung around the corner, holding his poles. He yanked off his hat and his red hair stuck up in every direction. "Everyone knows."

The tightening of her chest constricted more. What would people think about Dax and her together? Did they believe he would stay with her long, or only until he found someone more interesting? Even though that's not what she'd been talking about, the realization the ski patrollers knew about them, his friends knew, had her body freezing. She knew how they talked.

Dax stepped in front of the bench, blocking the boot, and put his arm around her shoulders in a protective move. "That's right. Me and Lexi. Who could believe it?"

Pursing her lips, she glared. Didn't he believe it? She punched him in the stomach. He barely flinched. After seeing his hard abs, she wasn't surprised. "Hey."

Why didn't he believe it? Was she not wild enough for him? Model-like enough? Her doubts drowned her earlier excitement.

Aiden considered them. "Taking a closer look, I can believe it."

"Thanks, Aiden." At least one of Dax's friends didn't hate the idea.

"You guys should come to Evan's party tonight. He rented a lodge in the mountains for the weekend. It's going to be a blast." Aiden headed toward his locker.

A ski patroller's party. The idea tempted. If everyone knew about her and Dax being together, they should present themselves together. Aiden believed in them. So would others. So would Dax. The party would be a place to introduce themselves as a couple. "The party could be part of my fun lessons."

"I thought we moved the fun lessons into the bedroom." Dax's voice deepened and quieted.

"Those lessons are fun." She grabbed his jacket and pulled him in for a kiss, right there in ski patrol headquarters, unable to resist, and as a bribe. She couldn't believe how bold she'd become. "A party might be fun, too."

"We'll see." He didn't seem enthusiastic.

If everyone already knew they were dating, why wouldn't he want to go with her to the party? She frowned. Maybe he believed she'd be no fun in the wild, social setting. Maybe he didn't believe in them as a couple, or believe they'd last.

He sank on the bench and put on the wired ski boot. Then, he put on his other boot. "Ready?" He wore his non-ski-patrol clothes of black ski pants and bright-green coat.

The nerves moved to her stomach, stomping and cramping in a weird rhythm. "You're sure it will stay on the boot?"

"Only one way to find out." He grabbed his helmet

and goggles with such strong confidence. "Let's go find an avalanche!"

She jerked back. "No. That's not the plan."

The plan was to hook up the prototype, and see how it withstood normal use. To see if the avalanche sensors worked with the force of a skier. To see if the place on the boot Dax had suggested was compatible with use and comfort.

"Just kidding." His lips twitched in a tease. He headed toward the back door of the locker room, where their skis were kept. "Let's go!"

He resembled a little kid heading to the slopes for the first time. She'd loved this excited, troublemaking-boy Dax from the day she started on ski patrol. Now she understood his depth, she loved him more.

Not the infatuation she'd had the past couple of years. Not the lust she'd experienced the last couple of weeks. Not the liking as she'd gotten to know him better.

Real, true, deep love.

The realization rocketed through her veins, causing her heart to pound.

Love.

He picked up his skis, and flashed her a boyish grin.

Boy, was she in trouble.

She took her helmet and goggles out of her locker, and slammed it shut. With her ski boots already on, she thumped toward the door. "Wait! Wait for me!"

They took the chair, and headed for the back bowls. The short climb showcased vistas of the resort and the Rocky Mountains. Towering peaks, bare-rocked crags, whiteness of the snow, and the tree line below. With the clear, blue sky, the view was breathtaking.

The entire experience was similar to their relationship. The initial build-up and fun lessons were similar to the slow chair ride. The straightening out of who was and wasn't dating who resembled the short climb. Standing on the precipice related to their first date, looking out at a bright future. And now, they were going to plunge down the cliff just as they'd plunged into sex.

Exciting, stimulating, thrilling.

"See the slope angle?" Dax pointed to a ridge. "We had to blast a few crevices out here the other day, to prevent avalanches."

Her thrills turned to chills. "We're not testing the prototype in an avalanche." The chills crept up her neck, making her shiver. "Today is about checking if the readings work during normal conditions."

"The guys were up here this morning. The bowl is in the resort. We'll be fine." He patted the top of her helmet. "At some point, the HAAWT will need to be tested in a real avalanche."

"Well, I'll have to find a crash test dummy." It wouldn't be her. And it wouldn't be Dax.

His laughter echoed around the slopes. "No need to worry now. One step at a time. Or one ride at a time." His intense stare told her he was talking about more than the HAAWT. "You ready?"

She perched on the edge of the bowl. Half her ski was on snow, the other half in the air. Kind of how she felt about life right now. Her invention was almost ready, but she had to find investors to make her dream happen. Her mother had started experimental treatments, but she didn't know if her mom would survive. She was dating Dax, but she couldn't plan on a future with him.

Sucking down freezing-cold air, she jerked her head down. It was now or never. "I'm ready."

"Yahoo!" He yelled, before jumping off the edge and landing in deep powder.

His perfect form didn't flounder or lose balance. He swished and took off through the waist-high snow.

With adrenaline streaming through her bloodstream, she pushed off with her poles. Her jump height was shorter, less perfect, still, she landed upright. Her muscles pumped, celebrating. Catching her balance, she swished to the side to slow her downward pace. The silky powder swooshed around her body. Her skis glided riding on satiny snow.

She turned right, then left, following Dax on the steep slope. Her muscles relaxed and she fell into a rhythm. Pushing herself to her limits stimulated and built her confidence. She was an expert skier, just didn't take risks anymore. She'd taken on the backcountry with Dax, something she hadn't done since her father's death. Except for ski patrol tryouts, when she'd been with dozens of other experienced skiers.

Her confidence blossomed, thriving in Dax's proximity. Yes, skiing was dangerous and risky. If precautions were taken it could be safe and exciting. Her invention would help insure other thrill-seekers' lives.

Dax waited at the bottom right before the chute entrance. His red cheeks and nose made him look more adorable. Or was that her looking through the lens of love? "That was epic."

She slid to a stop beside him, spraying snow into his face. "It was." Her nerve endings tingled. Adrenaline rushed through her veins. "How'd the HAAWT do?"

"I can't tell."

Clicking off her skis, she whipped off her helmet and set it on the ground. She got on her knees and wiped off the face of the device holding her breath the entire time. The needle twitched, proving it worked. The battery hummed.

A surge blasted through her. She let out an excited gasp. "It looks good! I'll have to run tests, but I think it works!"

Unable to contain her enthusiasm, she wrapped her arms around his knees. He tumbled to the snowy ground, chuckling. She crawled up his prone body and kissed his facemask. "It works!" She practically sang.

"Congratulations, Lexi." He lifted his facemask and kissed her on the lips. "Your HAAWT is going to be a huge success. *You* are going to be a huge success."

The pride in his voice banished her doubts, and turned her determination to steel. She was going to get an investor for her invention. Her mother was going to live. She and Dax were going to stay together and have a real future.

The loud music seemed to lower when Dax entered the room with Lexi on his arm. People stared. His stomach did an aerial. So sue him, because he brought a date to a wild ski patrollers' party. He usually came stag, and never went home alone. A few months ago, he'd been going home regularly with Phoebe.

This was a big step for him.

Lexi was a princess at a ribald street fair. Her red hair had been tamed into some sort of bun. She wore mascara and classy red lipstick. Her nose crinkled, as if she smelled something stinky.

Maybe it was him.

Because he did fit in here. Or at least, he had. He'd drank and danced and taken women to bed. He'd enjoyed himself. True, the scene had become too much the same. He'd drank less, and hung around with his buddies more. He'd arrive later, and leave earlier. The party scene had lost its fun.

He'd originally believed that was because Phoebe had left. One of the reasons he'd thought he'd been more in love with her then he had. But it wasn't because she'd left that he'd felt lonely, it was because he didn't belong here anymore. Not every party, almost every night.

He smelled spilt beer and body odor from the people dancing in the small living room. Why had he caved and brought Lexi? Because she'd wanted to come, and he found her requests hard to resist. And he'd wanted to show her off. Prove that they were a solid couple, and not a random hook-up.

"Coat?" He placed his hands on the smooth leather of her jacket and helped her take it off. Throwing the expensive coat on the edge of the couch or the bed wasn't appropriate.

"Thanks." She flashed a cryptic smile, before her

red lips flattened as she took in the scene. "What do the owners of the house think about this party?"

Weeks ago he wouldn't have given the dirty dancers, the making-out couples on the couch, or the beer pong being played on a pool table a second thought. Now, he cringed at the woman rubbing her ass into a guy's crotch, at the couple on the couch copping a feel in public, at the stains forming on the green velvet of the pool table.

"Don't know." But he did care. So did Lexi. One of the things that made her special. She cared about everyone. "Drink?"

At her nod, he took her hand and weaved their way across the room. A drunk woman bumped into him, not apologizing but giggling. In the past, he would have laughed and gotten in a grind or two on his way to the bar. Tonight, he used Lexi's coat to shield her from abuse.

It wasn't as if everyone was drunk and obnoxious. All the women weren't sluts. But compared to Lexi, they couldn't reach her status.

He'd rather be back at his apartment, holding her in his arms. His friends had insisted, saying he hadn't attended many parties lately because he'd moved out of the ski patrol dormitory, and was too busy studying. He'd ignored their taunts until Lexi had asked to attend. He'd tried to talk her out of it, even explaining what the parties were like. She'd insisted.

Pushing his way through the already-drunken crush, he tugged her toward the makeshift bar set up in the kitchen. Beer kegs took most of the floor space. Red cups, clean and used, littered the counter. Bottles of hard alcohol were spread across the small wooden table.

His foot stuck to the floor, making a squishy noise. He never should've agreed to bring her. Except these guys were still his friends, even if he'd moved on to a different place, emotionally. "What do you want to drink?"

Her shiny, heeled boots already had a spot on them. "Wine?"

"O'Donnell, dude. You're here." Matt, one of the somewhat-calmer patrollers, played the role of bartender.

"Hey." Dax didn't introduce Lexi, figuring they knew each other from ski patrol. "Got any wine back there?"

"You've become a snob since you moved out of the dorm."

"Not me." He didn't want his friends thinking he'd changed that much. He still wanted to be friends. "Her."

Lexi's perfectly-plucked eyebrows rose.

"I mean, the wine. It's for her." Shaking his head, he couldn't believe he'd mistakenly called her a snob. He was already getting into trouble, and they'd just arrived. His biggest fear was alcohol would make his friends' lips loose, and they'd tell some outrageous tale about his past behavior. Probably truthful, yet definitely exaggerated. And Lexi would dump him. "She's not a snob."

"Lexi Henderson." Matt fluffed his black hair trying to look nicer. "I haven't ever seen you at one of the ski patroller parties."

"I don't think I've ever been invited." Her prissy-sounding tone stood out among the drunken shouts and slurred words of most everyone else. What would the guys think?

"It's not an engraved-invitation-type of event." Dax slouched against the counter, showing his friend he fit in like he always did. Being sarcastic and casual.

"I can see." Her shoulders straightened, and her breasts shoved out in the tight sweater. "I guess when I heard whisperings of these events at work I should've dropped in."

"You should have." His friend's gaze glued to her breasts, and he wanted to punch him.

Instead, he snapped his fingers to get his friend's attention. He'd hate her coming here alone and the guys hitting on her. She deserved more than a drunk man slobbering. She deserved more than him.

"Your choices are beer, beer, or beer." Matt ogled her body, his leer running up and down its long length. "Or I can get you a fireball, or some other highly-intoxicating liquor."

Dax stiffened, trying not to show his offense. It was what his friends did, it was what he'd done. "Oh no." He couldn't picture her downing shot after shot.

"I'll try a fireball." She placed her elbows on the counter, and quickly lifted them off, probably afraid her sweater would be ruined.

"What? No." He wanted to protect her, not get her drunk. He liked her sober and smart when they made love.

"Yes." She shrugged her delicate shoulders, covered in a light-pink sweater with a prim collar. "I've never had a fireball before. I'll drink it slow."

Which is what he'd said about their relationship, and yet now he'd had a taste, he didn't want to go slow. Blood rushed to his head. Both of them. What was he thinking?

Matt handed Dax a beer, and her a fireball in a red cup. A big red cup.

With her dainty mouth to the garish plastic, she took a sip. She swirled the mixture in her mouth as if tasting fine wine and swallowed. "It tastes like a Red Hots candy."

"The alcohol will sneak up on you. Be careful." He did not want her getting sick. Not because he wouldn't take care of her, because he didn't want her to suffer.

"Sounds as if you speak from experience." A mischievous twinkle lit her expression.

He was speaking from experience, and he didn't want her going through a hangover and regret misery. He'd learned his lesson, and was always careful now, even if his friends didn't know. Acting the fun-drunk party boy was easy when he had his wits about him…because he wasn't drunk.

Surprised, he realized he hadn't fit in for a while.

He'd wanted to stay part of the group, especially after Phoebe left. He needed his friends around him to keep him happy. But the drunk kind of happiness had lost its shine.

"Don't tell me you're a wild party girl?" He hoped his tease added to the twinkle in Lexi's eyes.

It didn't. If anything, her gaze lost their sparkle. "No, and I'm not about to become one either. Does that disappoint you?"

"Not at all." Normally, he went for the wild party girl. They were fun, easy, and not into commitment. Just like him. With Phoebe they'd fallen into a pattern of hooking up at a party and going home together. It had been an easy, no-work-type of relationship. They never spoke of commitment, which was fine with him, until she'd cheated on him with her new boss. The shock had bowled him over so much he'd thought he'd been in love, even complaining to his brother. It had taken weeks to realize he'd been more upset she'd gotten bored with him first.

"O'Donnell, dude." Bode slapped him on the back, sloshing his beer and splashing Lexi's coat. "You actually came."

Dax used his sleeve to wipe the beer off the leather. "I said I would." He wasn't completely out of the party circuit. Dating didn't equate to death.

"You've been distracted lately." Bode's stare ran over Lexi as if she were a display mannequin, standing there for his perusal. "Helloooo, Lexi."

Dax cringed, and he hardened inside. Fisting his hand, he wanted to smash his friend's face. He'd never been jealous of Phoebe.

"Hello, Bode." Lexi's cautiously-polite greeting made him more comfortable.

"We should dance." Already wasted, his friend grabbed her hand and tugged her forward.

She stumbled on her heels, and Dax grabbed her other hand to save her from falling and protect her from his friend. "No, Bode."

"I'd rather dance than drink this." She handed Dax her red cup, and followed his friend into the crowd.

A cold wind blew inside his chest. A cold, lonely, bereft wind. He'd brought her to the party, he should be dancing with her.

If you could call what Bode was doing dancing. The guy jutted out his hips sticking his crotch too close to her. He ran his hands down her arms and across her hips. She tried to avoid contact. In the crowded dance space, she kept getting pushed up against him. Or did she enjoy the contact? She said she wanted to be fun and reckless. Was this part of the training? Is that why she'd agreed to dance with Bode? Is that why she'd agreed to go out with Dax?

His earlier concern hauled balls.

Compared to the other women wearing low-cut cocktail dresses and short, short skirts, Lexi's tailored pants and sweater made her resemble a nun. Yet, his body responded, watching her wiggle and strut. He was only hot for her.

Bode lowered his body into a crouch, shaking his butt. She followed him down, their knees bumping. His hand extended behind her and skimmed up her backside. Did he touch her ass?

Fury flared, and Dax's muscles tightened in a fighting stance. He tossed the coats on the counter and took a step, ready to grab Lexi and pummel his friend. He'd teased her about not acting wild when she danced and she was proving him wrong. Maybe that was her point.

Matt grabbed his sleeve. "Lexi looks like a rose in a field of weeds."

Yanking his arms back, Dax took a long sip of beer and didn't say anything to the observant remark. He didn't know what to say. Everything inside him floundered. What to say, how to react, what to do about Lexi.

"And you're dating her." His friend's voice held disbelief.

"Yep." He took another long pull.

"Not going to last long."

"Gee, thanks." He tried to contain his anger, using his usual brand of sarcasm. He couldn't. Twisting around, he grabbed Matt's shirt similar to how he wanted to grab Bode's. "Why do you say that?"

Realization hit Dax. He wanted his relationship with Lexi to last a long time. He could picture them living together in the future, raising kids. He loved her. Dropping his friend's shirt, he staggered back and leaned on the counter. His head spun, and it wasn't from beer.

He loved Lexi.

The spinning traveled to his chest, swirling around his pumping heart. The love radiated and warmed. He'd never felt like this before. Certainly not about Phoebe.

This was like floating in the clouds, and yet being weighted to the ground. To reality.

A reality of him and Lexi. Could it work?

Matt straightened his shirt, unruffled by Dax's action. "You're not good enough for her."

The spinning in Dax's chest moved to his stomach, making him sick. He wasn't good enough for her. She was smart and determined and brave. She worried about her mom and her brothers and her invention. He hoped she worried about him a little.

He wasn't about to admit his insecurities: not smart enough, not rich enough, not enough.

Act normal. Be casual. Don't show that your entire world has shifted. "Says who?"

"Everyone." His friend waved his beer toward the crowd dancing. "This is who you are. What you like to do."

The swirling made him nauseous. He did enjoy partying and taking risks. Tonight, he'd rather be home with Lexi. She sent him another glare from the dance floor. Would she be better off without him?

Doubts burrowed into his psyche. About him. About her. About them together. How could he love her, when he didn't know all of her? Like where she lived. That thought stuck in his craw.

And the word, love, caused his heart to tremble in his chest. Could this be real love, or what he thought he'd had with Phoebe. Would he get bored with the committed kind of life, or become annoyed with their rut?

His thoughts and emotions twirled like a tornado.

Or, the trembling thudded into his gut, she'd realize what a loser he was, and dump him. Then, where would he be? And what about his friends? They'd abandon him and his calmer lifestyle. He'd be alone.

"Lexi." Matt observed her moving awkwardly on the dance floor. "She's beautiful. Intelligent. Well-bred. Stylish." He snorted. "And kind of a prude."

She hadn't been a prude when Dax had made love to her. Not that he'd tell anyone. She'd been adventurous and generous. Fun. He'd loved every second, and couldn't wait to repeat the performance.

"I'm trying to be honest." His friend handed him another beer, as if he thought he'd need it. "She's too smart for you, and she'll figure it out fast."

Oxygen evacuated Dax's lungs. What *was* a woman like her doing with him? He was a ski bum trying to become a paramedic. Not a doctor or surgeon. She deserved better.

Lexi slithered against his friend on the dance floor, not appearing comfortable. Stepping away from her dance partner, she scowled at him again with a narrowed gaze. Maybe she was slumming it. Hanging out with him and his friends to prove her recklessness. Her dancing resembled a stick in the mud, although when she'd danced with Ryder Croft at the engagement party she had moves.

The green of jealousy flowed through Dax's bloodstream. Even though she'd called both of them playboys, Croft would be more her type. He was rich and socially-connected. He could afford to keep her in those designer clothes she wore.

Dax downed the rest of his beer. He liked to drink and dance and party. It was who he'd always been. He'd only been in a funk recently. Why wasn't he out there enjoying her, while he could? He wiggled his way to her and pushed his friend out of the way.

Her relieved expression soothed his ego. "Thanks for the rescue."

He was no knight in shining armor. Didn't want to be. There were a lot of women dancing who didn't need to be saved. If she wanted to be reckless, then she was getting everything she asked for. "Loosen up, *babe.*"

Chapter Fifteen

"Babe?" Lexi held onto her anger by a thin wire. *"Babe?"*

The generic nickname stabbed into a memory. Dax had never called her by a generic and sexist nickname before. Andrew used the monikers so he wouldn't confuse his various women. She believed better of Dax.

She'd been sending him a million pointed glares, begging him to come to her aid. He'd ignored her. Hurt had hardened into anger. She knew he'd been watching, because she'd catch his and Matt's glances between their laughs and joking around. Why bring her to a party, if Dax wasn't going to spend time with her? The point was to be seen together, to hang out together with his friends.

She enjoyed dancing. It's why she took classes at Quinn's dance studio. It's why she'd gotten on the dance floor with Bode. It hadn't looked as if Dax would ask. Better dancing than drinking, or so she'd thought. Bode's kind of dancing was pawing and groping and trying to grind. Wiggling, she'd tried to shake the guy's hands and his germs. She'd stepped one way and the other, wanting to walk away, but also wanting to prove she could fit in with Dax's friends. The crowded dance floor didn't give her much room to maneuver. She probably looked spastic and stiff, dancing out of reach. She wanted to dance out of the party and all the way home. Coming here had been a mistake.

Finally, she'd spotted Dax coming to her rescue. He'd wound his way through the crowd to her side. She'd wanted to hug him with relief because she didn't mind dancing close to him. Until he'd told her to loosen up and called her *babe*.

The wire frayed and snapped. The nickname wasn't cute and specific like the nicknames his brother Reed used. More like Andrew's *gorgeous* or *honey*.

"My name is Alexandria Henderson Cr—" She smashed her lips together and glared at Dax. In her anger, she'd almost told him her full name. "You can call me Lexi. Not babe."

When her mom had married Stephen Croft, he'd started calling her by her full first name, Alexandria. She thought it sounded too uppity, especially because of her new circumstances. She didn't want people to think she'd changed, so she'd insisted he and her new brothers continue to call her Lexi. Once she'd graduated from Highlands, she'd dropped the Croft portion of her name. Between Ryder being at the Powder Mountain Resort, and Jackson being out of town most of the time, most people hadn't made the familial connection.

Most of the revelers didn't pause at her outburst because the music was too loud. They continued with their dancing and drinking. Even Bode had moved on to harass some other woman.

"Alexandria, huh?" Dax took hold of her hands and yanked her up against his hard body. His normally cute smirk appeared stiff on his face. His sexual gaze examined her face. "You'd think I'd know that about the girl I'm sleeping with."

Slamming up against his body, she ignited, wanting him. But the words he spoke sent the flames straight to her face. "Shh!"

People might assume they'd slept together, but he didn't need to confirm it. Didn't need to talk about it. The flames burned inside her skin. Besides, she thought they were doing more than sleeping together. She thought they were a legitimate couple.

The reputation of the raging ski patrol parties had reached her ears before tonight. She'd never wanted to go, because getting drunk and hooking up with a random guy didn't appeal. If that was her not taking a risk, she was okay with the decision.

This one time, she'd hoped to show the patrollers that she and Dax were good together, that she could be fun and social, that she could fit in.

"Are you shushing me?" He did this exaggerated *no-you-didn't* finger wag as he turned her around to the music.

Coming to the party with Dax had meant having a safety shield. Until he'd watched Bode running his hands all over her and done nothing. That wasn't dancing. It was sexual harassment.

The back of her throat burned—a sure sign tears would follow. "This wasn't a good idea." She fought the tears. She didn't belong here. Maybe she didn't belong with Dax, either.

"You're not having fun." His head tilted and his mouth raised slightly in a pleased expression.

Did he not want her to fit in? He'd been resistant to coming to the party. She'd thought he'd been tired. Maybe he didn't want her to know how he behaved in the past. Maybe he didn't want his friends to see them together. Maybe he was embarrassed to be with her.

"I was having fun talking with you and Matt. I didn't appreciate how Bode danced." They turned in a slight circle again.

Dax's expression soured, and he pressed against her lower back, bringing her closer, more possessively. "I didn't like how he danced with you, either." His voice flared with jealousy, soothing some of her inner doubt.

If he was jealous, he must care. "Why didn't you interrupt us sooner?"

"Sorry." He placed his head on her shoulder and blew into her neck. "I was going to kick Bode's ass. Matt held me back."

His contrite tone smoothed the rough edges of her anger. "Does everyone always dance as if it's an orgy?" Had he?

"Pretty much." He lifted his head and kissed her on the cheek. His eyes glowed. "I'm sorry. I won't let you out of my arms the rest of tonight."

The sweet sentiment brought a grin, and her joy returned. "What if I have to use the bathroom?"

"I will guard the door with my life."

"I don't need a guard. I need a guy who cares." She slammed her mouth shut. Not the way to go, basically asking him what kind of feelings he had for her.

"I care." His tone husked, and his green gaze went serious. "I care deeply."

Everything inside her went soft. He cared. The word vibrated from her heart through her body. He more than cared. Her bones liquefied. Good thing she was already in his arms, because she would've fallen to her feet at his confession.

The music changed to a slow song. Couples formed. They swayed to the beat. With his arms wrapped around her waist and his head on her shoulder, she was in paradise. The loud guffawing and swearing, the shuffling couples beside them, the stink of beer and body odor disappeared. All she heard was the slow, romantic ballad. All she smelled was Dax's piney-fresh scent. All she felt was his body close to hers.

All she experienced was the rightness of the moment.

Until Phoebe walked into the party.

All Lexi's soft feelings fled.

Phoebe wore a tight, knit dress that clung to her hips and ample breasts. The low-cut top displayed more than it covered. Her boots wrapped around her calves and went up past the knees. The dress was so short, her bare thighs were exposed.

Lexi stiffened in Dax's arms, trying not to react. With his back to the door, he couldn't see his ex's entrance. Only she witnessed the way several men surrounded Phoebe, including Bode. She chortled at something he said and ran a finger down his cheek.

And yet, her laugh sounded harsh and fake. As if she wasn't the happy-go-lucky person she pretended to be.

Lexi stopped Dax from turning while they danced. She didn't want him to see how the other men reacted.

Matt brought Phoebe a drink, and she downed the liquid to cheers from her admirers. With her party personality, she fit in better at the party, with Dax's friends, with Dax.

Insecurity shuffled with Lexi's feet. She couldn't act that way, look that way. She didn't want to.

Swinging her long, black hair, Phoebe made a point of scanning the room. She stopped at Lexi and Dax on the dance floor. Lexi's pulse charged. Had Dax's ex-girlfriend heard he was dating someone else? Dating her?

Phoebe's eyes widened, and her expression fell flat. Her thin mouth lifted in a knowing smile. A winning smile. A confident, I-can-take-him-back smile.

Lexi's insecurities went from shuffling to an Irish jig against her ribs. Her defenses for keeping a man were non-existent. She didn't know the games to play.

Dax swung her around in a circle. His body froze.

And she knew he'd spotted his ex. Possibly the woman he wasn't over yet. Most likely, the woman who could take Dax away. Her body tightened, ready to fight. She wasn't going to give him back. He'd said he was over his ex, but doubts still niggled.

"Let's get out of here." He released her, and staggered back. His firm expression appeared shocked and possibly angry. "I'll grab the coats."

Her insides twisted. Confusion and fear braided, rubbing her newfound emotions raw. Curiosity about this woman, how Phoebe would affect her and Dax's relationship, became a pinch to the brain. "I need to use the bathroom before we leave."

"Okay. I'll meet you by the door. I mean, by the bar." His gaze glued to the far side of the room, where Phoebe stood with her male fans.

The fact he didn't want to stand by his ex set off all sorts of alarms.

The twisting on her insides got tighter and tighter the entire time she was gone. Maybe she and Dax should say hello together, proving they were in a solid relationship and Phoebe's presence wouldn't change anything. But what if it did?

He'd said he'd cared for Lexi, although no other declarations had been made. It was so early. Too early to have this type of disruption. This wasn't fair to her and Dax.

Coming out of the bathroom, she peered at the front door and didn't see her rival. She pivoted toward the bar, ready to put any uncomfortableness behind them, only to spot Phoebe and Dax hugging. He patted her on the back. The twisting inside Lexi's body went slack. Her heart, which had been beating rapidly, stopped, and dropped into a deep, dark hole.

Dax stared at Phoebe with a soft, sympathetic expression. Possibly love-torn.

The darkness surrounding Lexi's heart went pitch black. Was she going to lose him because of his ex's flashback? She pursed her lips and thickened her skin. Her body firmed. She refused to bow out. Their relationship was new, and she believed they had something to fight for. They had a spark, a solid connection. They deserved to have a chance.

She took a bold step toward them. She wasn't going to make a scene. She'd be nice and dignified. "Excuse me." *You have your hands on my boyfriend.*

"Lexi." Dax's green gaze widened. His voice sounded relieved, or guilty? His Adam's apple moved up and down. "You ready?"

She bit her lower lip. Was he mad or happy about her interruption? "Yes."

"Hello, Lexi." The other woman swiped at her cheeks and kept her eyes downcast. The confident woman who'd strolled into the party was nowhere to be found.

"Hello. How's Utah?" Lexi's lips rigidly formed words. She was determined to make pleasant conversation. What Phoebe and Dax did in the past together needed to stay in the past.

The woman's lower lip jutted out, clearly upset by the question, and Lexi didn't know why. "Good."

"How long are you visiting for?" She used her pleasant voice even though inside she worried about how long the woman would be in town. But if she had to worry about losing Dax, maybe their relationship didn't have a solid start.

Phoebe sized up Dax and then Lexi. "Undetermined."

The answer made her queasy.

"We're going." His mouth firmed, and he grabbed their coats. He didn't take Lexi's hand.

"So early?" Phoebe's tone went wicked. She

probably believed either Lexi wasn't fun at parties, or Dax was running. Possibly both.

His eyes flashed a panicked light, and she wanted to save him.

Stretching on her tiptoes, she nuzzled him on the neck showing she refused to give him up without a fight. "You know how it is when you can't get enough of each other."

A green arrow shot through her chest, because Phoebe would know exactly how it was to be with Dax.

Her husky laugh added to Lexi's internal torment. "Your little kitty has claws. Never realized that about Lexi *Henderson*."

The way the last name was emphasized sent a shiver through Lexi. Did the woman know? Would she blurt out her secret?

Dax put his arm around her shoulders and pulled her in close. "Night, Phoebe."

His act of possession lessoned Lexi's agony, as they slinked out of the party and got into the car. Their breathing was visible in the cold, making the air thick and tense. He shoved the keys in the ignition and jerked the car into reverse. The silence stretched. Her nerves went taut.

"That was interesting. Did you know Phoebe would be at the party?" Lexi tried to keep her tone light, pleasant, as if this was a normal conversation and not the possible beginning of the end.

The agonized pain returned, throbbing with a vengeance. She tried not to show her jealousy, not to show her fear of losing him. She had to remember, if she could lose him that easily, then what they had wasn't what she believed.

He'd been so resistant to going. "No."

Fidgeting in her seat, she tried to keep her voice light and learn more. "Phoebe looks good. Utah must agree with her."

"I'm not so sure." His cryptic comment demonstrated he knew more than he was letting on.

"Why do you say that?" Lexi waited to hear the news the woman was moving back to Castle Ridge.

"Found out the guy she was dating, and her boss, is married." His terse tone told her he didn't want to gossip.

Or he didn't want to forewarn Lexi. Except she needed to know what she was up against.

The car grew silent again. Dax pretended to concentrate on the windy mountain road. She knew he knew every curve and corner. Just like he knew every curve on Phoebe. The jealous thought stabbed. The woman had been upset while talking to Dax. And now she was single. Did she realize Dax was something good she'd given up and wanted him back? Lexi couldn't help wondering what had happened at the end of their relationship, and what the woman wanted to happen now. "What did you two talk about before I got there?"

"Nothing." His fast and flat answer proved there was nothing he wanted to discuss.

"You were hugging her." She tried to keep the panic out of her voice.

He glanced at her, as if sensing her upset. "Phoebe was upset. She wanted to talk. We were friends once."

Was that the truth, or was Dax foolish? Or did he think Lexi was naïve?

Patrolling with Dax, Lexi tried to keep her mind on the job, and not on the sexy man skiing in front of her. They were halfway through their shift, and had finished lunch. On the drive home from the party the other night, they hadn't talked much. She couldn't force the issue. He'd stated his relationship with Phoebe was over. Now, it was only Lexi's doubts holding them back.

She needed to trust him, and trust in their budding relationship. Which was difficult with her background.

Dax swished to a stop in front of a ski school group of young kids. He sprayed the instructor, and the instructor faked a fall. The kids laughed and Dax said, "If your teacher rides you too hard, as ski patrol officer I give you permission to spray him with snow."

Lexi chuckled, pushing her insecurities aside. She needed to take him at his word. She trusted him. If he said he and Phoebe were over, they were over.

She formed a small snowball. Lobbing the ball at the instructor, she joined in on the fun. "And throw snowballs, too."

Giggling, the kids dove to the ground and gathered snow to make snowballs. The instructor, still on the ground, got his own ammunition. The instructor tossed the next ball at Lexi. The kids followed.

Snowballs whizzed past her helmet. She ducked and covered her head. "Ah!"

Dax snapped off his skis and came to her aide. He threw his body in front of hers, taking the brunt of the snowballs. A snowball hit his well-padded torso.

"I've been hit." He grabbed his chest, and fell to the ground in a playful exaggeration.

Her laughter doubled. A vision of him playing with his own children, teaching them to ski and have fun, came to her mind. She could see this, see them together. A glimpse of what the future could be. Not that they'd always be ski patrollers. He'd be a paramedic, and she'd be marketing her invention.

No matter what happened, they'd always have their love of skiing and the mountains. She had to believe in her vision, in them as a couple in the future. She had to believe.

After leaving the ski school group, they took a chairlift and headed toward the backbowls. Clouds formed over the peaks, and the wind picked up. Fresh power had fallen last night. She took the lead, as they skied in deep powder toward the tree line. Where the chute started, they skied between the trees to the rope indicating the end of the resort, and the beginning of national forest land.

"This is why we need to check the ropes for damage." Lexi took off her skis, and tugged on the nylon rope. "Imagine getting here to mark the resort line, and the rope being ripped or torn."

"They could tie the pieces together. Patrollers should know how to make a knot." Dax took her hand off the rope. "Now, we have some privacy..." He pulled down her facemask and leaned in for a kiss.

Their helmets bumped.

"We're working." Her protest was weak, because she wanted the kiss. "Kissing is not part of protocol."

Digging his poles into the snow, he snapped off his skis and stepped toward her. He removed his ski helmet and placed it under an arm. "We're taking a break. We can do what we want on a break." He kissed her on the lips. "And I want to kiss you."

She took off her helmet and adjusted her braids. "If we're taking a break…"

His mouth devoured hers. She answered, meeting his passion with her own. She grabbed his butt and pushed him closer. They were due for a break. Through his ski pants she felt his hard-on, and his obvious excitement thrilled her. Undoing the zipper on her coat, his hands roamed across her breasts. She arched toward him, and sparks shot to her core. She wished they weren't working.

But they were on a break, and on a break they could do what they wanted, what they needed…

She pulled up his coat and shoved her hands down his waistband. It was too cold to undress, although a caress would keep both of them warm. They'd work twice as hard later. She jolted at the unusual thought. Being with Dax had made her more spontaneous and fun.

Her hands rubbed over the skintight Lycra he wore under his ski pants. He moaned, and she couldn't think anymore. She gripped his manhood between her fingers, remembering how it felt to have him inside her. She wanted to feel that good again.

A muted shout came from below, followed by a laugh.

"What's that?" He stilled under her touch.

"Kids doing tree runs." She kept massaging, not wanting to get back to reality. They were still on break.

"Why so close to the edge of property? I don't like it." His tense tone told her she wouldn't get him back into his frisky mood. "We should make them aware we're here."

"No!" Heat flared up her body. Embarrassed heat. "I don't want them to think anything happened."

He arched a brow and rezipped and buttoned his ski pants. "Nothing happened. I wish it had…"

"Stop." Her earlier excitement chilled. She couldn't believe she'd forgotten she was on duty, even if they were on a break. No kissing. No whatever else she was about to do. She zipped up her jacket.

The two kids ducked under the rope. Strictly illegal.

"We need to stop them." She stepped into her skis and grabbed her poles. Her limbs shook at what she'd been about to do, on duty, in public.

Dax's expression turned wistful. Like he'd ducked under the ropes plenty of times, and wished he could now. He stepped into his skis and grabbed his poles slower, as if uncomfortable, or not wanting to move.

She fixed her facemask and grabbed the radio. Even though she'd had a lapse in judgment, she took her job seriously.

He knocked her hand away. "What're you doing?"

"Reporting those kids. They're not supposed to go beyond the boundaries."

Their tracks through the trees showed the way the kids had gone.

"They're kids." After putting on his helmet, he skied to where the kids had ducked under the rope. "I did it all the time."

Her nerves stretched to the end. He'd been lucky he'd never gotten in trouble. She put her helmet on and followed. "It's dangerous. It snowed heavily last night."

Holding the rope up, he ducked under. "That's why we should follow them and make sure they're okay."

She froze. He'd already convinced her to take a *break*. She couldn't let dating Dax change her values. Taking more risks, okay. Being fun and adventurous, sure. "It's against the rules."

"For them. Not for us." He tapped the ski patrol logo on his jacket. "We need to check on their safety. If they climb to the Turret line, they could trigger an avalanche, which will endanger others."

The area was right above the backside, where hundreds of people were skiing and boarding. Even if they skied out there and found them, it would be too late to turn around. The only way out was down. And with the new snow layering on top of the old snow, the situation was precarious.

"The kids will be picked up where they exit and lose their passes." She pressed on the radio again.

"Losing their passes isn't going to mean anything if they die." His serious tone caught her attention, and she paused.

She remembered losing her father in an avalanche, of almost losing Dax. She imagined the parents' devastation if something happened to their kids and she didn't do everything she could to help.

The rules dictated they not go off-resort unless there was imminent danger. The danger was real, not imminent. The kids could set off an avalanche. They might not. But if they did, they could die.

"We're going to lose them." He jiggled the tight rope like waving a flag.

As tight as her nerves stretched, she balanced between right and wrong, leaning forward and back. Reporting the out-of-bounds skiers and heading to safety was what protocol dictated. If something happened to those kids, she'd feel responsible, because she hadn't been paying attention. Warmth flushed through her, followed by a wave of cold. If they hadn't been making out, they could've stopped the kids before they'd gotten away. Indecision tipped. Following them out-of-bounds, they'd be able to watch the kids and possibly keep them safe.

However, if one of them triggered an avalanche, they could all die.

"Lexi?"

A new thought struck like lightning. Sometimes a person had to break the rules to do the right thing. Jackson had said something similar. Dax had tried to convince her. She'd never believed it until now. Believed this was one of those times. Even so, she wasn't going to cross the line blindly. "Let me give base our location, probable descent path, and how many we're following."

The compromise was the best decision. Other ski patrollers would know where they were headed, so if she and Dax went missing, they'd know where to search. She and Dax would follow the kids, and make sure they stayed safe.

She headed under the rope to follow. The ungroomed snow stuck to her skis as she rounded a tree. He swished around, following the tracks the other skiers had made. Picking up the pace, they swiveled between trees and ducked under low branches.

He stopped at the edge of the tree line and took out binoculars. "They've already climbed up to the Turret line."

Breathing deeply, the cold air caught at the back of her throat. "It looks windblown."

"Yes. It does." He handed her the binoculars and unzipped his coat.

"What're you doing?"

"If I yell or ski toward them, and they see my ski patrol jacket, they might freak out and run, possibly triggering an avalanche." He shoved the coat at her, and she was too shocked to resist. "I'm going to join them."

"You'll freeze." Which wasn't her first concern, it was the only one she could articulate. "What if an avalanche strikes?"

"I have a beacon." He flashed a crazy-foolish smirk, making her fear double. "You better dig me out. Quick. And stay out of view."

She'd keep an eye on him. She wouldn't let him out of her sight. If he went under, she could pinpoint the last place she'd seen him. His life could depend on it. If she'd had the HAAWT, she'd feel better about their chances of surviving an avalanche. She'd survived one, and Dax had survived one. She didn't want their luck to end.

"Get out if you need to." His serious tone matched the situation.

She understood. The trees were no protection from the force of an avalanche.

He skied across the edge, using his poles to go faster. The path elevated slightly to a point with sharp, exposed crags. A drop-off where the kids stood, displayed the funnel they'd planned to take. Snow hung over the edge.

His arm muscles flexed through the ski sweater he wore. She shivered, thinking about how cold he must be, not to mention her other fears. Reaching elevation, he took off his skis and hiked the rest of the way to the crag. He waved to the two kids at the top and she breathed a little easier.

From her lower vantage point, she noted how the crag dropped into a deep funnel, before flaring out when it reached the tree line. Her location at the edge of the trees gave her a good view, while obscuring her from the top of the peak.

Each of the kids fist-bumped Dax when he reached them, probably congratulating themselves on how cool they were. She didn't think they were cool. They were idiots.

His hands moved, pointing at the cornice of snow, as if he explained the dangers. He stomped on the snow. The kids seemed to nod in agreement, and Lexi cheered internally. The kids were listening.

Dax pointed at the tree line. He must be telling them the best way to ski down without triggering an avalanche. They high-fived each other. One of the kids hung his skis on the edge of the crag. He made the jump and sailed between the rocky crags in the perfect location.

She followed his progress until the kid got near. Then, she stepped out from behind the tree and flagged him down.

"Are you okay?" She wanted to yell at how stupid he'd been. She held it in. They needed to get to safety first. "What's your name?"

"Walter." The kid watched his friend. "That's Gary."

Gary followed, taking the same path as Walter and reaching them easily. He was fine, too, and acted as if he'd been on an adventure. A risky one.

"Stay here." She put the binoculars back to her eyes.

Dax jumped off the crag. He landed perfectly and smoothly skied down the slope, traversing sideways to get to where she waited.

Tiny snowballs raced behind and caught up to Dax. The snowballs increased like a waterfall.

Her stomach dropped. Her knees shook. The signs pointed to the beginning of an avalanche.

Paralysis overtook her. Her body couldn't move, while her mind couldn't stop flashing pictures from her past when her dad died. Her muscles tied in knots. Feelings from the last time Dax had been caught in an avalanche suffocated her. She couldn't breathe. This time would be so much more devastating.

"What's going on?" Walter didn't understand the danger.

Cracks formed above Dax. Slabs of snow slid.

No doubt now.

"Avalanche." The word trembled between her lips and struck terror in her heart.

Dax understood the dangers. He tucked and skied faster, trying to get to the flank on the outside of the danger zone.

She'd promised to watch him, to dig him out if necessary. Except she had Walter and Gary to think about. Her job was to get the kids to safety. Pain radiated from her skin to her insides. Her duty told her one thing, and her heart another. If she hadn't slacked off on her job, they wouldn't be in this situation. The kids would've been aware of their presence, and not ducked under the ropes. They would've been safe.

But they weren't. And now she had to make up for it.

"Come on. This way. Fast." She dropped the binoculars, and they thudded against her chest, bruising her heart. "Let's go."

She was abandoning Dax. Abandoning him to his fate.

Leading the kids through the trees, she held the tears in. Her throat was dry and her muscles ached. It was a choice between losing four possible lives or just one.

Except it wasn't just one. It was *the one*.

Her heart cracked and bled. He was the one, and she might lose him.

Chapter Sixteen

Sensing a strange movement in the snow, Dax scanned behind him and spotted the sliding and roaring snow wheeling toward him.

Avalanche.

The sight slugged him in the lungs. The image was too recent and too familiar.

A panicked shiver snaked across his skin, and wrapped around his heart. Lexi couldn't get caught. The strings constricted. He fixed his gaze at her, willing her to escape.

She stood by the tree line where he'd left her, with the two boys. The strings around his heart pulled tighter. Panic for her screamed in his veins. "Get the hell out of here, Lexi."

Roaring jerked his attention behind him.

A fracture line cracked and formed. The high point was straight above him.

Don't panic. Observe and keep skiing.

The crack didn't appear to be deep. The staunch

wall wasn't wide. If he could ski more sideways than down, and ski fast, he could escape the avalanche.

What about Lexi?

His hope dove with his gaze. Her reddish-orange coat stood out between the trees. She needed to move. Now.

Adjusting his course, he tucked low.

He let the natural adrenaline flow, speeding him on. Guilt and worry were like a ball and chain holding him back. She'd been right about not going after the kids. He should've kept her safe inside resort boundaries.

If Lexi and the kids died, he'd have a tormented existence.

If he died, it was his own fault.

Icy particles of snow pierced his skin. His skis chattered on the rough snow. He plowed through. Using his edges, he cut across the slope.

The flash of reddish-orange heading back into the trees caught his attention. Relief rushed through his chest. Lexi was heading toward safety. She'd made the smart decision, unlike him.

He beat himself up, feeling every internal punch.

He couldn't think about his stupidity now. He fought gravity and the natural force of the slope. He fought himself.

Finally, he reached a spot outside the danger zone.

His nerves rioted with success. He bent at the waist to catch his breath. He'd done it. He'd raced the avalanche and won.

He forced himself to stand and look back. He noted the beauty of the avalanche. The snow sliding in patterns imitating a waterfall. The majesty of the crown. The force of the destruction. Mother Nature was powerful and unpredictable.

Just like love.

Urgency pushed past exhaustion. He needed to find Lexi and make sure she and the kids were okay. Make sure she'd reported the avalanche's location.

Weaving between the trees, he tried to find the path Lexi had taken. The branches scratched him. Anxiety ticked underneath his cold skin. The sweat from the workout had chilled him, and he didn't have a coat.

He was all kinds of stupid. He only wanted a hot hug from Lexi.

She was probably terrified for him. He could picture her trying to stay calm as she led the boys out of danger. The entire time, she'd be holding back tears of worry for him. Even though he was tired, he needed to find her fast.

He ducked under a branch, and spotted the top of the narrow chute leading back to resort property. If he couldn't find her, he'd grab the nearest worker with a radio and call to let her know he was okay.

Picking his way down the narrow chute, he slowed his normal pace. The scrape of his skis on ice jarred. He was tired, worried, and cold. Obviously not thinking straight. Panic at being caught by the avalanche changed to panic at not getting to Lexi quickly.

He broke through the bottom of the chute and rounded a bend.

And there she was. Safe. Secure. Beautiful.

A beacon. His light.

His heart gave a rapid *ba-bump* and lodged in his throat, so happy to see her alive. To be alive.

She stood at the end of a lower level tree run with the two boys. Out of her skis, she was screaming into the radio and hugging his ski patrol jacket. He couldn't wait for the moment when she hugged him. Unlike when he'd been dug out of the avalanche, this time he'd hug her back, kiss her back. Kiss her senseless.

Putting on a goofy grin, he swished to a spot near her. "No photographs, please."

Her mouth dropped open and her eyes were so wide they resembled pools of an alpine lake. He wanted to dive in. She dropped the radio to the ground and ran up the slight slope in her ski boots.

Anticipation of her hug and her love filled him with joy. He took off his helmet and held out his arms waiting for the best kiss ever.

She punched him in the chest.

Breath whooshed out of his lungs. Totally not prepared, he fell to the ground. His skis clattered and crossed.

"What the hell were you thinking?" Her face curled in a scowl. Her gaze shot angry arrows. "I've called out the entire ski patrol, and you stroll down here like you were strutting the red carpet."

He collapsed completely onto the ground, letting the cold snow cool his expectations. He'd been counting on a hero's welcome, and instead got slugged.

❋

Lexi's emotions churned and twisted. Relief, anger, love, and fury agitated inside her body. The last half hour had been pure agony, leading the boys to safety, knowing she'd left Dax behind.

Knowing he could die.

When he'd come down the chute she'd been so relieved, and then he'd made the stupid comment about photographs. As if this was a big joke. As if his life was a big joke.

Even laying on the ground, he appeared completely relaxed, showing no tension from the fact he'd been caught in an avalanche. His long hair spread out on the snow, carefree. His chin stuck up in the air in a no-care attitude. His arms lay to the side like corpse pose.

His brow furrowed, and his lips tilted into a grimace. "What did you hit me for?"

"Because you scared me." She wanted to shout. Her insides shredded with the aftermath of her fear. "I had to make a choice between you and those boys."

He lurched to a sitting position, showing maybe his casualness was an act. "Leaving was the right choice."

She knew her decision had been correct, but it didn't make it any less hard.

"Well, it didn't feel good." The shredding inside her waved in the wind, making her helpless. Completely at a loss as to what to do or say.

He snapped out of his skis and stood. Yanking on her arm, he pulled her into a hug and she melted into him. He was alive, and being in his embrace felt so good. So right. His strong body held hers upright. He gave her strength, even though he was most likely exhausted.

She wanted the hug to last forever, but knew it couldn't. She sighed. "Other patrollers are on the way."

"You called them." His resigned tone told her he expected as much from her. His arms fell away.

"I did." Her uncertainty returned. Why wouldn't he want the ski patrol's help? "They knew we were following the kids out-of-bounds."

"Because you had to call them." He hadn't wanted her to.

She'd compromised. "And I'm glad I did. Look what happened." Her justification didn't warm her as much as his arms.

"And I understand why." He stepped toward the boys, away from her. "Now, they need to get out of here."

Confusion swirled. The boys needed to be checked for injury by ski patrol, their parents needed to be called, they needed to be escorted to base.

"Gary. Walter. You need to go." The urgency in Dax's tone matched his pace as he slid toward them, a couple of yards away.

The kids' expressions appeared as confused as her.

"We need to confiscate their passes and call their parents." That's what protocol dictated. She stumbled and slid down toward them. She'd already broken the rules, she wasn't going to break more.

Dax put a hand on Gary's shoulder. "You guys understand what you did wrong?"

Nodding, both kids wore serious expressions. They'd been spooked by what had happened.

"Skied out-of-bounds," Gary answered.

"No."

She jerked. That's exactly what they'd done wrong.

"You didn't check the weather. You didn't have the right safety equipment." Dax pointed at his heavy pack. "A beacon. A shovel. Survival and first aid gear."

The kids' eyes widened. They seemed to understand the seriousness of the situation.

"Skiing out-of-bounds is fun." His lecture took another turn.

The wrong turn.

"You have to be smart and take precautions." He emphasized his point with a pat on Gary's shoulder.

"Yes, sir." He jerked his head down in a firm nod.

She hoped he meant it, and understood.

"Are we going to lose our passes?" Walter's voice trembled.

Dax contemplated her. The two kids stared with a pleading-begging expression. For locals, losing ski passes was a big deal.

She shifted in her boots. "It's the rules."

"My mom won't buy me a new one." Walter's sad tone tugged.

"We'll get kicked off ski team." Gary wailed.

"They'll end up hanging out in alleys and joining a gang." Dax smiled at the impossible scenario, and bumped his shoulder against hers. "Come on, Lexi. They've learned their lesson."

She wavered. Rules were rules, but they'd broken the rules, too. Dax had made good points to them about safety, and the boys were local, and she believed they'd learned their lesson. Everyone deserved a second chance. "All right."

"Yay!" The boys' yells cheered her.

She liked making people feel good. It reminded her of her mom, always upbeat and rallying people.

"Get out of here, before the other patrollers show up." Dax shooed them away, and then turned to her. He took both of her hands and his eyes lit up. "You did the right thing."

A twinge of misgiving shot through her. She hoped she did the best thing.

"Congrats, dude." Aiden patted Dax on the back, once they were at ski patrol headquarters.

Unfortunately, word had spread fast because of Lexi's frantic calls to base. Everyone on staff knew.

"O'Donnell! Henderson!" Chuck didn't sound relieved. "Get in here."

Dax rolled his eyes and struggled to his feet. Sure, they'd broken a couple of rules, but they were safe, and those kids were safe. He considered Lexi, sitting across from him on the bench of the ski patrollers' locker room. "You still mad?"

She bit her lower lip. Her red cheeks brightened. "I wasn't mad. I was worried."

"Sorry."

"And you acted so cavalier about the entire thing."

Acted being the key word. He'd been just as worried about her.

"O'Donnell! Henderson!" Their boss yelled again.

They didn't have time to have this discussion now. He held out his hand, hoping she'd take the gesture as part of his apology. To prove they were going to be okay. He held his breath.

She placed her cold hand in his. Squeezing, he helped her to a standing position. They didn't talk as they trudged toward Chuck's office.

"What the hell were you two thinking?" His anger boomed through the small room. Leaning on his desk, his lips snarled. "Ski patrollers do not go outside the boundaries, unless there's immediate danger, especially when avalanche danger is extremely high."

Dax took the stance of a defensive back. "There was immediate danger to those kids. They could've been killed."

"You could've been killed." His boss slammed the desk with his palm, and Lexi jumped. "Protocol is to report them, so we can monitor when they exit through the chutes and suspend their passes."

Lexi squirmed and tried to pull her hand from his, as if she didn't want to be in alignment with him. The withdrawal punctured his already-wounded pride. He clasped her hand tighter, not wanting to let go.

"I know the current conditions." Even in a defensive position, he took the ball and ran, controlling his need to lash out. "The kids could've triggered, and been caught in, an avalanche alone. They wouldn't have known to go for the flank. The kids would've continued to ski down and been unable to beat the avalanche. With us going after them we stopped a tragedy."

"You caused an avalanche." Chuck's expression went red. He fisted his hand and pounded it on the desk.

"Barely." Dax scoffed, holding his temper. Why didn't these people get it? Skiing was a risky sport.

Skiers took risks. He'd taken risks. It was part of the fun. Not saying they had to be stupid. Precautions could be taken like being properly equipped. Those kids hadn't been and he'd lectured them at the top of the mountain. Maybe they needed a class for that. "No injury. No foul."

"Nobody was hurt. Or buried." Lexi's timid voice barely infiltrated through the thick cloud of their boss's anger. She jerked her hand from his.

Leaving him to defend his actions alone.

"This could've ended a lot differently." Glaring, Chuck's brows drew together.

Dax stepped forward, slightly in front of her blocking her from most of the boss' anger. "It didn't." Firming his lips, he spat. His own anger hammering at being reamed for a successful mission. "We're fine. The kids are fine."

His boss smashed his fist into his other hand and ground it into his palm. "Did you confiscate their passes?"

Lexi dropped her gaze to the ground. "No."

The boys had reminded him of himself at that age. He'd promised the kids they wouldn't get in trouble, and instead Lexi was getting in trouble. He scrunched up his face.

Chuck's cheeks puffed. "You broke rules by following them outside the boundaries, triggered an avalanche, and didn't take the kids' passes?"

Contemplating Lexi's bowed head, Dax pulled in his defensiveness. It had been his decision to go after the skiers, and his fault they hadn't gotten their passes taken away. He should be the only one getting yelled at. He'd dragged her into his mess. "A small avalanche."

"Chuck." Her submissive tone warned Dax to be prepared. "At the time," She glanced at him with a contrite expression. "it seemed a good idea. Considering the avalanche risk, we shouldn't have followed those kids."

Her words slashed into his gut. She'd agreed to the solution. Granted, it had taken persuasion, but she'd come around to his way of thinking. And while she hadn't exactly blamed him, she punted in his direction.

He took another step forward. "It was completely my fault, boss."

"How could you go along with O'Donnell's stupid ideas? You know better."

He sunk lower. Did Lexi think his ideas were stupid, too?

"We didn't follow protocol." Which meant Lexi thought he was wrong. "And we should've taken away their passes."

The slashing opened a gap inside him. She'd agreed with the boss and not him. She believed he'd been wrong. He'd thought he'd convinced her his plan was the right way to respond. That if they didn't make friends with the kids and lead them out they would've done something more dumb. He thought she'd support him.

The only stupid person was him for believing she'd back him up. "Those kids would've triggered the avalanche sooner, and been in danger if we weren't there." He'd take the blame, except he wouldn't go down without a fight.

"We'll never know." Chuck sank into his chair. "Your insubordinate actions will have to go in the report."

Dax's shoulders lowered, wondering how this would affect his paramedic training. This would go in Lexi's most-likely perfect record, too. She was going to be upset.

"We're sorry, Chuck." Lexi's voice matched her frown. "It won't happen again."

While he felt bad for her tarnished record, she should've stuck up for him, and what they'd accomplished as a team. Even if not by the rule book, what they'd done had been right. No one was hurt, and the kids had learned a valuable lesson.

That's what a team did. That's what couples did. That's what people who loved each other did.

Chuck tapped his fingers on the desk. "It won't happen again. Since you two are now going out, you won't be scheduled to patrol together anymore."

Probably best if they didn't patrol together, if she didn't believe in Dax's tactics. His stomach churned back to animosity, and he wheeled around to stomp out of the office. He'd thought she believed in him, believed in his abilities and his brain. They get in one sticky spot at work, and he discovered she was just like everybody else. His parents, who forced him to go to college, his sister, who never took him seriously, his friends, who believed he wouldn't amount to anything.

He thought Lexi was different. He thought she'd seen him differently.

"You're still on safety committee together." Chuck's final declaration was a knife to the back.

Great. Patrolling less and doing a boring task. If he thought Dax wasn't safe, why put him on the safety committee? He stormed toward the locker room. The paperwork could wait. He wanted away from this place, and he wanted a beer.

"Dax, wait!" Lexi called.

He kept going. He didn't want to deal with her betrayal right now.

She grabbed his sweater and tugged.

The tiny tug wouldn't have stopped him, even so, he flung around, ripping her fingers off his shirt. "You didn't stick up for me in there."

Her gaze dimmed, and her mouth formed a little bow. "We were wrong."

Pounding his fist into the locker, he couldn't decide who he was more angry with: her, his boss, or himself. "What we did was right, even if it wasn't by the books."

"It was against the rules. The rules were written for a reason." Her rigid tone had him pivoting around to make sure she believed what she was saying.

She stood with her legs shoulder-width apart. Her hands on her hips. She stood tall in a righteous stance. Her lips formed in a determined line. And her eyes, her eyes were narrowed into slits, boring into him and alighting his chest ablaze.

She didn't get it. Even after the fun lessons and trying to take risks and dating a guy like him. She couldn't change or react without a rigid set of rules. This incident was the perfect case study, and she'd failed.

Or maybe he'd failed to teach her. "Sometimes you have to take a risk and go with your gut."

Lexi greeted her mom and kissed her wan cheek. Mom's face was so gaunt, her skin appeared to be sliding down. She wasn't looking better. She was looking worse.

Everything inside Lexi scraped, jarring her. Anxiety about her mom was a constant weight and a constant worry. "How're you feeling?"

"Fine." The word scratched out and her mom winced.

The blood in her veins pooled at her feet. "Are you sure?"

"Doctor says pain is to be expected." Mom's thin arms led to skeletal shoulders. She'd lost more weight in the days since starting the new medication. "What's going on with you?"

Lexi fiddled with the white hospital sheets and pillow, trying to make her mom more comfortable. "I'm meeting with Andrew tonight."

Mom's chin tilted, and she winced again.

Lexi's cringed at her mother's misery, and pressed the call button. "I'm calling the nurse." She'd call the doctor later and find out exactly what was going on.

Her mom didn't protest. "Your ex-fiancé, Andrew?"

"That's the one." Trying to use a lighter tone, one brushing off concern, she knew seeing Andrew wasn't a big deal. She was completely over him.

"Why? Andrew wasn't nice to you when you were dating." Mom acted similar to a bear protecting her cub. Unfortunately, she resembled a skinny guinea pig.

"He's working for a major Wall Street investment firm, and says he has investment leads for the HAAWT." Doubts niggled inside Lexi, yet she needed to grasp any opportunity to find financing.

Frowning, Mom lifted her hand, reaching out. She cringed, closing her eyes, and dropped her arm. "Do you believe him?"

Lexi's college-aged self would've said yes. She'd been gullible and naïve. She was older now, more experienced, less-easily impressed. She took her mom's frail hand in hers. Her mom knew how often he'd lied in the past. So did Lexi. "He must know people at corporations because of his job."

"I understand your reasons for not talking to Jackson, but your HAAWT is no longer a wild dream or a college project." Mom's voice grew stronger, filled with pride. "If your brother knew how far you've come, he'd be interested."

Lexi's pride meant something, too. "He'd still look at me as his little sister and not take me seriously."

Mom's hand squeeze was so light it was barely a flutter. "You've got a prototype and test results. He'll have to take you seriously."

"Like he takes Ryder seriously?"

Mom's fierce expression dropped. She knew Lexi was right. "Ryder is figuring out life. He'll do something wonderful soon."

Lexi loved how her mom defended each of them, believing in them and their merits.

Letting go of her mom's hand, she took a step back.

She went to the sink and added water to the flower vase, trying to decide how much to confide. Turning, she faced her mom. "I was thinking about asking Dax to come to the meeting with Andrew."

Her mom's eyes widened. "You've told Dax who you really are?"

She bristled. "I am really Lexi Henderson."

Mom's gaze narrowed, and she used her lecturing expression. "You know what I mean. Have you told him you're a Croft?"

Lexi's stomach roiled. If she took Dax to the meeting, she'd have to tell him about her past and her second last name. He'd gotten her in trouble at work, could he get her in more trouble knowing the truth? The more she reflected back on the incident, she realized he was right. They'd done the right thing by following the kids and letting them go. Why ruin their entire ski season and high school sport for one mistake?

"Not yet. If I take him to meet Andrew I'm sure the name Croft will come up in conversation." Because one thing was definite, Andrew enjoyed talking about the Crofts and their wealth.

"So you'll tell Dax. Before tonight. Before the meeting." The challenge in her mom's voice was clear.

The roiling heated into a boil of indecision and wariness. Andrew had done a number on her, taking her trust and confidence and smashing it into pieces. She'd been rebuilding both over the last couple of years, but was she willing to take a chance on Dax? If she invited him to the meeting she had to tell him in advance. They'd already had too many misunderstandings. He was angry about her not defending him to Chuck. If she loved Dax, she should trust him with her background and her name.

Jerking her head down, she decided. "Yes. I'll tell him. He gets off his paramedic training shift soon. I should go."

She was rewarded with her mom's approving smile.

Her confidence boosted, pushing her forward. Giving her mom a quick kiss goodbye, she scrambled out of the room and through the corridors toward the paramedic's room. The entire time, Dax's words echoed in her head.

Take a risk and go with your gut.

Lexi had been trying to do just that. She'd taken a risk by dating Dax. She'd taken a risk by agreeing to her mom's treatments. She'd taken a risk by scheduling a meeting with her ex-fiancé to discuss investment opportunities. She'd taken a risk following Dax off-resort and almost been caught in an avalanche. She had to consider every angle.

She took a big, shaky breath. Now, she was going to take another risk. Two, actually. To prove to Dax she could go with her gut. She was going to invite him to meet with her and Andrew, sharing part of her past and part of her future—her invention. And she was going to sit him down and tell him her last name. Right now.

Shifting from one foot to the other, she waited by the paramedic program director's office. They hadn't spoken since leaving work yesterday, both mad at each other. She'd clung to her righteousness like a cloak, and he'd seemed more angry than just because of a simple dressing-down by their boss.

She'd realized later, a ski patrol team should have had each other's backs. It had nothing to do with them dating. It was about mutual respect and knowing he could count on his partner. She'd broken the code.

Visiting her mom had given her the gumption to make a bold move, a risk-taking move. You only lived once, and her mom was proof of how short your time on Earth could be. So, she was here waiting for Dax.

He emerged from the office with stubble on his cheeks and his hair messy. Her fingers itched to mess up his hair more. She wanted to see him smile.

She bit her lower lip. "Hi, Dax."

He slid to a halt. His gaze ran over her. His cold expression caused her belly to flip. "Lexi."

Maybe this wasn't a good idea. She twisted her fingers together, and gathered her courage. "I wanted to apologize for not sticking up for you with Chuck. Not sticking up for us."

He pursed his lips, not in a forgiving expression. A sour one. "That's okay. I probably tarnished your perfect record."

"It's not perfect."

He arched a disbelieving brow.

"Okay, it was perfect. But that's all right. Perfect can be boring." As she spoke, the realization smacked her. She'd lived a perfectly boring life. She'd had no excitement until Dax.

"I'm sorry." Silence stretched between them. He glanced at her, and then toward the exit. She stared at the ground. "Am I forgiven?"

He seemed to consider. "Am I? For making you go against the rules."

"Of course."

The tension between them lessoned.

He wove his fingers with hers, and swung their clasped hands high. "I thought you'd agreed on the plan. I was counting on you to back me up."

His action was carefree and relaxed. His tone sounded tense.

"I did agree." The actions had made sense at the time. "Faced with Chuck's anger, I cracked. It's hard for me to break the rules."

Dax mouth widened in a big, gut-twisting smile. "But you're learning. Thanks to my excellent tutelage."

They both chuckled.

She pushed herself to move forward. First the apology, then telling him the truth. Another risk. "What're you doing now?"

He ran his fingers through his messy hair trying to straighten it as if he didn't think he looked perfect. He was always perfect to her. "Just got off paramedic training, and headed to ski patrol."

"Oh." Her shoulders slumped. She'd been so focused on telling him the truth, she hadn't considered he might be busy.

"The life of a working man." Was that pride or chagrin?

She couldn't tell, and wished she could read his mind. "Do you have time for coffee?"

"I'm barely going to make it on time, and Chuck's not very happy with me at the moment." Dax's wiggling eyebrows hinted at a tease, not blame.

"I understand." Did she ever. Maybe he'd have time to get together before the meeting with Andrew. The rushed circumstances wouldn't be ideal, but she needed to tell him her last name before he met her ex-fiancé. "What're you doing tonight?"

Dax leered and wiggled his eyebrows again. "What have you got in mind?"

Blushing, she knew what he had in mind. The idea tempted. "Not what you think. I've got a meeting with a contact who might have potential investors for the HAAWT."

"Great news." His enthusiasm was a balm. He believed in her project.

"I'd love for you to come with me." Not very professional to have her boyfriend tagging along on a business meeting, except she wanted Dax there for his support, his perception, and to act as a shield.

"I've got a big test tomorrow. I really need to study after I get off work." His shoulders slumped and he frowned, appearing disappointed. "I'd really like to go. Maybe I can put off studying—"

"Studying is more important." Her own disappointment coursed through her bloodstream. She'd wanted to tell him the truth about her name, and wanted him there for support, yet she understood. She couldn't blurt the truth in the few minutes they had in the hospital corridor. "Never mind."

"You'll do great." He grabbed hold of her hand and squeezed. It was this silent communication she appreciated most. By touch, she could sense their connection. "Call me after your meeting."

Leaning down, he kissed her goodbye and dashed away.

Before she could make plans to meet with him privately and tell him her truth.

Chapter Seventeen

Dax flipped another page in his textbook, and his thoughts flipped to Lexi. She'd be meeting with the contact who knew potential investors right about now. He'd been honored she'd asked him to attend the meeting, since besides helping her tinker with location for the device he hadn't been a major part of her invention. He turned another page and tried to focus.

On the pages. Not on Lexi.

She'd appeared anxious about the meeting, really wanting him to go. He wasn't sure why. She knew every aspect of her invention from the idea, to the original design, to the testing. Although, he'd rather be at a boring business meeting than studying. Especially if Lexi was sitting beside him.

The words on the page blurred. He needed a break.

He relished the practical training and wanted to become a paramedic. His grades so far were passable. If he wanted to do well and get a good job as a paramedic, on the mountain or in town, he'd need to do more than pass the tests. He wanted to ace them.

A knock sounded at the door.

Lexi.

His mood brightened and soared. If anyone could rejuvenate him and encourage him, it was her. Maybe her meeting was done and she had good news. He hurried and opened the door.

His soaring mood nosedived. It wasn't Lexi standing at his door, it was Phoebe. "What're you doing here?"

They hadn't spoken since the party. He'd assumed she'd headed back to Utah, not giving her any further thought. She'd tried to entice him at the party, and played the sympathy card with tears. Until Lexi had come back from the bathroom and claimed him. He'd enjoyed the experience. He liked the idea of belonging to her.

Phoebe's long, red leather coat hung off her shoulder. Beneath, she had on a tight sweater and slim pencil skirt. In the old days, he'd have been wondering what she wore underneath. Now, he wanted her gone.

"Not much of a greeting." Tilting forward as if she might fall, she kissed him instead.

Shock infiltrated through his senses. So shocked, he let her waltz right past him and into the apartment.

Still holding the door open, he swiveled toward her. "How did you find me?" He'd never told her he'd moved into an apartment.

"It's a small town. People gossip." Her laugh gnawed on his nerves.

"What do you want?" He crossed his arms and braced the door open with his foot. He didn't want people gossiping about her visit.

Over-emphasizing her swaying hips, she moved back toward him. She draped her arms on his shoulders and tilted in close. "You, darling."

The smell of hard alcohol tickled his nose. "Have you been drinking?"

"Just a little. Little shots." Giggling, she stumbled, pressing her body against his. Her warmth did nothing to heat him. "I was at the Castle Ridge Lodge bar with the patrollers, and you weren't there." She pouted.

He pushed her away, trying to keep his space. "I've got to study." He'd heard about the gathering, had several texts to join, and he'd ignored them.

She went to trail a finger down his cheek, except it turned into a poke. "Studying makes Dax a dull boy."

He slapped at her hand as her finger went lower, past his chin and across his pecs. "Then why would you want to hang out with me?" She probably couldn't understand reasoning in her current state.

She tossed off her coat and untucked her shirt. "I can make you fun again." She tried to pull her top over her head, exposing the red, lacy bra beneath.

"The door's open." He didn't want that kind of fun, not with Phoebe. He yanked her shirt back down. "You really need to go." He picked up her coat and handed it to her. "How'd you get here?"

"Bode dropped me off."

"Why would he leave you?" Irritation jetted through his system. Bode knew he was dating Lexi. Dax hadn't talked to Lexi about exclusivity, even though he believed they were headed in that direction.

"I told him I was planning to spend the night." Reeling, Phoebe stumbled toward his bedroom.

His irritation pulsed into anger. He ran after her. "No. You need to leave."

"You're going to kick me out in the cold night?" Her pout became even more pitiful. In the past, he'd wilted at her pout, giving her whatever she wanted. Now, he realized the pout was a ploy.

A ploy that affected him, just not in the same way. Although Castle Ridge was a safe town, he couldn't kick her out while drunk. If she sat down for a minute she'd probably pass out and he'd never get rid of her. "Where are you staying?"

"Here."

"No." He needed to think. "I'll walk you back to your friends at the bar."

He regarded his open books and sighed. The break would help clear his head and his irritation at Bode and Phoebe. Dax would escort her to the bar, make sure she was okay, and leave.

Lexi had had enough of Andrew. He'd reminisced about their past. He'd leaned in too close. He'd fondled her knee under the booth at the Castle Ridge Lodge bar. He hadn't talked about financing investment opportunities through dinner or now during his insisted-upon post dinner drink. She gripped the stem of the wine glass so tight she thought it might break. At least when Dax was avoiding work he was honest.

Her heart tugged. He should've been with her tonight. He would've kept Andrew focused and his hands off. She also understood how important studying was to the paramedic program and was proud of Dax for saying no.

Andrew's brown hair puffed up in a way showing he used too much product. His beady eyes examined her every move. "I've got a penthouse apartment in Denver, with a great view of the mountains." His bragging tone annoyed.

She really didn't care where he lived, or how much money he made, or when he'd make partner at his firm. They'd broken up two years ago, and hadn't kept in contact. At one time, she'd cared about everything he did or said. Now, she didn't care at all, except for the promised contact information.

Her gaze drifted toward the bar, where a few ski patrollers hunkered near the end. She'd only agreed to meet with him because she'd been pushed by Jackson's attitude. She needed to find an investor, and was willing to explore any avenue. "What about the list of companies you texted me? Can you give me contact names and numbers?"

Andrew covered her hand gripping the glass stem. "I don't understand why we ever broke up."

Disgust curled in her stomach. How could he not? Her mouth dropped open and she pried her hand free. "Because you loved my money more than me."

His actions and attitude had shaped her relationships since. She hadn't told Dax about her connection to the Croft family, for fear it would change what they had together. For fear her money would come between them. Dax didn't seem to be a money-grubbing type, and yet there'd been a few instances where'd he'd mentioned how poor he was, or if he had money what he'd do. She'd been waiting for a sign to share her entire self with him, a sign money wasn't important and they had a future together. Him attending this meeting would've been the push she needed. Except he couldn't come.

"Not true. I did not love your money more than you." Andrew's voice didn't hold conviction.

Distracted by the noise at the bar, she gave up arguing. It was an old discussion that didn't need to be rehashed. She was here for a different purpose. "I thought we scheduled this meeting to discuss your ideas for finding investors for my invention. If you don't have any ideas, or contacts, I should leave."

The only reason he was aware of the HAAWT was because he knew about the invention in college. He'd said he could help. Another risk she'd taken. And most likely another failure.

"Why don't you go to your brother?" His flippant, this-is-easy-to-fix-with-your-money tone dug into her.

"No." Her irritation came out swift and sure. "I told you. I want to do this on my own."

"Darling." He grabbed her hand again. "Why make it difficult? Use your trust fund, or ask your brother for the money."

"I don't get my trust fund yet, and I need a company with manufacturing facilities." She snatched her hand back. This is one of the reasons they'd broken up. He thought using Croft money was easy. He didn't understand her need for independence. She stood up. "If you are unwilling or unable to help find investors, then this meeting has ended."

"Lexi, wait." He stood and gripped her upper arm with a light, unmanly pressure. "What about us?"

An electrical current shot up her spine. She jerked her arm from his hold. "There is no us."

"I've got a list of possible investors. I'll write them down now."

"Email me." Rounding the corner toward the bar, a familiar, husky laugh caught her attention. Phoebe, half-wearing a long red coat, clung to Dax's arm. The earlier electrical current sizzled. Lexi's knees went weak, and she halted near the hallway toward the bathroom. He handed the woman a glass of clear liquid, and took a sip from his beer mug. He had his head turned away, speaking to Bode.

A frisson of hurt sizzled through her body, and ended in a pulsation of pain. He'd said he had a test tomorrow, and couldn't go to the meeting with Lexi. Yet, he couldn't say no to Phoebe. The pulsing pain throbbed into fury. He was out partying with his ex-girlfriend.

Or was she, Lexi, his ex?

They'd never talked about exclusivity. But they were sleeping together, her heart wailed. They'd gone out in public as a couple. Their boss understood they were dating. Why didn't he?

The internal wailing echoed in her empty chest. She felt lost and alone. Gullible and naïve. All the things she'd believed she'd grown out of—one moment brought it crashing back.

"Lexi?" Andrew came up behind her with his coat. "What's wrong?"

Having him here reminding her of her past mistakes didn't help.

"Nothing. Let's go." The urge to confront Dax pounded through her. Fear of making a fool of herself was greater. This was one risk she wasn't willing to take.

Lexi stabbed the phone, deleting another text from Dax. She didn't care if he was late to work at the ski patrol base because he'd taken longer than expected on a test. She didn't care he wanted to know how her business meeting went last night. She didn't care he'd spent the evening with his ex-girlfriend and not studying.

She didn't care. She didn't care. She didn't care.

Shoving a tub full of carabiners back on the shelf, she slashed another item off the list. The sooner she got done with the safety inventory, the sooner she could be off the committee, the sooner she could be rid of Dax. She didn't sleep around. And she didn't sleep with men who slept around.

"Hey." The scourge of her thoughts swaggered into the small supply area. His blond hair was tucked under a knit beanie. His roughly-shaven cheeks gave him a rogue appearance. His red eyes pointed to having had a little too much to drink last night. "You didn't answer my texts."

She couldn't ignore him at work.

"I've been busy." She swallowed against her dry throat and blinked forcing the tears back. She dragged out another bin of carabiners. "I assumed you'd been busy, too." The cattiness in her voice should've been obvious.

"I have. Studying, classes, training, work." He slumped against the rough wood table and closed his eyes. Tired, dark shadows showed beneath. Must be from drinking and being up all night with Phoebe. "I'd ask for time off at work, except I need the money with rent to pay."

"I'm sure your brother would let you pay late." Lexi shifted in her seat, uncomfortable with a discussion about money. She always hated when people thought she should ask her brother for money. Like Andrew.

"I couldn't do that." Dax's eyes flew open, and he sounded offended. "I made a deal."

She appreciated how he didn't want to take advantage of his brother. And understood. And yet, he'd broken his word by going out last night instead of studying.

He sidled along the table beside her. Using a finger, he twirled her braid around his finger. "How'd the meeting go last night?"

She snatched her hair back. "How'd your studying go last night?"

"Awful. I think I did poorly on the test." Him being upset about the test riled her. It was his fault he'd done badly.

She tossed a carabiner back in the bin. The metal clanged on metal and spiked her ire. "That's what happens when you're too busy partying."

His red-rimmed eyes opened wider. "Excuse me?"

Standing, she stomped to the other side of the table,

unbelieving he tried to continue the pretense. "I was at Castle Ridge Lodge last night." Using her finger, she stabbed in the air toward him. "So were you."

His mouth opened and closed, realizing he'd been caught. He moved around the table, closer to her. "I was only there for a few minutes. One beer."

She moved away from him in rejection. Jealousy burned through her anger in a green fire. "And one vivacious Phoebe hanging on you."

"Oh, Lexi." His tone softened and he rubbed his knuckles down her arm. She couldn't help the automatic tingle spreading along her spine. "It's not what you think. I was only at the bar because of Phoebe."

The tingles along Lexi's spine shattered into tiny arrows that pierced through her body. The hurt traveled through her escalating the agony. She leaned away and took a step back.

Her devastation must've manifested on her face, because his expression cleared. "No. That came out wrong." He stepped toward her and gripped her arm. "I wasn't with Phoebe. I was trying to get rid of her."

Lexi's eyebrows rose with her skepticism. "Really?"

A desperate gleam in his gaze willed her to listen to his ridiculous tale about Phoebe showing up drunk. "I couldn't kick her out in that condition. So, I took her back to the bar where her friends were."

The story sounded plausible, definitely something Phoebe would do. Lexi wanted to believe. Her insecurities wound in her stomach and pulled tight. Dax had never looked at her until she'd kissed him. He'd never been interested in quiet, non-risk-taking Lexi.

His grip tightened. "Why didn't you say hi? Come over and yell at me in the bar? This could've been cleared up, and I wouldn't have worried about you not answering my texts."

Dax was worried? Stunned, she calculated in her mind. Did he have the same insecurities about their relationship?

She clung to her righteousness. "I didn't want to make a scene."

"Not a scene. A clarification." His grip slackened around her arm. "You don't believe in us."

His disappointment dampened her anger. In a way, he was right. She didn't believe in herself being able to keep Dax interested.

"Is there an us?" She needed to know. "We've never said anything about being exclusive."

"And you'd like that?" His voice lilted in a tease.

Hope tugged her forward. "You're so charming and flirtatious and out there."

A smirk slipped on his face. "Thank you, but I don't understand what flattery has to do with us."

Her face heated, feeling silly for causing a scene and for not approaching him at the bar. "I'm none of those things. I'm quiet and studious. Not willing to take risks or be very social. An inventor."

His expression grew serious. "I like the quiet, studious Lexi." His steady tone assured. He wasn't flirty or charming. He was real, and he liked her for being real. "And an inventor takes risks."

He was right. She'd taken risks with her prototype. Maybe she could take more risks personally.

Unfortunately, the rejections for funding kept

piling up. George Webber wouldn't respond, and Andrew hadn't been helpful, except for supplying a few names. He was trying to worm his way back into her life. "Not a successful inventor."

Dax put his arm around her shoulders in a half hug. "What happened at the meeting last night?"

"Besides the guy hitting on me? Not much."

His body stiffened. "So I'm the one who should be jealous."

"Hardly." She was so over her ex-fiancé. With Dax, she knew he didn't want her money, because he didn't know about her wealth. She'd find the perfect opportunity to tell him she was a Croft. A place where no one could eavesdrop and she'd have time to explain. "Andrew is my ex-fiancé and I have no interest in him romantically."

"Ex-fiancé?" Dax's shocked tone scared her. "I didn't know you had one of those."

"In college, and he's not important."

"That's a relief." Dax swung her around to face him, keeping his arm around her shoulders. She was glad he didn't worry about her ex. It was a sign he'd take the news of her last name well. His gaze bore into hers, and his sudden seriousness had her heart revving. "Because I want to be exclusive, too."

Her heart revved higher. "Really?"

"Just you and I."

The high revving swirled into an internal squeal. Yes!

He placed his lips on hers, sealing the deal with a kiss. She swooned, wishing it wasn't in the middle of the afternoon at work.

Breaking off the kiss, he gave her a quick hug. "We'll have to celebrate our new status sometime soon."

"I'd enjoy that." She found it hard to keep her hands off of him. To get her mind back on work and cool her internal temperature, she tugged out one of the buckets filled with radios.

They settled into their tasks, charging and cataloging the radios.

"Last night, Andrew emailed me a few names who I contacted first thing this morning, and have already gotten negative responses." Frustration crawled across her skin. "I really believe the HAAWT has great potential. I can't find anyone willing to listen."

"I listened, and I think it's great, even though I'm not a safety gear guy." Dax's lips looped in a smile, and he indicated some of the equipment in the supply room.

"Maybe you should do the pitch for me." Only half-joking, she was getting desperate.

"It's your invention." He wanted her to get the glory, she could tell.

She hummed. He believed in her invention and he believed in her. It was a sign. The sign she'd been waiting for. She was going to tell him about her name. But when? She needed to figure out the best way to explain.

He rapped his knuckles on the top of the bin. "Have you tried Croft Industries?"

Choking, she gripped the edge of the table to steady herself. Her head spun. She should tell him. Right here, right now.

He held up a palm in a stop and hear me out sign. "They're local. You know Ryder Croft, even if he's not involved with the business. He's a big skier, too." Dax's eyes glowed as if sensing success. "They'd be perfect."

Her knuckles turned white. "No. No. I don't think they'd be a good fit."

She didn't have her speech practiced, her explanation why she hadn't told him earlier memorized. Now wasn't the time. This was an important disclosure, and she couldn't just spit it out.

"Why not?" His expression fell. "Croft Industries has manufacturing, real estate, technology."

Listing their various businesses, he became more and more animated. While she got more and more worried. The spinning in her head moved to her belly. Her mother had told her she needed to tell Dax the truth. She'd been thrown by him being with Phoebe last night and Andrew's presence. Lexi needed to get Dax off this subject. A distraction. She thought of the tickets in her bag. "Would you go to a charity event with me tomorrow night?"

"A charity event?" He blanched, as if she'd said something about visiting aliens, not attending a ball.

The perfect plan for telling him her news came to her. "For the hospital."

Before the ball, they'd meet, and she'd explain everything and her reasoning for holding out so long. Then, they'd go to the event and celebrate their love.

They worked companionably late into the evening trying to get the job done. They shared stories from childhood as they checked serial numbers on radios.

They discussed happenings around town, and around the world. Dax knew a lot about different cultures. He hadn't traveled as much as she had, but he read a lot of books. They joked and laughed.

The entire time she'd gotten hotter and hotter. Her thoughts had grown wilder and wilder. She wanted to show how much she cared. Show him how she'd changed and grown. Show him how good they were together. She loved him and always had. Maybe now wasn't the time to speak those words. It might be the time to demonstrate. Her nerves quivered with anticipation. Everyone had left for the night. Chuck had said goodbye. The resort was closed. The ski patrol base was locked and empty.

Except for her and Dax.

Strutting toward where he leaned against the wood table, she ran a hand along his neck and shoulder. The caress ignited the desire on a slow burn the entire shift.

The murky green of his orbs brightened.

Feeling brave and scared at the same time, she trailed a finger across his bicep and moved to his shoulder. She traced his carved muscles from his pecs to his abs. His eyes went wide when she fiddled with the drawstring of his sweatpants. A man in sweats wasn't usually attractive, yet on Dax, they clung to his narrow hips and showcased his package.

A growing package.

He was interested. "What're you doing?" He grabbed her hand, skimming his waistline.

"We're alone." Her voice dropped to husky, and she sloped into him, hinting at her desire.

He peered out the door toward the office and locker room. "Someone could walk in."

She stepped between his legs and pressed against him. Her core warmed. "The doors are locked. We'll hear them before they see us." She wiggled her eyebrows, letting her recklessness have full rein. A recklessness she never knew she had until being with Dax.

"Lexi." He drew out her name, appearing frustrated and turned on at the same time. "We shouldn't."

Chuckling, she slid her hand inside the front of his sweats. "You sound like me. Like the old me."

"You'll ruin your perfect record." He heaved out a breath when she ran a finger along his smooth penis.

Her lips teased into a smile, while her core throbbed. The urgent need racing inside her couldn't be denied. "You already ruined my perfect record."

"True." The lilt in his tone told her he was almost convinced.

She needed to thoroughly convince him. Licking around his ear, she whispered, "I've heard make-up sex is amazing." Wrapping her hand around his shaft, she moved up and down.

He groaned and wrapped his hands in her braids. "We're not fighting."

"We were earlier." She pressed her mouth to his, needing a small taste. "And I'm sorry for not approaching you and asking what was going on last night."

He returned the kiss, running his tongue along her seam. "I'm sorry for not texting you to tell you what was going on."

"I'm sorry for not responding to your other texts." Using her tongue, she opened his mouth and dipped inside. Tasting and savoring.

His tongue tangled with hers unable to resist any longer. Joy sung through her veins. She pressed her breasts against him, and her hands continued to move in an up-and-down motion. She was ready for him.

He broke off the kiss to chortle. His head quirked. "I'm sorry for not saying…sorry?" Shaking his head, he appeared desirous and confused. Just the way she wanted.

"Nothing to be confused about. We're both sorry. Fight done. Sex begins."

Flabbergasted and totally turned on, Dax loved Lexi's aggressiveness. She was a different woman. No rigid rule-follower now. And while he loved the old Lexi, this new, tiger-like woman had his balls blue in seconds.

Hurriedly, she removed his sweats and underwear, and threw them on the floor. He yanked off her sweater and sports bra, and tossed them on a shelf. She tugged off his sweatshirt, and ran slim fingers down his bare chest.

Each slide of finger was a streak of fire, scorching his skin.

Following her rushed movements, he cleared the table of radios. The clatter of them falling made her jump and laugh. He grabbed one of the emergency blankets and laid it on the top of the table. Hurried and hot was one thing. Cramped and uncomfortable something else.

He unsnapped her jeans and wiggled them off her round hips and down her long, long legs. His heart pounded. He loved her legs. He loved her.

He'd realized his love days ago. Should he tell her? Now?

"Dax?" She tugged on his hair, pulling his face up.

She resembled a fiery-haired goddess. Her passionate sapphire gaze dove deep into him, as if she could see into his soul. Her high cheekbones resembled famous sculptures they'd discussed.

Her red lips, lips that had kissed the entire length of his body, pouted. "Something wrong?"

Everything was perfect. She was perfect.

"No, no." He picked her up and set her on the table.

Her long legs draped over the edge, spread in invitation. His cock twitched. Her ivory skin glowed. Her bare hips with the perfect amount of roundness led to a small waist. A waist he could fit his hands around. Her right-sized breasts fit perfectly in his fingers.

"I need you now. Want you now." Her desperate tone had him tipping over her, wanting her now.

No finesse. No warmup.

"Condom." He bent down and scrambled for the jacket he'd hung on a chair. "Got it."

"Hurry." She reached for him.

Ripping open the foil, he rolled the rubber on in haste. The pace and ill-advised location excited him even more. Every brain cell clicked off. Every body part tingled and heated.

Staring at her glowing expression, he asked, "Are you ready?"

"I'm always ready for you." Love and passion glowed on her face.

He sunk into her, letting her warmth surround him and lost himself inside of her, not knowing where he ended and she began.

Chapter Eighteen

Dax rubbed his sweaty hands together. He'd taken a quick shower after his paramedic shift, thrown on his best khakis and polo shirt, and dashed to the Croft mansion on the outskirts of town. He still smelled of antiseptic and death.

A dark cloud hung around him. A child had died in the ambulance on the way to the hospital this afternoon. As an EMT, he'd applied his skills to help. His colleagues said he'd done everything according to procedure, that he'd done the best he could to save the child's life. Maybe his best wasn't good enough. In a life-or-death type of job, maybe *he* wasn't good enough.

Gaping at the ostentatious foyer of the Croft home, he certainly wasn't good enough for this place. A crystal chandelier hung from the frescoed ceiling, putting him in the spotlight. The sharp crystals pointed, practically screaming he didn't belong here. Not in this house and not delivering this presentation.

His pulse sprinted, and nerves jittered in his stomach.

The shiny marble floors reflected his guilty and nervous expression. He'd lied to Lexi to make the appointment, cancelled their plans to meet before the charity ball. He didn't enjoy lying, but she'd been so adamant about not contacting Croft Industries, while he believed they were the best option to invest. As a symbol of his love, he was going to deliver a Croft Industries investment on one of their silver platters to Lexi.

"Dax O'Donnell?"

He jerked his head up at the rough voice.

Jackson Croft wore a tuxedo, similar to the rented one sitting in Dax's car. Croft appeared comfortable. He must wear a suit every day. His dark expression bore down on Dax in an unfriendly demeanor. The man hated him on sight.

Sticking his hand out, Dax's palms were sweaty. "Yes, sir. I mean, hello. Nice to meet you."

Croft wasn't much older than him, yet he acted old. Mature and knowing. As if he could find Dax's faults.

The billionaire took his hand in a perfunctory gesture. "This way."

He followed the man through the foyer and a second grand hall. Surreptitiously, he sniffed under his pits, hoping his nerves didn't cause him to stink worse. He was determined to help Lexi find an investor for the HAAWT. Feeling terrible for missing the meeting with her jerk ex-fiancé the other night, he'd called Croft secretly. Why get her hopes up if he got a firm no?

But he hadn't. Croft had insisted they meet this afternoon.

"Thanks for meeting with me so quickly." Dax used a professional and friendly tone, one he used with parents of injured kids on the slopes.

"Come in." Croft opened a set of double doors, leading to a spacious office.

The dark cherry-wood-paneled walls had built-in bookcases filled with books, awards, and expensive marble and iron statues. A large, formal mahogany desk sat in the center of a round carpet. Several flat screen monitors sat on the desk, blocking the framed photos behind.

Between the grand foyer, art work in the halls, and now this office, the house must've cost a fortune.

Dax whistled internally. "Nice house. Do you live here alone?"

"No. It's the family home." Croft settled in the plush chair behind the imposing desk. His frown said he didn't want any personal questions. "Take a seat."

Fine with Dax. He wanted to keep the meeting short and to the point. Once he got Croft's interest, he'd turn the entire thing over to Lexi. And maybe he wouldn't be terribly late for their date.

"What have you got?" The billionaire glowered.

He squirmed in the tiny chair on the other side of the desk, trying to calm his nerves. Reaching into his unprofessional backpack, he pulled out the presentation he'd printed from Lexi's computer. He'd only made one change near the end. Figuring if the billionaire liked the prototype, he and Lexi could celebrate. And if he was rejected, she'd never know.

"I'm looking for investors in a new skiing and boarding safety product. It's called the HAAWT. The device will save lives." The papers he held weren't in color or in a formal binder. Lexi probably would've made the package pretty. He hadn't had time.

Croft's brow furrowed and his lips pursed in an angry shape. "How do you know this? Has it been tested?"

The skeptical tone made Dax uneasy. The man seemed ready to reject without hearing a word.

"It hasn't been tested in an avalanche." He and Lexi had had a fun day taking the device through its paces on the mountain. "It has been tested under normal conditions on the slopes and in labs."

"How will I know if the device actually works?" Croft pitched forward on his desk. The glare from his gray eyes cut through Dax.

He flipped to the page with test results. "As you can see here, the lab tests prove—"

"I don't care about tests." Croft ground the words out barely holding onto his patience. "I care about real-life scenarios."

Good thing Lexi wasn't here to experience this strange and unprofessional behavior from Jackson Croft.

Dax fumbled with the pages of the presentation. His nerves clobbered his stomach. "Once I get investors, I'll be able to—"

"Why haven't you tested the device?" The challenge sliced him, making him feel like a chickenshit.

Which he wasn't. He held onto his irritation because he was trying to sell the man. "Well, avalanches are dangerous."

"Which is the point of this invention. Is it not?" The

billionaire was having a snit. He appeared to want to strangle Dax right there in his office.

Bewildered, he sat back in the chair. No wonder why he'd never wanted to go into business. He didn't appreciate the emotional power play. With trembling fingers, he held up the presentation papers again. "If you'd let me get through my presentation I can show you the facts and figures."

Croft jerked to his feet, sending the chair flying backwards. He scowled with a thunderous expression. "You've wasted enough of my time."

And the mighty Jackson Croft kicked Dax out.

The noise from the charity ball drifted through the hospital hallway. Lexi's long dress skimmed the shiny floor as she made her way to her mother's room. Her mother, who'd insisted she and her brothers go to the event to represent the family, had asked her to stop by and model her gown.

The glittering aqua dress had a tight bodice and a long, full skirt. Sequins clustered around the V-shaped neckline in swirling patterns. The sleeves had cut-outs at the shoulders. The dress made Lexi feel like a princess. And Dax was her prince.

Except he didn't know she was a princess. Guilt made the crown heavier.

They were supposed to meet at the Castle Ridge Lodge for drinks before heading to the hospital together. She'd prepared her speech on how to tell him the truth about her relationship to the Crofts. All day her stomach had been tied in knots at how he'd react. Once she explained her reasoning for holding back he'd understand. He'd have to understand.

Until he'd stood her up.

Okay, he hadn't actually stood her up. He'd called and apologized and been vague about an extra shift and needing the money. Her stomach pulled tighter. Everything would be fine. She'd wait for him near the door with a beer in hand, tug him into the hallway and explain.

"You look beautiful, Lexi." Her mom lay in the hospital bed, appearing even more pale.

"You don't." Her pulse scampered. She couldn't put her finger on it, but something was wrong. She'd called the doctor and he'd said everything was going as well as expected. "How're you feeling?"

"A little weak and tired." Her mom's hand fluttered, waving off the concern. "The doctor said the medication would have side effects."

"You mean besides the pain?" Her ribcage tightened. "Have you called him?"

"I don't want to bother him. He's going to the event tonight, too."

Most of the doctors and hospital executives would be attending the ball. Even Paul, the paramedic program director would be there. And Chuck, too. They both knew her other last name, and she'd begged for secrecy from the start. But tonight, as a couple, they'd assumed Dax knew. The urgency to get to him first pumped through her bloodstream.

"Mom." Lexi moved beside the bed and took her mom's thin hand, wanting to press home the point. "You're supposed to report any changes to your health."

"I will after the event." Her mother's gaze scanned behind her. "Where's your boyfriend?"

Lexi might not have called Dax her boyfriend, even so, her mother knew his importance. "He had to work late, so I'm meeting him here."

Her mother beamed. "You're going to have a wonderful time."

She twisted her hands together, similar to the knots twisting in her stomach. "If he's not furious at me for not telling him I'm a Croft."

Her mother's smile slipped on one side, almost a sag. "I thought you were going to tell him earlier today?"

"He took another shift at work." Or something. "He's a busy guy."

"Once you explain about Andrew's actions, he won't be mad." No matter how ill she felt, her mother always had a kind word or a pleasant way to look at things. After Lexi's real father died, her mom had been heartbroken, and yet continued with a sunny disposition. Same for when Stephen Croft died.

Lexi had been devastated both times, and had retreated farther into herself.

Sadness drifted through her anxiety. "I hope so. I wish he hadn't taken the extra ski patrol shift because he needed the money. Then I could've told him before the ball, not at the ball."

"Life plays out in miraculous ways. Sometimes life's surprises are light and happy. Other times, they are sad." Mom's tone turned serious. She pulled apart Lexi's hands and squeezed, although the squeeze was weak. "You are a strong woman, and are never given a challenge you can't handle."

The poetic words sounded like a prophesy. Lexi understood what her mother said. She found it hard to believe one hundred percent.

"I'm not interrupting something, am I?" Ryder strolled in, wearing a designer tuxedo with a tie-dyed tie. His bland expression told her he was happy to interrupt, always wanting to know what was going on. He kissed her mom on the cheek. "I'm here as directed." He hated black-tie events. "Where's Jackson?"

"I haven't seen him." Lexi checked her phone and saw the email from George Webber. Clicking on the link, she quickly read his brief message. Her lungs constricted. A rejection. He wasn't interested in meeting with her, or hearing about her invention. She sighed. This was not shaping up to be her night.

"Something wrong, honey?" Her mother could always read her. "Is it Dax?"

"No. Nothing." She couldn't worry about the rejection now. Tonight was about telling Dax the truth, and cementing their relationship, so they could move forward.

"You two have fun tonight." Her mom's eyes drifted closed. "Take a picture."

Lexi hoped it was only tiredness. Between the suffering her mom didn't complain about, the lost weight, and weakness, she had to wonder what else was going on. Maybe she should stay and call the doctor herself.

Her mom's eyes flashed open knowing her thoughts, and showing her inner strength. "Go."

"We will." Lexi kissed her mom on the cheek. Her eyes burned. "Love you." Her voice sounded scratchy with the held-back tears.

"Ready?" Ryder whispered, because her mother was already asleep.

Nodding, they headed down the hallway.

"Do you think Mom's okay?" His worry betrayed by his tense tone.

"She says she is." Lexi wanted to believe, but she didn't. Her stinging eyes burned hotter.

"We have to take Mom's word for it." Ryder didn't seem to believe what he said.

Lexi hoped Dax didn't see her and Ryder arriving at the event together and automatically assume the worst. No need to worry unnecessarily. Dax wouldn't get there until near the end of the cocktail hour. She'd find him and a private spot to tell him.

It sounded so simple, yet she knew this would be difficult.

To take her mind off her message, she thought about how he'd look dressed in a tuxedo. A thrill scattered her nerves. She couldn't wait to see him and kiss him, and tell him her name.

The hospital auditorium had been changed into a winter wonderland. Giant snowflakes dangled from the ceiling. Snowmen and women dotted around the exterior of the large room. Tables were decorated with lighted snowballs for centerpieces. A band played lively music on stage. The perfect setting for her and Dax. Maybe tonight she'd tell him she loved him, too.

In for a penny...

"I'll see you later." She wanted to separate herself

from her brother. She waited near the entrance, while Ryder cut a path directly to the bar.

Shey Webber greeted him with a big kiss on the lips.

Lexi pulled her chin up. She hadn't realized her brother and Shey were an item. They looked good together, even though he was a playboy, and Shey was a serious businessperson and heiress.

That's how Lexi wanted to look with Dax. As if they belonged. Because she believed they did. Excitement traveled her spine. Once she came clean about her real last name, there'd be no secrets between them. He wouldn't care she was rich, or be after her money. They could move forward as a couple. Become more serious.

Because he liked her for her. They could fight and make up, with great sex. They could discuss and disagree. Once they each spoke of their love, they could plan a future.

Lexi couldn't wait.

Dax tugged at the rented bowtie. The strip of cloth choked. Or maybe it was the too-shiny, rubbery shoes, or the wide cummerbund cinched around his waist. Men always talked about monkey suits, and this one made him feel like a gorilla in a zoo.

Probably because everybody stared, knowing he didn't belong at this hoity-toity event. He tugged at the tie. It was similar to how Jackson Croft had made him feel. Why would Lexi want to attend? The way she'd been dressed at his sister's engagement party, she'd definitely fit in. She would shine similar to a diamond, even with these rich snobs.

He took the stairs from the regular hospital floors to the auditorium, where the event was being held. His mind still churned from the meeting with Croft. If the guy hated him on sight, hated his idea, why had he agreed to meet with Dax?

All he wanted was to see Lexi, and pull her into his arms. Maybe after a drink or two, they could abandon this gig, and go back to his place. His blood heated at the thought of taking her to bed. He was ready to confess his feelings, though why she wanted to date him, he didn't understand.

Entering the auditorium through a side door, he kept the image of heading back to his apartment in his mind. In under an hour, he could be in bed with a naked Lexi. He grinned. Spotting the paramedic program director talking to his ski patrol boss, he gave a wave. He didn't stop to say hi. He knew once he saw her, everything would be better.

And he was right.

His heart stopped when he caught sight of her standing near the main doorway. Her fiery red hair was pinned up in a bun, yet it acted like a beacon. He couldn't wait to take the pins out and run his fingers through the curly strands. Her blue dress molded to the upper half of her body, displaying her curves. Curves he was intimately familiar with. The silky bottom half of the dress hid those gorgeous long legs. He could imagine running his hands beneath the material and on her skin.

Her eyes connected with his and her face glowed. He glowed inside, because he'd made her happy. He wasn't sure why she cared for him, but he was so glad she did. She glided toward him and the dress appeared to caress her body. She moved like royalty.

"I'm so glad you're here." Relief sputtered in her voice.

He took hold of her hands and felt their shaking. He wanted to hold her close and turn the shaking into passion. "Were you worried I wouldn't come?"

"No. Of course not. Don't be silly." Her speech seemed rushed. "Do you want a drink?"

"I want to dance with you." Desperation trembled through him. He needed to hold her.

"Dance?" Her gaze zoomed around the room. "Now?"

"Immediately." He nuzzled her neck with his lips, demonstrating his need.

He sensed the shivering desire go through her body. "I thought we could go somewhere to talk."

"Why talk when we could be doing this?" He swung her around into his arms, and moved toward the dance floor.

Sighing, her body relaxed. Her gaze shifted around, as if afraid someone might stop their progress. He wouldn't let that happen. Her body fit with his. Her scent wove around him, taking away his earlier worries about not being smart enough or good enough. She made him feel right.

Everything felt right as long as she was by his side.

Being in Dax's arms was heaven.

And he'd looked like an angel in his tuxedo. His long, blond hair had been tamed for the evening, floating around his shoulders. His broad shoulders were emphasized in the suit. His tall, trim body had glided toward Lexi as if his feet weren't touching the ground.

She drifted on a cloud in his embrace. The music wove around, cocooning them in their own world. His hand at her lower back sparked through her dress. His body pressed against hers, a little closer than was appropriate. She didn't care.

He'd noticed her nervousness and had asked. Because he cared. More than cared. She was sure.

A happy trill sang in her heart. Everything was going to be okay. One dance to give her confidence, then she'd take him outside and tell him.

The other dancers circled around. The music played on.

"How was your day?" Nice and simple small talk before the big reveal.

His shoulder dipped beneath her hand in a too-casual shrug. "We had a DOA this morning."

Dead on arrival. Sincere sadness drifted through her for the victim's family and Dax for witnessing. "I'm sorry."

"In our job it's to be expected." His cavalier attitude was fake. She heard the stress under the tone.

She appreciated how he already thought of being a paramedic as his job. He was compassionate, and accepting of the facts of life, and death. "It is part of the job."

"Once you find an investor for the HAAWT, being a paramedic and ski patroller won't be your job for long." His gaze flashed with what hinted at a guilty secret.

She didn't know if that would ever happen. Webber's earlier rejection stung again. "I don't know. George Webber declined to meet with me."

He rubbed her arm with his knuckles in a caring stroke. The movement sent waves of desire vibrating through her. He kissed her forehead and her nose. The slight touch of his lips didn't satisfy.

She lifted her head and leaned in. Their eyes connected in a knowing, wanting, glance. He bent his head and took her mouth.

The kiss tasted like the beginning of a new chapter in their life. His mouth pressed against hers with a longing, making her quiver. A longing communicating something deeper.

"Excuse me." Jackson's uptight voice interrupted their lovely kiss.

She didn't want to be bothered by her brother. Her blood pressure spiked. Her brother, Jackson Croft. Her body tensed. "Jackson?"

Dax's mouth dropped wide. He squinted at her and back at her brother in what appeared to be a he'd-been-caught expression.

Angry lines wrinkled her brother's forehead. It was an expression she saw frequently. He took a swig from his Champagne flute. "We need to talk."

"Now?" She didn't want to talk to her brother, she wanted to continue kissing Dax.

"You know Jackson Croft?" Dax's unsure and confused question made her realize what was at stake. He shook his head. "Of course you do, your families are close."

She'd been too confused from the kiss to pretend or deflect.

"Know her?" Jackson gripped her upper arm pulling her completely away from Dax. "I'm—"

She wasn't a toy. Using her elbow, she nudged her brother. "Jackson, this is Dax O'Donnell." She introduced them between tight lips. She needed to get him away and tell him before her brother blew it.

"We've met." He held out his hand to her brother.

"Met?" Worry spasmed in her gut.

Her brother ignored his outstretched hand and continued to glare. "I can't believe you're dancing with this guy." The disgust in Jackson's tone was overpowered by contempt.

Stubbornness turned her spine to steel. She didn't care if her brother didn't like Dax, she did. "He's my boyfriend."

He dropped his hand ignoring the snub. "I didn't tell Croft when I went to talk to him about—"

"About *your* product." Jackson's fingers dug into her arm. His disapproving expression caused her pulse to beat faster.

Something wasn't right. How had Dax met her older brother? Did he already know who she was? Her mind scrambled. "A product?"

"He pitched an advanced avalanche warning trigger device."

An avalanche exploded in her mind. The meaning rushed and roared. *No!* Her brain shattered into bits and pieces, shooting shards of ice that pinned her with pain. Her hand flailed to her forehead, trying to hold in the hurt. Dax would never steal her idea. She trusted him.

His eyes glittered with guilt. His mouth pinched into culpability.

The shards of ice dug deeper, making her cold. Frigid. Dizziness swirled in her head. She staggered back, so glad Jackson had a grip on her arm to keep her from falling.

Jackson pulled her closer, in a protective-older-brother stance. "Lexi, O'Donnell stole your prototype and pitched the HAAWT as his own."

Chapter Nineteen

Jackson's accusation stabbed through Dax's midsection. The agony radiated outward. That was what happened, but the billionaire hadn't let him finish the presentation. The man had kicked him out of the office before he'd had a chance to share the real inventor's name.

"I wanted to tell you in person, Lexi." Croft continued to hold her arm and Dax wanted to rip the hand off his girlfriend's skin. "But you were already at the hospital."

Her eyes shined with tears. Her mouth stayed open in a constant, round *O* of shock. She believed every word Croft said without giving Dax a chance. The torment numbed his body.

"You stole my idea!"

The music stopped and her accusation screamed through the room. Everyone stared. Shey and Ryder moved closer. Paul and Chuck, and a number of other hospital executives, stopped their conversations to listen.

"No." Dax held up his hands in a calming gesture. He didn't want to have this discussion in front of a room full of strangers and two of his bosses. He wanted to take Lexi in his arms and kiss away her expression of devastation and anger. He wanted to comfort and explain. "It wasn't like that."

"I believed you liked me for me." Her hurt tone sliced into him. He did like her for her. He loved her. "Not for my wealth."

Shaking his head, he tried to make sense of her words. "Wealth? What wealth?"

The room grew more silent. He skimmed their expressions. Ryder lowered his head, as if he knew a secret. Chuck and Paul glanced at each other in conspiracy. Shey angled her head in surprise. What did these people know that Dax didn't?

"It wasn't my money you were after." Lexi stepped forward and grabbed the lapels of his rented tuxedo. "It was my invention!" She shoved him.

Stumbling, he noted her furious expression, at Jackson's contempt, at Ryder's amusement. Their families were close, real close. Her mother had a different last name. Ryder was visiting his mother in the same hospital.

Dax finally figured out something everyone else had known. Lexi had played him for a fool. His blood heated. "You're related to the Crofts."

"She's my sister." Jackson leered as if Dax was an idiot.

Because he was an idiot.

She'd lied to him the entire time they were dating. Everything fell into place. Her discomfort when he talked about money. Her designer clothes. Her refusal to take her idea to Croft Industries. Her love for Ryder—her other brother.

Anger pulsed at Dax's neck. She'd never invited him to her house, never even told him where she lived.

The pulsing increased. He fisted his hands. Jackson insisted on meeting today because he knew. Knew they were dating and wanted to dig for dirt on Dax.

"Was this some kind of test?" He glared at Lexi and her older brother. He'd never been very good at tests. And he'd failed this one spectacularly. Anger plunged in his veins now. His heart thumped to the furious beat. "You don't think I'm good enough for you."

She angled her chin up. "Not if you're a thief and a liar."

Her words struck, imitating strong fists. He'd never lied to her, except not telling her about today's meeting. "I didn't steal your prototype. I was trying to help." His nails dug into his palms. He refused to unleash his anger in front of these people. He'd already made a fool of himself. "I figured I'd pitch the idea and if Jackson liked it, I'd let you carry on from there."

"Right." Her sarcasm spiked Dax's rage.

Why was he the one explaining his actions?

"I did it because you didn't want to go to Croft Industries and now I know why." His rage roared like a wild bear being attacked. He hadn't done anything wrong. But Lexi? "I might not be good enough for you, but I never lied about who I am."

Swiveling on his slippery, rental shoes, he stormed

away. He didn't have much in life, except he had his pride. His bosses had witnessed the shameful incident. He'd been called a thief and made a fool. The Crofts were major donors to the hospital, and the paramedic core. He'd never graduate and get a job in this town. He might as well say goodbye to his career as a paramedic, goodbye to Lexi, goodbye to his future.

Each of Dax's steps stomped on Lexi's chest. His betrayal cleaved into her, making her want to double over in torture. She stood tall. She wouldn't retreat or surrender. She wasn't that girl anymore. He'd stolen her prototype and tried to sell it to her brother. Now, he walked away from everything they'd had together.

But what did they have? A few nights of passion. A few weeks of fun. A lifetime of memories.

Memories that would hurt and haunt.

A chilly fog surrounded her.

Sure, she'd omitted the fact she was a Croft, but once she explained why, Dax should've understood. Doubts wormed their way into her head. Maybe she should hear him out, let him explain his intentions.

Her hand urged to reach out, yet she kept them clamped at her sides. She'd been tricked like this before, by Andrew. Had she been blinded by love again?

"It's okay, Lexi." Jackson still had a grip on her arm, still being the overprotective brother. "He's not worth it."

The fog morphed into a wall of resentment. Jackson

had no right to tell her who was worth how much. "How would you know? You've never had a serious relationship. Never cared about anyone enough to feel heartbreak."

His stony expression would normally make her cower.

Instead, she stood taller. "I'm sorry I said that, Jackson."

He'd had to be tough. He'd kept the family business running after his father died, even though he couldn't graduate from college.

"No. You're right." He let go of the grip on her arm and his hand fell to his side.

Ryder sprinted from Shey's side and hurried to them, gripping his phone with white knuckles. "We gotta go." Something about his expression had Lexi's chest spasming. "It's Mom."

Lexi's lungs screamed. She'd noticed something was wrong with her mom earlier this evening. She should've said something to a nurse, but she'd been too nervous about the evening.

With Jackson on one side and Ryder on the other, she ran through the hospital hallways like a zombie. She'd lost Dax, the man she'd loved secretly for years. She'd lost the dream of him helping with her invention. She'd lost everything.

She couldn't lose her mother.

They arrived at her mother's room to find chaos. Doctors and nurses crowded into the room, surrounding the bed. The machines' incessant beeping grew louder and louder. The acrid smell of blood and antiseptic.

And the silence from the woman in the center of it all.

"Mom!" Lexi lunged toward the bed, agony spearing through her center.

"Lexi." Jackson grabbed her arm, his tone intense. "Stay out of their way."

Ryder pulled her into a hug. He smoothed her hair trying to comfort. "It will be okay."

"No!" Nothing was going to be okay. She could sense it. Tears blinded. Her throat burned, and she gasped, trying to swallow her despondency. "Mom."

"She wants to speak to you." The doctor, wearing a white coat over his tuxedo, cleared a path to the bed. "There's not much time."

Lexi's body trembled, and her knees gave out. Her pulse charged so fast she thought it would spurt out of her body. With Jackson and Ryder's support, she moved toward her mom. Her brothers by her side. She held her breath, afraid of what she'd see. She wanted to remember her mom how she'd been, not how she was now.

Her mom's face was pale, yet had a yellowish tinge. The area around her eyes was swollen and red. Her lips were dry and cracked. The change during the hour was extreme.

"Children." Mom's voice was so low, they leaned closer to hear. "I love all of you."

The words touched Lexi's bleeding heart. "I love you, Mom. You're going to be okay."

Jackson and Ryder exchanged a glance of skepticism. They didn't believe Lexi.

"I am going to be okay. No more suffering. Or medicine. Or hospitals." Mom coughed, and a trickle of blood leaked out of her mouth.

Horror leached out of Lexi. She couldn't breathe.

A nurse swiped the blood off her mom's face, even so, it was too late. She'd never get the image out of her head.

"I'm going to be with your fathers." Mom's expression became peaceful, even while her body was being wracked with pain. "And I want each of you to be happy. To live your lives fully. I'll be watching from above."

As an angel. The image reminded Lexi of making angels in the snow, how the act had given her courage to take the next step with Dax, to be brave, and take a risk.

Mom shifted pinning Ryder with her gaze. "Ryder, it's time you got serious. About life. About a job. About a girl."

Her brother pulled his mouth in a tart expression. He didn't appreciate her suggestion. Mom must not know about his secret relationship with Shey Webber. Or maybe she did.

"Jackson," Mom's voice grew stronger, knowing she had to be tough on him. "You need to get less serious and have fun."

Her older brother's eyes went wide, caught in the middle of Mom's target. His lip curled in disgust. No way was he ever going to change his ways.

"And my little Lexi," Mom's tone softened. She focused with an odd clarity. "Don't use your past as an excuse to hide from your future."

The profound words wrapped around Lexi's cold heart like a hug. Taking her mother's hand, she stared back and watched the light in Mom's eyes go out. "Mom."

The machine buzzed in a long, flat noise. Lexi jolted. Her mother was gone.

"I'm sorry." The doctor used his palms to close her mother's eyes.

She sunk to the tiled hospital floor in her beautiful dress. The folds of silk surrounded her, yet she experienced no comfort from the caress. Realization started slow, with the numbing of her toes and legs. Her mom was dead. The numbing worked its way up her body, stopping at her hollowed-out chest and dry throat. Her head spun and her heart clenched.

A lone tear dripped, running down her cheek and dropping off her chin. The one tear hit the aqua of her dress, staining the spot darker. The spot spread, similar to her devastation.

Her mom was dead.

Everything inside Lexi muted to dark and empty. Loneliness wallowed inside. She bent at the waist and gave in to her anguish. The tears wouldn't stop.

The hospital hallways were one long tunnel after the other. Dax kept following the light, hoping to find comfort from the familiar. Hoping his fear of the whitewashed corridors would overwhelm his devastation of losing Lexi. Wandering up and down, he tried to keep the emotions under control, tried to stay numb. He loved Lexi, and he'd lost her.

Or had he ever really had her? The numbness frizzled with sparks of anger. She'd probably considered slumming with him a lark. He hadn't even known her real last name.

He untied and ripped off the stupid bowtie. He'd worn the monkey suit for her, and wondered why she'd want to come to the charity event. Now he knew why. He'd thought it weird, and yet didn't want to question his good luck at having her, knowing she was special and he was not.

Remembering her slip-ups made him angry at himself. The way she sipped wine and laughed when he'd suggested Croft Industries. Her fancy clothes, and how she moved as if a debutante. Probably because she was a debutante. She'd made him a fool. The shame boiled in his blood.

If he'd known her full last name he never would've flirted with her, never would've suggested fun lessons, never would've made love to her. He would've been too intimidated.

Just like he'd been intimated by her brother Jackson. He'd called Dax into his office resembling a principal about to lecture a rowdy school boy. He'd never gotten to the point of exposing who the real inventor was. He kicked at the shiny linoleum floor.

Wheeling around the corner, he ended up in Emergency. The place was crowded for a Thursday evening. Maybe facing his fear, the numbness would end, and he could consider the rest of his life. Without Lexi.

He flashed his badge and entered into the Emergency rooms, with the curtains cordoning off the various beds. Machines beeped, doctors and nurses talked, patients moaned.

"Avalanche…" a man said behind a closed curtain.

"Were you carrying the proper safety equipment?" Another man asked.

"We had everything, including a float device. The avalanche hit so quick we didn't even know it was happening until after the snow was on top of us." The first man sniffled. "I couldn't activate the device fast enough." A distressed cry. "I got separated from my friend and he was buried alive."

If they'd had Lexi's invention, the man's friend would be alive.

The man's distressed cries shook Dax to the core. He might be mourning the loss of his relationship, but this man was mourning the loss of a friend. Even if he couldn't be with Lexi, he wanted to make sure her prototype came to market. She deserved it. Backcountry skiers and boarders deserved it.

He might not be good enough for her. He might not make it as a paramedic. But he could test her device in real-life situations as investors had requested. He could use a video camera and his phone, intentionally trigger an avalanche, and record the device working.

The shaking halted and his body firmed.

Even though she didn't trust him, and believed he'd stolen her project, he believed in her and the HAAWT. And he was going to prove the prototype worked.

In the early morning, Lexi sat in the chair in front of Jackson's desk wearing old sweats. This was the chair her mother had favored when discussing things with Stephen Croft, and later with Jackson. Her lilac scent lingered in the air, and she took a big sniff. A tiny whiff of pine blended with the lilac reminding her of Dax. She'd cried most of the night, unable to sleep. Early-morning light crept into the study, and she dreaded the daylight.

In the daylight, she'd have to face the fact she'd lost Dax and her mother on the same night.

Blackness invaded her soul. Her heart cracked into irreparable pieces. Not only was her heart broken, she was broken.

When Jackson told her Dax had stolen her idea, she didn't want to believe. Then, Dax had realized her last name and had felt betrayed. And she couldn't go after him because of her mom.

Guilt had blame parading in Lexi's mind. She'd known something was wrong. She should've stayed and called the doctor, even if her mom didn't want her to. She'd been so excited to see Dax dressed in a tuxedo. Of being held in his arms while they'd danced. Of telling him the truth about her family—excited and scared.

Her muscles tightened, remembering Jackson's interruption and Dax's guilty expression. Instead of having the night of her life, she'd learned he'd pitched the HAAWT to her brother, pitched the idea as his own. Lost her mother and Dax.

At least her mother wouldn't witness her embarrassment and heartache. Wave upon wave of grief overtook Lexi, yet her eyes stayed dry. She didn't think she had any tears left. Hugging her legs, she curled into a ball on the chair.

The sun rose. She heard their housekeeper moving about the house. Cramps inundated her legs. How long she sat there, she didn't know.

Stretching, her foot knocked a folder off the desk and papers fell out and scattered onto the Aubusson carpet. Papers looking suspiciously like her presentation. She caught her breath. Falling to her knees, she reviewed the familiar, bullet-pointed text. The graphics cut through her gaze. Dax had stolen her prototype and her presentation.

Determination charged through her. She might be down, but she wasn't out. She owned the patent. She'd make the HAAWT happen. She just wasn't sure how, right now.

She flipped through page by page. He hadn't changed a single word. Must've copied it from her computer when she'd worked at his house. Possibly when she'd been sleeping after making love.

Her stomach soured. Except it hadn't been making love. It had only been sex. Sex so Dax could take advantage of her and steal.

Coming to the presentation's conclusion, featuring the reasons why investing in the HAAWT would be good for a business, she turned to one last page.

An added page.

A page spelling out who the real inventor was. Who'd developed and built and tested the HAAWT.

Lexi Henderson.

Chapter Twenty

Dax checked the cameras, making sure they were set to record and go live on social media. One was placed on his helmet, and the other on his chest. A third camera, his phone, was on a selfie stick he held in front of him. He'd abandoned his ski poles at the base, but still carried the other basic avalanche equipment. Once he triggered the avalanche, he wanted people to view what happened from every angle.

A strong wind blew across the top of the backcountry bowl, blowing snow upwards. The incredible view from the top of the cliff featured mountain peaks, evergreen trees below, and a frozen lake in the distance. He loved this view. Loved the mountains. Loved Castle Ridge.

Loved Lexi.

First thing this morning, he'd taken the lifts as far as he could, ducked under the resort rope, and hiked to the top of the ridge. He hadn't told anyone his plan. His goal was to prove Lexi's HAAWT worked and could save lives.

Save his life.

An interesting combination of nerves and adrenaline skittered across his skin, similar to how he'd felt right before a high school ski race. Most people would consider his actions risky and insane. To him it was necessary.

He believed.

Believed in her invention. Believed in her. And he was going to prove both.

Readjusting the helmet so the cameras caught every important angle, he took a deep breath. He waved at his phone camera. "This is Dax O'Donnell and I'm *hawt*." With nervous laughter, he stretched out the last word. "Just kidding. I'm testing the HAAWT."

The cornice he stood on had formed from windblown snow, building out at sharp angles. This particular cornice creaked and cracked, imitating his bones as he prepared for the ride of his life. He'd picked this spot knowing the likelihood of an avalanche was high, because they'd happened in past winters. If he triggered one on purpose, the chances would be one hundred percent.

Part of his job as an avalanche expert on ski patrol was to assess the avalanche danger, and if needed, use an avalanche cannon or dynamite to set one off so it would be safe for skiers later in the day. Tests were performed: measuring slope angles and orientation, snow metamorphism, hand pit test, compression and extended column tests to check whether the area was safe. This morning, he'd tested for unsafe.

The conditions couldn't have been more perfect for an avalanche.

A chill tickled his spine. A warning for danger. He didn't need a warning, because he knew the location was dangerous.

But he believed in the HAAWT.

The cliff he stood on faced leeward and was wind-loaded, therefore only a fragile bond had formed. It had snowed overnight, laying a heavy layer of new snow on the partially-melted old snow. The crags funneled into a chute that would keep the avalanche directed between the two walls.

He cleared his throat so he sounded professional. "This is a live test of the Henderson Avalanche Advanced Warning Trigger prototype, or HAAWT, created by Lexi Henderson," he coughed. "Croft."

Holding back a shiver, Dax focused on his mission. He wasn't cold. The shivers were from excitement. This was going to be the thrill of his life, and he needed to consider possibly the end of his life. He didn't think so, though. Not after reading her notes and playing with the prototype.

He gave the date, time, and weather. There were probably other things he should mention for the test, but he didn't know the scientific methods like Lexi did. Twisting his lips, he ignored his ignorance. He did know how to use social media. "This test is being recorded and broadcast live."

He hoped it wasn't broadcasting his burial. It wouldn't. He knew the prototype worked.

He believed.

"I placed the dynamite below the crown, and it's

attached to this trigger." He held up the dynamite trigger in his left hand.

Beholding the bluebird sky, he sent up a prayer. The gusts of wind slowed to a caress, giving him faith. Taking a risk, a thought-out and calculated risk, was worth it. He believed in Lexi's device, and he believed in her. He loved her even though he hated how she'd lied to him about her last name because she didn't believe in him. Didn't trust him.

"I love you, Lexi," he spoke into the camera. There, it was out. Staring down at the cliff he planned to jump off, he took another deep breath.

No tricks or fancy moves. The charge was set. He planned to leap and press the button to trigger the dynamite. Then ski fast. He knew he couldn't outrun the avalanche. He could get a head start.

His muscles contracted. This was it. The final moment before the big bang.

"I believe in you, Lexi. I believe in the HAAWT." He jumped.

The weightless sensation of being airborne for a second burst through his body. He tightened his legs and bent at the knees, preparing for impact. His skis hit the side of the mountain on the wall, and his body absorbed the shock. A surge of adrenaline erupted in his system as he controlled his downward progress. With a confident finger, he pressed the button connected to the dynamite.

No doubts or regrets, because he believed.

The explosion deafened.

With a shout, he skied fast down the chute.

The snow billowed chasing him.

Crushed and roared and rumbled.

He hustled and hoped the HAAWT had time to sense the ground's movement to initiate the float avalanche airbag.

If not, he would be buried and his body wouldn't be found until Spring.

The hospital machines were silent. The medication smells absent.

Lexi's mother gone.

She and her brothers had met with the doctor this morning to discuss what had gone wrong. In his office, the doctor had talked about the risks, her mother's advanced stages of cancer, her age. Lexi hadn't wanted to hear. So she'd left the meeting and wandered to her mother's private hospital room with a sluggish gate.

The room had been cleaned and sanitized, waiting for the next patient. Nothing of her mother's remained. Not even the flowers she'd brought the other day.

"You know she's in a better place." Jackson's delicate tone was the exact opposite from when she'd woken him early this morning.

"I know."

"Ready to go?"

After discovering the presentation Dax gave, she'd marched to her brother's bedroom and demanded an explanation. Jackson said he'd insisted on the meeting because the idea had sounded suspiciously like hers. He admitted he hadn't given Dax a chance to finish, and never read through the presentation left behind. Jackson had been too angry.

Her stance softened. He'd been angry for her. He was her big brother, and he always protected her. At school, when the kids had picked on her for being brainy. At dances, when the girls had insinuated she didn't belong at the private school because she wasn't rich. He'd even stood up to her mother, when Lexi had wanted to join ski patrol.

Meeting with Dax had been a form of protection. Jackson was trying to protect her from unscrupulous men and business associates. He understood what had happened between her and Andrew.

Dax was nothing like her ex. Guilt for holding out on him for so long, for not believing in him, strangled in her throat. She needed to apologize and see if they could salvage their relationship.

Nodding, she traversed the hall with her brother. "You know, Dax was only trying to help me."

He hadn't stolen her idea, he'd been trying to help find an investor. He believed Croft Industries was the right place for the HAAWT.

He was right. Croft Industries *was* the perfect place for the HAAWT to be developed, produced, and marketed. Because just as the device was her baby, Croft Industries was her family, and she'd been too stubborn to realize.

"I know." Jackson's agreement surprised her. "The presentation was impressive."

"More than the presentation." Her resentment caused her voice to harden. Originally, she'd never wanted people to believe Croft Industries invested in her idea because of her connection. After Jackson's initial scoffing, she'd been reluctant to show him her progress or the final prototype. It was time to release her stubbornness, so the device could come to fruition with the right company. Croft Industries. "The prototype has been tested in labs. Manufacturing the device can be bid out. We can make the product cost effective. Most importantly, the HAAWT will save lives."

"I like the name. Any way to work a C into it?" He bumped his shoulder against hers.

She became animated and could barely hold in her excitement. "C for Croft?"

"Of course." His superior tone carried a light edge.

"We can negotiate the final name in the contracts." She wanted to squee with delight, but her excitement was tempered by her recent loss. Her *baby* was going to be born, and yet her mother wouldn't be around to share the experience.

"Lexi!" Quinn, Dax's sister-in-law, rushed down the corridor. Her tight expression exhibited fear. This wasn't a dance emergency.

Nerves swooped through Lexi. "What's wrong?"

Her friend slid to a halt. She huffed and puffed. "It's Dax."

Her nerves skidded and crashed into her stomach. "Is he okay?"

"Look." Quinn held out her phone, showing a live feed.

A skier was in the off-resort backcountry, taking a steep line. Lexi recognized the area known for avalanches. A loud plume of snow billowed against a clear blue sky. An avalanche.

The angle switched to a camera in front of the skier. The green coat jumped out at her. Dax's coat. She gasped. Anguish spread through her chest. "What the hell is he doing?"

Quinn's hand shook, holding her phone. "Dax triggered the avalanche with dynamite to test some new safety device."

Lexi exchanged glances with her brother. His expression held shock and concern. She could only imagine her horrified look.

"Reed recorded the whole thing. And Dax is broadcasting live."

Her heart tried to burst from its constraints. "So Dax is alive?"

"I don't know." Her friend's eyes shined with unshed tears. "Reed called ski patrol, and headed to the ski patrol headquarters."

With her heart pumping, she took several short breaths. She couldn't lose her wits. Too many things to do. She had to get out on the mountain and help find Dax. "I've got to go."

She hurried to base and got dressed.

"What the hell do you think you're doing?" Chuck entered the ski patrol locker room, yelling, making Lexi jerk.

Reed followed on his heels, not letting the ski patrol boss out of his sight. His tight face and red eyes showed his anxiety.

Ignoring them both, she continued strapping on her first aid pack and zipped up her ski coat. Pushing her wild emotions back, she tried to sound calm and collected. "Going to find Dax."

"The avalanche rescue team has left." Chuck's reasoning wasn't going to work.

Her resolve firmed. "I'll catch up to them. More hands are always needed."

"You're dating the victim."

Victim? The word went off like a bomb in her chest. "Don't call Dax a victim."

The bomb burst into fragments, embedding in her lungs and abdomen and skin. The misery spread across her entire body. She couldn't lose Dax.

"Let her go." Reed's sharp voice startled her. "I'd join her, if I could." He couldn't ski with his injury.

Lexi went through a mental checklist, double-checking her equipment and supplies. Shoving on her helmet, she grabbed her gloves.

"Protocol states you aren't allowed on the rescue team." Chuck's firm tone stopped her.

For a second.

Her resolve firmed into concrete. She whirled about to stare him down. "Screw the protocols."

The words flowed out of her, knowing she was right. Normally a rule follower, this wasn't time to go by the rules. Dax would be proud of her. She was proud of herself.

She left the locker room, and snapped on her skis. Fault and responsibility weighed heavily on her. Dax had taken the risk for her to prove the HAAWT worked.

She couldn't lose Dax like she'd lost her father, right after losing her mother.

She rode one chairlift after the other. Usually, she chatted with her chair companions; this time she was silent, too afraid if she spoke only crying would come out. Getting off the last chair, she couldn't stop her crazy thoughts flying off in scenarios going from bad to worse.

She skied off-trail, winding her way through the trees. Each trunk represented an obstacle she'd worked her way past. Her strict-rule following and not taking risks. Her stubbornness to access the Croft money. Her belief Dax could never love her. She'd changed her mind on all of these issues.

Ducking under the rope, she followed the other ski patrollers' path repeating the mantra.

The edge of the slide was littered with tree limbs and rocks. Seeing the power of the avalanche sent a shockwave through her system. The destruction from the top of the crag, where Dax must've skied from, to the bottom of the slope overwhelmed her comprehension. She'd helped rescue avalanche victims before, and she'd survived one. Never had she seen such devastation.

Her heart clutched. *She couldn't lose Dax like she'd lost her mother.*

A group of ski patrollers stood about twenty yards farther up slope. Doing nothing. Anger exploded with the force of an avalanche. They'd already given up on trying to find Dax, believing he was already dead. Her breath hitched. She refused to believe it. She couldn't lose him without telling him she loved him. She didn't care if this was a fling to him, or he was mad at her for lying.

But if he was mad, why would he pull such a crazy stunt for her? He'd taken a risk for her future, and she wanted to make it *their* future.

"What're you doing standing around?" Her scream of agony echoed through the mountains. "We need to find Dax! Start digging!"

An order, when she'd never ordered anyone to do anything in her life. Another way Dax had influenced her for the better. She wasn't going to be a wallflower anymore, not with her life or her invention. Or her love life.

The patrollers stared, as if she was crazy. Maybe she was. Loss did strange things.

"Get moving!"

Bode's smirk skewered into her. Aiden's slight smile soothed the pain. Matt's grin threw her entire world off-kilter. How could they be happy when they might've lost a friend?

Their bodies separated, the red from their ski patrol coats provided a perfect contrast to the bright green. A second explosion occurred inside of her. This one resembled an explosion of blooming flowers in spring, a riot of bright colors. Dax emerged from the center of their huddle. The flowers brightened her insides, creating a garden of happiness.

His blond hair gleamed, the sun shining a spotlight. His green eyes shined. His lips raised in a quirky, one-sided smile. Dax's smile. He beamed shining a light on her. Her entire body heated.

He was alive.

The image of her kissing him the last time he'd been caught in an avalanche flashed in her mind. She wanted to do so much more. Nerves bunched and then fluttered, like butterflies leaving the flower garden growing in her midsection. Possible rejection was palpable.

With no risk there's no reward.

Tossing her poles, she snapped off her skis and ran to him.

"Life is too short and you have to take risks for what you believe in. I believe in you. I believe in us." The fluttering butterfly wings brushed her insides, sending tingles of anticipation and dread. She dropped to her knees. "Dax, will you marry me?"

Chapter Twenty-One

Dax's chest thudded.

Marry?

The concept was foreign. He hadn't gotten around to thinking of marriage yet. His pulse raced, sending extra blood to his brain. The idea titillated. He loved Lexi. Heck, he'd risked his life for her. Blood pounded from his brain to his heart—his melting, overloading heart. With Lexi, marriage would be an adventure.

This was so crazy. They'd only been dating a few weeks, and they'd had a furious fight last night. And yet, crazy described him perfectly, and now it described her. He'd pushed her to take risks and he loved her even more.

Bode's face scrunched with disgust. Dax didn't care what the guy thought. Aiden's body tensed, standing on his tiptoes waiting for the answer. He seemed thrilled at the idea. Matt glared, obviously jealous. The entire group of patrollers continued to stare, with expressions of suspense.

Staring at Dax. Staring at Lexi *still* on her knees.

All the air whooshed out of his lungs, and he found it difficult to breathe. More difficult than when he'd been caught in the avalanche and swimming his way to the top with the help of the HAAWT. How could he leave her in suspense so long? He loved her.

Through craziness and fights. Through bad jobs and big brothers. Together, they felt right.

He bent down and pulled her into his arms, loving how her warm body fit his, loving how her unique scent wrapped around him. Simply loving her. "Yes, I'll marry you."

She didn't react for a second, as if in shock. Then, her body softened against him, gluing herself to his heart. She gazed up and her eyes glowed with happiness.

And he realized, he'd put the look there. And he wanted to do it again and again. Forever.

The crowd cheered and clapped. The sound was only background noise, as he tugged her closer and leaned in for a kiss.

When their lips touched, fireworks went off in his head and reignited the fire in his soul he thought had been extinguished by her lack of faith in him. The fire burned bright, like their first kiss after he'd been rescued from beneath an avalanche. But this kiss was so much better. And this time he hadn't been buried beneath the snow.

That thought ignited another fire, a different kind of excitement. Breaking off the kiss, he couldn't wait to tell her the news. He gripped her upper arms between his gloved hands. "It works. The HAAWT works."

The patrollers hadn't dug him out from beneath the snow. He'd been standing along the side of the slide, continuing to record the test results, when they'd found him.

Her just-kissed lips lifted into a dazzling grin, making him believe he could conquer an avalanche or the world. He'd meet with Paul and Chuck and grovel to get his job back and be reinstated for paramedic training. He'd start the backcountry avalanche preparedness classes and sell his students the HAAWT. He'd do anything and everything for her.

Her smile slipped into a flat line. She slapped him on the upper arm. "What were you thinking, testing the HAAWT?"

"Guess the honeymoon is over." He couldn't stop the tease, it was part of his personality.

She clung to him and didn't laugh. "My mom died last night. I thought I'd lost you." Her desperation clawed at Dax's lungs.

"I'm so sorry." His excited heart dipped into his gut. He hadn't known her mom had died. He wrapped her closer in his arms, holding her super-tight, never wanting to let her go. Wanting to protect her from harm. Had her impulsive proposal been spurred on by the loss of her mother? Doubt stabbed, imitating ice shards. He couldn't handle losing her. "That's not why you proposed, is it?"

"Of course not." She slanted away to study him. Her eyes shone with love, yet he could see the sadness around the blue edges. "I love you, Dax O'Donnell. Love you with all my heart."

"And I love you, Lexi Henderson Croft." He twisted his lips into a tease wanting to see her smile. "Love you so much that even if I couldn't have you, I'd ride an avalanche for you."

She rewarded him with a soft, knowing tilt of her mouth. "Sometimes taking a big chance is worth the risk."

He didn't know if she was referring to triggering the avalanche or her proposal, but he had to agree. They'd taken a risk for love and they'd won.

Epilogue

Dax wiped his sweaty palms against his suit jacket. He wasn't nervous, more excited. Maybe a bit anxious that Lexi was ready for this big step.

Marriage.

Standing at the front of the chapel, he stood with the minister and his wife, who would act as the only witness. The Las Vegas wedding had been planned in two weeks, in secret. They'd told no one. Lexi acting rash was a concept he was still getting used to, just like he was getting used to being successful in his paramedic class. Another month and he'd graduate.

He stood a little taller. Life was good. And their private wedding felt right. Just the two of them exchanging vows to each other. They could have a large reception after they sealed the deal.

The canned organ music filled the small chapel and Lexi stood at the end of the long aisle. Her fiery red hair flowed under the short veil. The short white dress hugged her curves and showcased her long legs. Sighing, he couldn't take his eyes off her. She was more than a pretty package. Intelligent, funny, brave, and all his.

Until the minister coughed and choked and gurgled. The man's face was as red as a tomato. Moving his lips, he grabbed his throat with both hands.

"Are you okay?" Dax's gaze darted between his gorgeous bride strolling down the aisle and the minister collapsing beside him. "Can you speak?"

The minister's wife put a hand on the man's shoulder. "He can't breathe." Her voice screeched.

Dax didn't panic, he assessed, doing what he'd been trained to do. The confidence he'd gained over the last few weeks flowed naturally in his blood. He might not have the certificate, yet, but he had years of experience as an EMT. And he had a woman who believed in him and his abilities. A woman who'd helped him believe in himself.

The minister put one hand out and braced against the table behind him. His eyes bulged from his sockets and his mouth gaped open.

"Oh my." Lexi's waltz turned into a run. Her high-heeled shoes scraped on the white runner. "What's wrong?"

"He's choking." The minister's wife took the bible from the man's hand. "He just ate a mint."

Dax wanted to give Lexi the best wedding possible. Something memorable, not morbid. The minister would not die on his watch.

"I'm a paramedic." Not quite, but he didn't have time to go into the exact details. And Lexi wasn't dressed for the maneuver.

With his front to the minister's back, he placed his

arms around the man's chest, fisted his hands and pushed up below the minister's ribcage. He did the Heimlich. Once, twice.

A large mint flew out of the minister's mouth. The man coughed and breathed heavily. "Thanks." The minister's voice scratched.

Dax released the now-breathing man and helped him sit on the short dais.

"Darling." His wife kneeled beside him, concern evident on her face. "Are you okay?"

The minister nodded, clutching his chest.

"Is he all right?" Lexi reached the end of the aisle, breathing a little heavily. Her breasts moved up and down in the tight bodice of the gown.

"Yes." Dax nodded. Confident in his abilities and his future. A Heimlich maneuver might be simple, but he'd assessed the entire scenario, stayed calm, and proceeded by the book. "Are you going to be able to go ahead with the ceremony?"

That was important. He'd taken a couple of days off work to fly to Las Vegas with Lexi. She'd wanted to get married as soon as possible. They only had the weekend and he wanted it to be perfect.

"Yes, of course." The minister straightened.

"Don't rush." Dax took Lexi's hand in his. He could wait a few minutes. They might only have the weekend in Vegas, but they had the rest of their lives together.

"You saved my husband's life." The wife's gratefulness pumped his confidence higher.

Lexi's eyes sparked with love and devotion. And trust. "And, you saved our wedding."

He had.

He'd saved a man and his marriage. He'd grown and conquered. He'd fallen in love with the most amazing woman. A woman who trusted and believed in him.

Just as he believed in himself.

"I'm fully recovered." The minister stood. "Are the two lovebirds ready?"

"I am." Lexi's wide smile seared Dax's heart.

He couldn't stop a tease. "You mean, I do."

Read on for excerpts from other books
in the Castle Ridge series.

Dear Reader,

I hope you enjoyed *The Playboy Switch*. If you enjoyed the book, please consider leaving a review at your place of purchase. Word of mouth is crucial for any author to succeed so she can continue bringing you more stories you love.

And don't forget to join my newsletter for a free book. You'll also get the latest book news, sales, and contest information. You can join at www.allieburton.com

Allie

The Billionaire's Ploy
A Castle Ridge Small Town Romance, Book 5

by ALLIE BURTON

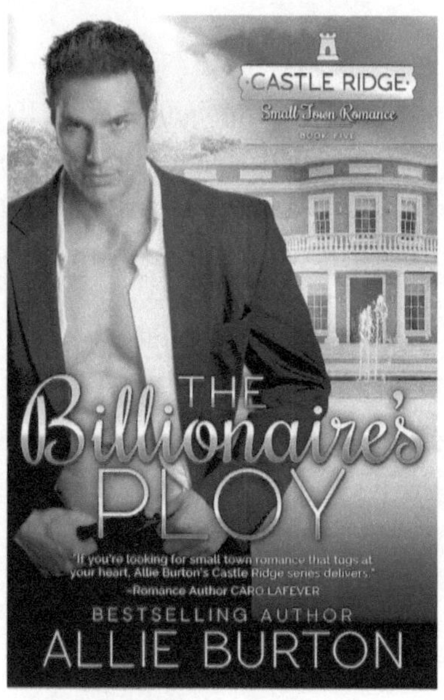

All's fair in love and business.

Billionaire Jackson Croft refuses to let anything interfere with his merger and marriage plans. His merger. His brother's marriage. When Emory Barrington returns to Castle Ridge and catches his younger brother's attention, Jackson needs to take drastic steps to stop the flirtation. Even if it means using himself as bait.

As a child Emory was infatuated with the younger Croft brother, so when he invites her to a party she can't resist. Until Jackson interrupts their dance, tries to bribe her, and then steals a kiss. A kiss that vibrates to her soul.

To make up for the attempted bribe, Jackson offers her a job decorating his Denver penthouse. She's just starting her interior design firm and can't turn the business away even if it means working closely with the billionaire. The project turnaround is fast and the attraction between Emory and Jackson grows faster. She believes she sees the real man beneath the façade, but when she learns of his double-dealing her heart can't take the betrayal.

In this take off on the *Sabrina* story, can deception lead to love?

EXCERPT:

"The party is tonight. You should come." Ryder's invitation had Emory's stomach clutching.

All of her teenage fantasies about attending one of the Croft events burst into an explosion of light. Joy shot through her entire body setting off tingles of excitement. *Ryder Croft invited me, Emory Reese Barrington, to a Croft party.*

Geez, quit acting like a child. She shouldn't be impressed. She'd been to lots of fancy parties in Spain. She was a special guest at a Vizconde's party. Her thoughts soured. One of many of his special guests.

"You're inviting me to your sister's wedding reception? Isn't it a bit late to RSVP?" Except he wasn't inviting Emory, he didn't know who he spoke to.

"There will be hundreds. One more person won't be noticed." He took her hand and rubbed his thumb against her skin. "We could dance."

She practically swooned. Clutching the coat tighter between her hand, she imagined holding Ryder in her arms while they danced, of him walking her through the elaborate gardens like she'd seen him do with other girls, of him kissing her.

Ryder would be disappointed when he found out her name, but for now, for this one moment in time, she could be special to him. "I'd love to."

"Great." An uneasiness slid into his gaze and she wondered if he was picturing the woman he'd planned to propose to. He turned away and opened the trunk taking out her suitcase.

"Hello, Emory." An even deeper masculine voice rumbled.

In a panic, she pivoted around at the greeting. Her fantasy to pretend for a little while longer died by two words from the scary, older brother. She'd hoped Ryder wouldn't learn who she was until tonight at the party. When she was dressed up and looking her best.

She straightened her shoulders. It was too late now. "Hello, Jackson."

Wearing a suit and tie on a Saturday afternoon, he strolled from his boring sedan parked ahead of them. His brown hair had been slicked back from his forehead in perfect grooming. A couple of new lines had formed on his forehead. Because he never had fun, his only interest being the family business.

"Emory?" Ryder raised his brown eyebrows into high arches. He hadn't figured out who she was after spending thirty minutes in her company.

Her spirits lowered. Had she been so unnoticeable

as a kid? Jackson had recognized her immediately.

Jackson signed off on a clipboard a worker gave him, barely glancing at her. "How was Barcelona?"

She angled her chin surprised not only that he remembered where she'd gone, but that she'd been gone at all. Their paths didn't cross frequently in the past, on purpose. She'd avoided him and his scary and overbearing attitude. "Good."

The work experience had been great. The personal life not so much. But she wasn't going to go into detail. Not with Jackson.

"Emory?" Ryder's jaw dropped.

"Your mother is going to be glad you're home." Jackson looked at her and then at his brother. His gaze went quizzical. "Good to see you," he said before heading up the stairs and through the front door.

"Emory?" Ryder shook his head as if trying to get her name straight.

Disappointment speared through her chest. Her fantasy had ended sooner than expected. They weren't even going to have drinks together. "I suppose your invitation to the party has been withdrawn now you know who I am."

"No." He shook his head again still appearing shocked. "No. Of course not."

She raised her brows. "Are you sure? Do you still want to dance with the housekeeper's daughter?"

He waved a hand in front of his face and his expression cleared. His gaze roved over again as if assessing her shape. "This is the twenty-first century."

Her stomach squirmed with misgiving. That wasn't really an answer to her question.

The Heartbreak Contract
A Castle Ridge Small Town Romance, Book 6

by ALLIE BURTON

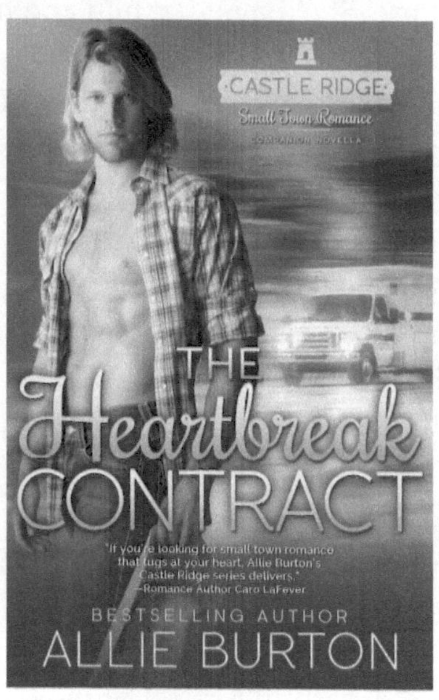

Love on the dotted line.

Self-made sports and entertainment agent Vivienne Tucker knows no one in the frozen town of Castle Ridge is going to melt her heart. No one can. She's been on her own for too long and while her skin might appear soft, she's as tough as nails.

Paul Bradford is a devoted family man to his younger siblings, whose heart and life belong to the town he grew up in. He's not used to taking time for himself or relationships, but after an anonymous one-night stand, he can't forget the ice queen who heated at his touch and ignited a passion he thought he'd lost. Until the next day when he spies her kissing someone else.

Vivienne never expected to see Paul again until she discovers he's the older brother of her newest client. An older brother who doesn't approve of her client's career choice. An older brother who stirs up desire she's tried so hard to forget.

When her client is involved in a possibly career-ending accident, Vivienne and Paul must put aside their differences and work together. But what if working together makes them both re-think the heartbreak contract they'd agreed upon?

COMING SOON IN THE CASTLE RIDGE SERIES!
The Marriage Merger
The Runaway Royal

Did you miss the first few books of the Castle Ridge series where Dax is first introduced?

Excerpt from

The Romance Dance
A Castle Ridge Small Town Romance, Book 1

by ALLIE BURTON

A slow sashay to desire.

After being abandoned by his fiancée and his fans because of a disfiguring accident, former classical pianist Reed O'Donnell returns home to hide. He's pieced his life back together becoming a landlord and remodel construction specialist, but shies away from a social life.

Ex-ballerina Quinn Petrov moved to Castle Ridge and invested her money to start a dance studio with plans to put down roots. She wants to get involved in the community to promote her business and make real friends, not the acquaintances she'd made in New York. When she meets her secretive and sexy landlord, she's intrigued but he always seems to be hiding behind a mask.

Reed can't stop the attraction he feels toward his new tenant, but she's beautiful and outgoing, while he is not. When his younger brother begs him to help impress Quinn, Reed can't say no. Using the musical language of love, he woos Quinn for his brother, but when his own mask slips will he reveal his secrets?

In this modern take of Cyrano de Bergerac meets Beauty and the Beast, Quinn and Reed dance their way into each other's hearts.

EXCERPT:

Quinn lay on her back and scooted farther under the sink. The warmth from her body slid along his skin, sending tingles of attraction to his loins. Her long leg lay next to his damaged one. Perfection next to destruction. Reed was a grotesque monster next to her doll-like body.

"What do you need me to do?" The soft lilt at the end of her question sent a shiver up his spine.

"Point the light at this joint." He handed her the flashlight and the beam swung around. He'd have to show her the joint. Reluctantly, he took her hand and guided it into position. Locked together, her delicate hand hid the scars on his. He didn't appear so hideous.

"Is this good?" Again, the sexy lilt playing to his lust.

"That's what she said." His brother Dax chimed in, and pounded on the top of the sink. "Ba-dum-bum."

Fever flushed through Reed at his brother's lame joke. He hadn't heard his brother come in. He dropped the wrench again.

The tool fell and smacked Quinn on the forehead.

"Ouch." She held her other hand at the spot.

"Oh, shit. I'm sorry. Are you okay?" He stroked her forehead where the angry bruise formed. "Dax! What're you doing messing around? I wanted your help, not a comedian."

"I'm fine." Lifting her arm, she rubbed her forehead. Her upper arm smashed against her breasts, making them jiggle and pushing them up higher in the low-cut camisole.

His cock noticed, hardening into a bigger shaft. He tightened his muscles, trying to control the anger surging inside him. As well as other things. He didn't want this attraction, and he certainly didn't deserve a woman so beautiful. And he'd hurt her. "I'm sorry. My idiot brother surprised me."

"You asked me to come. What's going on down there?" His brother peered under the sink. "Is this a new, kinky way to—"

"Dax, dammit." Reed shoved himself out from underneath the sink. Reaching back around, he held his hands out for Quinn. She placed her slim hands in his. Like a monster, his ugly, scarred hand swallowed her tiny one. The earlier image of her hand making his look better slipped away. He had too much ugliness to cover up.

He helped Quinn out. "Thanks."

"You called me." Dax took her elbows and helped her to her feet. A knight helping an injured princess being held captive by a monster. His sexy smirk enhanced his handsome face. "Who is this beautiful—" His gaze traveled the length of her body. "—and wet woman?"

Reed stiffened and clenched his hands into fists. His little brother shouldn't be ogling her. Not with her perky breasts sticking out of the soft silk material, not with the way the wet cloth clung to her slight curves and hugged her hips. He grabbed Quinn's wet robe and held it in front, covering most of her. "Here."

Her relaxed, answering grin showed she wasn't concerned with how much of her body was displayed. As a dancer, she was probably used to people staring at her. "I'm Quinn Petrov."

His brother's charm was already working. Annoyance pulsed at Reed's temples.

Besides their green eyes, it was hard to tell Dax was his brother. Dax had longer, blond hair while Reed's was dark and curly. Dax's lanky and able body was the opposite of Reed's thick trunk exterior and his limp. Dax's fun attitude toward life contrasted with Reed's darker views.

"Bro, why didn't you tell me about your new woman?" His brother gave an exaggerated wink, trying to embarrass Reed.

If Dax stayed in town longer than his ski patrol shift, he'd know who Quinn was. "She's not my woman." He sounded grouchy and short, and he hated himself for it. This woman didn't matter to him. Not what skimpy clothes she wore, or who she dated. "She's my tenant."

"Interesting." His brother's eyebrows rose and lowered in a more-than-interested action.

"I should get changed." Quinn's soft smile had his insides twisting. "Nice meeting you, Dax."

"I'll be seeing you around." The suggestiveness said more than his words.

The twisting inside Reed's gut pulled tighter, watching Quinn's wet backside sway out of the bathroom. He couldn't pull his gaze away from the mesmerizing move.

"Getting out of bed was worth it for the view." His brother's face took on a wolfish expression. "I want to be a landlord, if I can have hot tenants like her."

"Stick to blowing avalanches up." He wanted to blow up. At his brother, at Quinn, at the situation. He never should've called Dax. "Help me finish fixing the leak."

Dax crouched down by the sink and picked up the flashlight. "So what's going on between you two?"

"Nothing." Reed climbed back under the sink, with a caulk gun in hand.

Why would his brother think he'd have anything going on with a woman as beautiful as Quinn? He hadn't dated anyone since his fiancée. He only socialized with his family, rarely talked to anyone else except his construction clients.

"It's the middle of the night." Using a suggestive tone, his brother pointed the light at the pipe connection. "You're dressed in only shorts. She's in a sexy nightie."

He strangled the caulk gun like he wanted to strangle his brother. "Shut up, Dax. Nothing is going on between Quinn and I."

Dax wiggled his eyebrows. "Then, you won't mind if I ask her out."

a small boy from drowning she exposes herself and her mutant abilities to Chase, a budding investigative reporter.

Now, he has questions. And so do the police.

Once Pearl discovers her secret identity, she learns she's part of a larger war between battling Atlanteans. A battle that will decide who rules the oceans. A battle raging between evil and her true family. Will she find a way to use her powers in time to save a kingdom she never knew existed?

This is the start of a young adult fantasy action adventure novel series. "Free sweet summer young adult paranormal with death-defying underwater rescues."
– Reviewer

About

Soul Slam

Soul Warriors, Book 1

by ALLIE BURTON

An ancient Egyptian amulet.
A pharaoh's soul inside demanding she obey.
A double cross that ends with a curse.

On her first heist to steal an ancient Egyptian amulet, sixteen-year-old Olivia inadvertently receives the soul of King Tut…and the deadly curse that comes with it. And Olivia's not alone at the museum.

A member of a secret society, Xander believes it's

his place to inherit King Tut's soul and justly rule. He knows nothing about the society's evil plan to control the world or the curse. Now, he must deal with the female thief who stole the amulet.

When the two teens find themselves up against the secret society, they reluctantly join forces and must figure out how to end the curse before it turns deadly. On the run and unable to touch because of the curse, Olivia and Xander develop a connection during their quest.

As the mystery surrounding the amulet unfolds, Olivia and Xander fall for each other. But is love enough to save them and the world from destruction?

"If you are a fan of Rick Riordan books about a quest with love and history thrown in…this is for you!"
– Hooked In A Book Review

Other Books by Allie Burton

CASTLE RIDGE SMALL TOWN ROMANCE SERIES
The Romance Dance
The Christmas Match
The Flirtation Game
The Playboy Switch
The Billionaire's Ploy
The Heartbreak Contract
The Marriage Merger (*coming soon*)
The Runaway Royal (*coming soon*)

LOST DAUGHTERS OF ATLANTIS SERIES
Atlantis Riptide
Atlantis Red Tide
Atlantis Rising Tide
Atlantis Tide Breaker
Atlantis Dark Tides
Atlantis Twisting Tides
Atlantis Glacial Tides

SOUL WARRIORS SERIES
Soul Slam
Tut's Trumpet
Peace Piper
Cleo's Curse

Find all of Allie's books on her website.
http://www.allieburton.com/books.html

Allie Burton has always been a reader and writer. She wrote her first novel at the age of twelve when she was stranded at a hospital by a snowstorm. Receiving her first romance from her grandmother, she fell in love with the genre. As an adult, she read young adult books with her own teens and was excited to find something fresh and new. Now, she writes both.

Having so many jobs as a teen and adult became great research material for the stories she writes. She has been everything from a bike police officer to a professional mascot escort to an advertising executive. She has lived on three continents and in four states and has studied art, fashion design, and marine biology.

Allie is a member of the Society of Children's Book Writers & Illustrators and Romance Writers of America. She loves to ski, golf, and run. Currently, she lives in Colorado with her husband and two children.